"Growing up and being trans and aliens, oh my! *How to Get over the End of the World* is one of those rare novels that combines razor-sharp wit with a courageous and tender heart. With pitch-perfect accuracy and fearless honesty, Hal Schrieve evokes the raw wild magic of queer and trans adolescence with characters that are at once astoundingly realistic and delightfully larger than life. Ferociously intelligent and relentlessly authentic, this book has all the makings of a queer cult classic."

—KAI CHENG THOM, author of *Fierce Femmes and Notorious Liars: A Dangerous Trans Girl's Confabulous Memoir*

"Hal Schrieve has proven hirself a virtuoso of vital, immediate trans storytelling. *How to Get over the End of the World* is a brave salvo against anodyne trans YA, richly populated by messy, earnest, colorful characters. You'll love them, loathe them, and fall in love with them all over again. Trans kids are under attack. *How to Get over the End of World* will show them how to fight back."

—PEYTON THOMAS, award-winning author of *Both Sides Now*

"*How to Get over the End of the World* would have been phenomenal and necessary even without the science-magic: queer and trans teens, playing in bands, falling in love, raising hell, fighting and friending and living radical lives. But, there *is* science-magic. Aliens and telepathy and *vibes*. This is the book we need right now."

—MICHELLE TEA, author of *Black Wave*

"*How to Get over the End of the World* feels wholly original—a punk rock opera that finds a way to blend sci-fi, coming-of-age, and inspiration that maybe we can fix this messed up world. No one writes the contemporary teen voice better than Hal Schrieve."

—COLLEEN AF VENABLE, author of the National Book Award–longlisted *Kiss Number 8*

"A story exploding with voice and vulnerability, *How to Get over the End of the World* is electric and soft and honest and powerful and left me buzzing. I've never read such a raw depiction and reflection of my trans and queer identities, and I'm beyond excited for young readers who'll get to read this book and feel seen by Hal's words. Simply magical. Very gay."

—KACEN CALLENDER, author of the National Book Award–winning *King and the Dragonflies* and the bestselling novel *Felix Ever After*

HOW TO GET OVER THE END OF THE WORLD

a novel

HAL SCHRIEVE

TRIANGLE
SQUARE
books for young readers

SEVEN STORIES PRESS

NEW YORK · OAKLAND · LONDON

Seven Stories Press
140 Watts Street
New York, NY 10013
www.sevenstories.com

College professors and high school and middle school teachers may order free examination copies of Seven Stories Press titles. Visit https://www.sevenstories. com/pg/resources-academics or email academic@sevenstories.com.

Library of Congress Cataloging-in-Publication Data

Names: Schrieve, Hal, author.
Title: How to get over the end of the world : a novel / by Hal Schrieve.
Description: New York : Seven Stories Press, Triangle Square Books for
   Young Readers, 2023. | Audience: Ages 13-17. | Audience: Grades 7-9.
Identifiers: LCCN 2022059331 | ISBN 9781644213018 (hardcover) | ISBN
   9781644213025 (ebook)
Subjects: CYAC: Interpersonal relations--Fiction. | Telepathy--Fiction. |
   Visions--Fiction. | End of the world--Fiction. | LGBTQ+ people--Fiction.
   | LCGFT: Novels.
Classification: LCC PZ7.1.S336544 Ho 2023 | DDC [Fic]--dc23
LC record available at https://lccn.loc.gov/2022059331

Printed in the USA

9 8 7 6 5 4 3 2 1

Chapter 1

ORSINO

The ship is spherical, like a pink pearl in black space. It flashes in and out of my dreams. The dreams have been happening for two years, and they're getting more frequent, which Robin is worried about. It feels as if the aliens are getting closer.

Tonight, they were talking to me.

I was on their ship, but I was also in the middle of a forest fire.

The forest burned. I could hear the goats behind me, screaming. They weren't burning yet, but they could smell the smoke too. I couldn't save them.

The ship was broadcasting a message.

You are a sentient terrestrial being sensitive to psychic speech. If you understand this message, please indicate an affirmative.

It flashed like a caption over me in symbols I didn't recognize, but then the meaning came across in these drifts.

It's not like reading.

I couldn't indicate an affirmative, because I can't control anything in dreams.

The smoke was making it hard to breathe. I was running toward the road. I couldn't see the big blue car in the driveway. In the dream, my dog-mind registered emergency. The car was supposed to be there.

We are transmitting data to your stardate.

The long wormlike bodies of the beings in the ship crawled across my field of vision, obscuring the driveway. They had lots of eyes; they operated their screens with their long, flexible tails. I could see them inside the flesh-like walls of their ship at the same time as I felt the hot earth scalding the bottoms of my feet.

The underbrush was alight.

Ferns, grasses, old logs, new saplings. Trees fell, bringing with them fresh waves of towering flame. My fucked-up cracked paws hit the ground painfully as I ran toward the line of warm asphalt.

Blood was leaking from my mouth.

We split time to speak to you, because you have the sensitivity needed to listen. We need you.

I wasn't outside anymore. I was in a house and the walls had come down on me. A huge block of cement was on my back, pushing me into something sharp. I could smell smoke again.

You are our forerunner. We need you to change time. We need you to live.

Saltwater stung my tongue. I was on a beach. I had come there from the road, from the farm. The sand was slick with oil. I looked down and on the rocks were dozens, hundreds of dead fish, dead birds black with it. Their eyes rotted inward.

We are where you will be. We need to speak to you. Do you understand?

The pink ship flashed, and the worms' tails made noises, and screens flashed the unreadable text. I couldn't tell if I was still a dog or a person. My feet were stuck in the mud and the tide was rising. Plastic bags pushed against my face and eyes. My heart jerked, pounded hard, and my hands slipped. I was looking at the surface of a planet under a smoky, red sky. My head was pressed against metal.

Do you understand?

The voice was too loud, too close. My throat was dry, but I screamed.

"Shut up!"

The plastic bags weren't there anymore.

The wormlike being with many eyes looked up at me. I felt sure that the being could see me.

We were floating far above the earth, orbiting the moon.

"Orsino, bro," Jukebox said. "Wake up."

The light was off, but the hall light shone through. Jukebox was standing in the door, their shadow stretching towards me across the thin carpet. They were wearing a pair of my sister Robin's underwear; their scarred, tattooed chest was bare. Their hair stood up on end. I was half-on and half-off my mattress, my face pressed into the carpet.

"Hey," I croaked.

"Thought you might need help," Jukebox said. "It's four in the morning."

"Did I wake you up?"

"I've been up trying to write. I heard you screaming."

"Sorry," I said. My neck felt weird.

"I wasn't writing anyway."

Jukebox came over and sat on the end of my bed. The colored ink on their chest was purple and blurry in the dark, but I could still see the wolf tattoo on their arm staring at me as they handed me a cold washcloth with their other hand.

"You're here. You're okay. It's not real."

I shut my eyes again and saw the ship recede into the distance, the dog running through the fire, paws hitting hot ground.

"I think it *is*," I said. I pressed the washcloth to my face. I was surprised I could even talk. I still felt my cracked paws and bloody teeth, felt the plastic in the water over my face and the men with knives cutting me. My heart was beating in my ears. I felt electricity crackling, everywhere. Same as last night, and the night before. I felt an urge to look outside. I knew that something was happening to the sky.

"This kinda stuff feels real," Jukebox said.

I shut my eyes again and saw the shadows shake, the spaceship descend and ascend towards me. "It doesn't go away."

"I dream about Ghost Ship every night," Jukebox said. "The fire going up. People screaming. It feels really really there, really close. But it's over. Even if it doesn't feel over. Your stuff with your dad and the dog and the . . . well, the spaceship."

"I still think my stuff is really the future. There's Agatha, but there's this fire too," I said.

Jukebox's face was half-dark, half-lit-up from the light in the hall. They nodded at me.

"They told me that they need me," I said. "There are these beings, this light, and they're showing me that there's a bad past and a bad present, and a bad future coming too, where the fires just grow and there's death and floods and plague and then . . ." I stopped. "This . . ." I couldn't speak any more. "They said they need me to change it. I don't know how."

"I'd take a cold shower if I were you. You dunk all the way under the water, real cold, and it slows your heart rate way down."

"Thanks," I said.

"If that doesn't work, I have weed."

I rolled over onto my mattress and pushed myself up, staring at the floor for a second as my vision spun. I nodded at Jukebox, to show that I heard them. I pressed my face into the washcloth again. It was cold and smelled a little bit mildewy.

Jukebox and I stood up at the same time, and they looked for a second like they were going to hug me. Instead they slapped me on the back. "I hope you get more sleep, bro," they said as they left. "If you want any weed, let me know."

I heard Jukebox murmuring something to my sister in the next room as I went down the hall past my mom's door. I could see the yellow light on in the kitchen down the hall. Mom must still be working on her chemistry homework. I hit the light switch in the bathroom fast, not wanting to see shapes in the dark. The tub's never been caulked, because our landlord's cheap; in the three months we've lived here, a little ring of mold has grown up around the edge. I wiped at it with a tissue to get the moisture up before I ran the water. I sat in the tub and turned on the shower head so the water ran cold. I could still see the fire when I closed my eyes. My jaw was still chattering. I ran my hands over my belly, felt the hair growing there, touched my feet. I didn't touch my chest.

I looked up out of the bathroom window and saw that the sky outside was a bright, unearthly violet. It shone like the wall of a tent being lit from the other side by an enormous purple light. I blinked; it did not go away.

I looked away from the window. I stood in the cold water and scrubbed myself down with the thin washcloth. My body was wrong; the ways it was wrong were various, but one of the main ones was that I wasn't a dog. In my room, I dug through my drawer and found my ROSWELL shirt with the bleach stains and the pants I had cut with kitchen scissors.

"Oh, you made coffee," my mom said when I set the cup down next to her on top of her textbook. "Thank you." She had on her scrubs already—these were ones printed with cats in different colors. "How did you sleep?"

"Fine," I said. I looked toward the window.

She looked at me. "I can hear you, you know."

"It wasn't any worse than usual." I wondered why Jukebox was the one to wake me up and give me a washcloth, if Mom had heard me too.

"We have got to figure out some meds for you. They have to make something that's gonna calm you down." She chugged her coffee and ran her hands through her hair, trying to make it lay on one side. She cut her hair the week we moved to Tacoma. It's turning gray, but not super fast.

You just see it on the edges. "And we gotta get you a new therapist. It's been three months since Dorothea retired, and I can tell it's getting worse for you. For a while there I thought things might be getting better."

"Jukebox said maybe weed would help," I said. "Some people use it for trauma stuff."

Mom sighed. "Yeah, I mean, if it works, that's one thing. But I don't want you just dependent on weed forever. I mean, look at Jukebox."

I rose to the bait. "What's that supposed to mean?"

My mom gave me a no-bullshit-here look. "Hey. I've done a lot of fucked-up stuff, said bad stuff, I know. But you *can't* look at that girl and say everything's all right with her."

"Them," I said.

"Them, whatever. My brother was kind of like that, you know. Up and down, all hyper and then all depressed. *They* got a lot going on. I think *they* need therapy or stabilizers or something, not just weed. You, too."

I shrugged. "Maybe I can get a white noise machine. Then you won't get woken up when I yell."

"That's a horrible solution," my mom said. "That's a non-solution." She sighed. "You're going to do your online homework today, right?"

"Yeah," I said.

My mom left to go to her nursing residency at the hospital, and I took a minute and checked my phone. My latest piece had gotten 970 likes. I looked at some pictures of pit bulls at a local shelter that had wide silly heads and big eyes and sketched a couple; my next picture was going to be a bunch of them in a circle, like the Matisse of the women dancing. I sent a couple sketches to Robin so she would see them when she woke up.

Robin texted me back right away. She must have been awake already, staring at her phone in her bed. *Thanks for dog pics, they rule! Remember, show tonight. We need ur help hauling J's gear soon so we can get back to their house and set up.*

I remember, I said. *Gonna go collecting rn.*

There was a pause. *Jukebox says can you get a possum skull for their altar,* Robin texted.

I didn't text back. I could imagine the way they would say it aloud to my sister, in my sister's bed, the pillow half covering their face, smiling crookedly.

I checked my notes again; someone had asked me to draw their boyfriend's snakesona. It wasn't porn stuff, so I messaged back saying okay. I could make a living just drawing stuff like this, if I wanted to.

I threw on a coat and pulled on the sneakers that had started fraying at the top, then grabbed trash bags from under the sink. The sun was still barely up as I locked the door behind me. The sky was no longer purple.

When I was little, our dad would try to take us hunting. I was bad at holding the gun steady. I only killed a deer like, twice. But when my dad killed something, I would always help him clean it, cut it up, cure the meat, hang it. My dad would save deer skins. There were people who made stuff out of deer leather that he could sell them to. He cleaned and kept the bones of a lot of deer. He taught me to clean the bones too. It was a slow, exact process, and I liked knowing it. I liked watching as all the layers of stuff that made a creature alive were stripped away, and you could see each layer, and see the stuff inside changing. Part of the way he taught me involved letting the animal's body—or its head, if it was big—soak in a bucket on the edge of our property, sealed in so other animals couldn't eat it. You'd open the bucket and this enormous stench would come out, and you would see if the skin was ready to come off.

When I was eleven or twelve, I started looking for road-kill and dead animals in the woods, and I'd take off the meat and clean those bones, too, to keep. You learn a lot about animals by seeing the way they work inside. Since we lived next to a long stretch of rural road in southern Washington, there was a lot of roadkill. I started making art out of the bones. I would paint pictures of them, then paint the skulls themselves, then take them to a spot in the woods I liked, and hang them up. My dad helped with the bigger animals.

Now I do it for myself.

Tacoma is spread out over industrial areas and down-town and the residential towns around it, so the wild animals congregate along certain fault lines, near strips of green. There's a hill near our apartment covered in trees, overlooking the Sound and the warehouses. The hill was too steep to level as they built the highway. It goes down and then there's a little drop and you hit the road. I find animals near there. The roadkill is mainly stuff like raccoons, dogs, cats, squirrels. Some rats. I like the rat skulls. I hide them in a box now because Jukebox's bandmate Stacey asked me if I would make a necklace of them for her, and I think that's gross. The rat box has some little blue rhinestones glued to the top, so my mom knows it's special and doesn't throw it out. When it's full, I don't know what I'll do with it. I can't hoard bones in our apartment forever.

When I collect, I walk around with rubber gloves and two bags. One for trash, and one for animals. A couple times people have gotten freaked out seeing me putting just animals into bags, so I make sure to do trash too, and take it up to the dumpsters. That way I'm serving the community or whatever.

The roadkill hill is also a hill where some guys live in tents. They're homeless. One of them's named Matt, but I only know that because he asked me for a cigarette once. Sometimes I wave at them. One of them has a bike he does cool tricks on. If he ever said hi to me, I would be his friend.

The first thing I found that morning was a dead crow, wing bent and leg flattened on the side of the road, even before I got to the roadkill hill. I passed the Asian food market and the salon and the weed store and the blocks of buildings that look almost exactly like ours, because they were built by the same developer forty years ago. All of the buildings in my part of town look like shit. I smelled distant smoke from someone making a woodfire, or maybe having a barbecue.

I found a frog, too, but it was too flat to move.

Since I first started getting the visions, stuff happens when I touch roadkill. When I find an animal, it comes up, gets closer. I can feel the animal, see little bits of its dreams and nightmares and memories, feel the parts of it that haven't really gone yet. The feeling of its feet on the ground, and the anticipation of food, sleep, day.

I wrap the animals in my bag as gently as I can. I try not to get the fur or the blood on my clothes, since my mom won't do my laundry anymore.

I touched the frog, looking at its green belly and red blood on the asphalt on the edge of the road. I looked at the shape of the road, the way it curved around the bend. Cars rushed by. I picked up the frog. The life of the frog flashed in front of me—a tongue, an eye opening and shutting, the pounding of the roadway. Its last feelings, and also its feelings from the day before it died.

I turned my face up toward the empty gray sky.

The pink pearl of the ship spun against the clouds. The cold sun gleamed on its starboard belly. It cast a shadow over the freeway.

My legs dropped out from under me, and I felt a heavy jolt through my tailbone, where my tail was growing. My hand clutched the slime of the dead frog. The ship spun, curling in and out of clouds like it was an ordinary thing, normal in daytime.

And the dead frog somehow accelerated.

I saw not only this dead frog but the frog that had laid its egg, and the egg, blazing in my head. My heart sped up. I saw lines of frogs, layers of frogs, dripping back through time, frogs in their thousands growing legs and eating and swimming in green water since before the road was here. Frog life was paced with cycles of life and death, small devastating moments of fear and night and unsafe morning light; the frog's joy was in survival. But there had been a first frog here; there was a time when there were no frogs. All the frogs remembered.

I felt a tremor through me, cold and electric.

I searched in the sky for the ship, but it was no longer there. Now I saw a sudden reach of white ice that stretched up toward the thin bluish clouds. The road was not there beneath it. This was what had been here before frogs, as the frogs knew: a sheet of ice covering the whole world. It loomed above me, blue and transparent, thousands of feet of slow, heavy ice.

I blinked, and it disappeared. The road, and the frog-guts, pounded against my tailbone.

The ship was not above me anymore. The cars were back, their frightening speed juddering through me.

I looked in the sky the whole way back. Just white space. I told myself it was a dream that had stuck with me.

"Hey, roadkill king," Robin called to me as I came up the road again with my bag. She was standing on the porch barefoot in her black skinny jeans and white tank, her buzzed head wrapped in a towel. "We're leaving in a minute. We're gonna get lunch on the way."

Chapter 2

JAMES

I got two texts just before the first bell rang on the first day of school.

Ian's text read: *Should I break up with closet case? At the end of my damn rope.*

Opal's text read: *Just had a WEIRD convo with Barb. Apparently NATALIE IS LEAVING??????? LIKE TO MOVE TO PHILADELPHIA?? AND OUR POSITIONS ARE GETTING CUT?? DO YOU KNOW ABOUT THIS?*

I didn't reply to Ian's text.

To Opal, I texted: *I know nothing about anything.*

I smoked a bowl in my car and thought about what reflection and renewal actually meant to me. It *was* almost Rosh Hashanah. I was wearing my new spiked collar.

I sat in a haze through English, US History, and Spanish 3, red-eyed, in relative peace. I told myself that Opal was being melodramatic. Barb gets the dirt on everything before we do, but I figured Opal was confused. At lunch I made a beeline towards where Opal was sitting at our usual table on the very edge of the cafeteria. Their hair was bright orange, which was a change from last week. Their bright yellow backpack was hung over the back of their wheelchair, covered in pins from shows we'd been to last year.

Noah, who was on his way to the trash can with his left-overs, whistled over at me as I went.

"Hey, Judy, nice spikes!"

I was different this year. I gave him the finger and slammed my little plate of horrible cafeteria salad down next to Opal.

"What the hell was the text from Barb?"

Opal groaned, looking up from their phone. "So, okay. HIV government funding or whatever has I guess dried up for some kind of reason, Gemma says, so Gemma told Barb that our youth educator positions are gonna get canceled after the gala in winter. But Gemma's just doing that out of spite, probably. Natalie hired Mickey without telling Gemma or the board I guess? And the funding got cut, so we don't have money for Mickey's position. And now Natalie told Gemma she's leaving to move and work at a shelter in Philadelphia, and Gemma told Barb that it's because Natalie knows our budget's screwed and doesn't wanna deal, and that's all I know. So now we're like . . . hiring a new executive director after the gala."

I impaled a parmesan-y leaf. "Are you absolutely for sure this is happening?"

The Compton House is named after the riot some trans and gay people had in Compton Cafeteria in San Francisco in 1966. It does support groups for baby gays and baby trans kids and we also do education for nonprofits and schools and churches that want to not be totally homophobic. Opal and I work there now as youth educators for a stipend of three hundred dollars a month. Mostly we organize filing cabinets and sometimes we do a condom workshop or a genderbread man workshop. The groups there saved my butt when I was thirteen. I'm getting tired of it.

"Well, they're still paying us real nonprofit dollars to plan workshops until December," Opal said. "But like, I keep thinking about what other programs they're gonna have to cut with no budget. What about the itty-bitty gays that are like eleven right now? They need somewhere to go. We can't let Compton House *die*."

"It's gonna be okay. It won't die." I wasn't sure if this was true, but what the hell could I do about it if it was? "How's Barb?"

"Dyed her hair pink. She's seeing this trans guy, which is weird, but I guess he's fine with the gender implications or what have you. We're rewatching *Buffy* together, which is cool."

"Are the rats gone?"

"Singular rat. It is deceased." Last week Opal had been down in the garage sorting the stuff they took out of their aunt's house and had seen a giant rat run under Barb's truck.

"That's a relief."

"Yeah, for sure," Opal said, digging into the tempeh whatever. "We can't have shows in the basement if the rats eat my drums."

I was finishing my salad when Ian burst through the cafeteria doors wearing the silver crop top he bought at the mall with me in May and the pleated skirt he'd gotten at the thrift store a month ago. I was glad to see him wearing stuff like that. He'd been too nervous last spring. The top hugged his wide shoulders and thick arms and shone in the white lights of the cafeteria.

"Silver crop top!" I yelled.

"It's too cold for today, I'm freezing. Girl, how are you? You keep posting depressing things on your finsta?" He's allowed to say Girl to me because I'm gay and so is he. Gay *she* is fine too.

"Oh, I'm just stoned and dropping out," I said. "How are *you*?"

Ian made a face. "I was working doubles all week last week trying to save money, and Tristan said he would bring me a snack and hang out, and we planned it three times and he flaked three times, and now he says I can't talk to him at school still."

"So dump him," I said.

Ian stuck out his tongue. "I know I asked, but I don't *want* to."

"You've been fucking for over a year and he doesn't say hi in public. Are you just addicted to being treated like shit, or what?"

"The swim team is homophobic. He's scared."

"He doesn't have to totally avoid you. It's so toxic."

Ian shrugged and stretched his arms. "We went to Sasquatch together, and *that* was good. He gave me that necklace, you know?"

"So he got a two-for-one deal on St. Christophers' medals and thought of you."

Ian's infinite tolerance for Tristan's bullshit gets *infinitely* on my nerves.

"Ugh. You're so mean to me," Ian said. "The window was open in English and I was like, close it, and Ms. Regan was like, blah, fresh air. I'm gonna shrivel up if it's this cold all September."

"You'll live."

Ian grew up in Florida. He says that his mom has never forgiven his aunt for persuading her to move here, because of the weather. Though she hasn't left yet. Ian and his mom moved here when we were ten, after his parents got divorced. He'd left all his friends back in Miami. My parents had just gotten divorced at about that time, too, and I'd gone kind of weirdo tomboy and lost all my horse-girl friends. He was fat and girly and had Sailor Moon sneakers that he wore every day. I wore one black sweatshirt all the time and wore my hair in a horrible, constantly disintegrating ponytail. We'd talk about wolves or manga at recess; we made a comic together about a vampire named Ace Spade.

"You smell like weed," Ian said.

"I wear my stink with pride," I said. "420, baby."

"Earth Crisis would give me shit just for condoning your nonsense."

"Earth Crisis would give you more shit for quitting veganism to eat bacon."

"Earth Crisis is straight bros and I am not bound by their strictures, but I appreciate their zeal for radical sobriety.

I think if we all really loved pigs and chickens and didn't intoxicate our bodies to avoid the horror in the world, some good things might get done."

Ian is straight edge because he read about how Kristen Pfaff died of a heroin overdose on Wikipedia after Opal played us their vinyl of *Pretty on the Inside* when we were fifteen. He cried about it for two days. Opal told him about straight edge punks and Limp Wrist just to shut him up, but then he took it really seriously. He got annoying about me smoking weed that year. We had a fight about it and I made him read an infographic about how weed helps people with anxiety. I think these days he's downgraded it from "dangerous health hazard" to "annoying dumb habit."

If I am a stoner and Ian is straight edge, and he likes stupid jocks, why are we friends, you may ask. A good question, but not one without an answer. Besides the fact that we are bonded by the experience of being weird-queer in cow land, Ian likes *Barbarella* and *Tank Girl* and *The Voyage Home*, which are my three favorite bad/good movies, and he doesn't mind when I want to watch them over and over, and he doesn't mind when I dump my complaints about my dad on him, because he also has complaints about his dad. This is the sign of good friendship. He also texts me when I am sad. He knows a lot about music.

Also—he is hot.

He has eyes the color of mahogany cabinets in an old house, and brown hair that makes a curly halo with gold undertones when he grows it out. He's my height, but fatter, with big, round shoulders. His skin is really . . . *smooth*.

When we went to the beach once over the summer I realized I stared at him all the time—the few hairs on his chest, the freckles on his back, his round stomach getting golden in the sun, his happy squint that furrows his whole face. He talks like a girl, but like sort of a tough, street-smart girl. He's avoided getting beat up in high school partly because I punched someone for him in ninth grade and partly because I think people have a sense that the only reason he hasn't punched someone is because he'd destroy them in one blow, like One Punch Man. I like the way his body moves. He has freckles and moles all down his arms. He gives good hugs.

Opal's take is it's definitely good that me and Ian aren't ever going to be together, because it means that we are ninety percent more likely to still talk after we graduate. But I still have a playlist about him, and I've memorized the four moles that make a crooked line down his neck. Desperate, you might say, but I'm not. I am pining artfully, which is different. I can learn from the experience of unrequited desire for a cis gay boy, and it will make me wise. Many people are completely stupid the first time they find a boy they like. I will go into life already having loved, lost, and learned to deal.

"Why don't you ask Mr. Mermaid if he wants to Ariel it up with you this weekend at the OVID-Rocketpizza show downtown?" Opal took out their lunchbox, which was the same Hot Topic brand tin thing they'd been carrying around since ninth grade.

"Oh, that's actually a good idea." Ian pulled out his phone. I looked across the room toward where the swim team sat with the other athletic people. I could pinpoint exactly the moment when Tristan's phone lit up. He stopped smiling and started texting under the table.

I felt my mouth scrunch.

"How is practice with the Rocketpizzors?"

"Same old." Ian stuck out his tongue. "Ken and Devon are dicks."

"I can't wait for you to roll out the gold leopard print glam rock," Opal said. "This town needs some new fucking energy. All the shows are the same people or touring bands where someone's an abuser."

"That's *not* true," Ian said. "There's lots of fun stuff if you go to places other than Le Perv and Goat Mansion. Come to Clown Barn sometime."

"God, venue names really all suck," I said.

"Clown Barn is an amazing name for a venue," Ian said. He looked down at his phone, and then over to the side of the cafeteria where Tristan had been sitting. Tristan was gone. Ian got to his feet. "Better than Red House. Hold on, gotta go sort out logistics for this weekend with Mr. Closet in the orchestra practice room."

He left me and Opal sitting there, staring at each other. We exchanged a look.

"He is *never* going to break up with him," I said.

Opal gave a helpless shrug.

"Whatever. I have to pee." I got up and threw my paper tray away, then looked around. It was time for the biggest event of my school year thus far.

In Washington State, it is illegal to discriminate against trans people in schools. You have to let us use the bathroom of our choice. In theory. For now. But until I got top surgery this past summer, I never tried. I probably could have passed where nobody knew me. But I'd been around these schmucks since first grade, and I'd gotten enough shit from people just trying to get them to use a new name. I can handle conflict, but not when my bladder's full. Instead, from freshman year through junior year, I peed in the nurse's office, at the back of the first floor. Which is a real pain, particularly if someone else has recently been in there throwing up.

I opened the door, unleashing the stink of five hundred teenage boys' rank piss, and went in to hunker down over a toilet. I realized too late that there was a group of boys laughing right next to the stall I was in. My urethra contracted. I smelled chemical fruit, and realized Evil Noah and his friends were vaping by the urinals.

"Judy?" Noah said. "I can see your boots."

"You're not allowed to fucking vape in here, dipshit," I said through the stall.

"Man, I think I hear a girl peeing," he called. I heard his friend Trevor laugh. There was a pause. I saw Noah's feet in front of my stall. I felt my heart speed up, just a little. But fuck that. I flushed, yanked up my pants, and squared my jaw.

"Pretty fucking gay of you to be listening to people peeing," I said. "Get the fuck away from the door, Noah."

He laughed.

"I'm serious, dude."

"You're not supposed to be in here. This is the men's room. What are you doing in there, cutting?"

I opened the door into his body, hard. The dirty metal made contact with his chest and hip. He stumbled backwards.

"Fuck off, Noah," I said. "You can suck my *fucking* dick."

Trevor laughed at me, his vape pen in hand. He was blocking the sink, so I left without washing my hands.

Olympia is a haven of queer culture. It's also right next to deep red rural bullshit country. Two things can be true.

Chapter 3

IAN

Until I go to college, I have James and Opal.

Opal introduced me to Nick Cave and G.L.O.S.S. and took me to my first punk show. James got suspended in freshman year for punching Morgan Stern when she wrote IAN HAS AIDS in big font on the whiteboard. Morgan cried and said James knocked her tooth loose, which made it a whole big deal until her friend Gabby snitched and said her tooth was loose from a volleyball tournament and then Morgan said she was just joking.

I *had* Tristan. Past tense. It felt good, the first three or four times we had sex, and then bad-but-good, the next six months where he told me I was hot via text about eighteen times a day but never talked to me in person, and then bad, when he stopped telling me I was hot as much and didn't start talking to me. But he still fucked me. He would text like, *meet me at St. Martins,* and we'd go talk and walk in the woods and he'd kiss me at some point, and then we'd fuck in his mom's car. Mostly he topped me or I sucked his dick. A couple of times he let me top him, but he didn't really like it, he said. It's a really weird thing, to be having a secret affair. It feels pathetic and gross. Sometimes I wished that Tristan was older, or married, or something, so there would be a good reason for him avoiding me other than that he didn't want to embarrass himself in front of his friends.

Sometime around the last week of August, driving Tristan home, I realized I didn't really have him anymore. I only had the times we made out. Those times were good, but they weren't worth the other shit. And then, coming back to school and seeing the looks on James and Opal's faces every time I mentioned him, I realized I had to do something about it. James and me were each other's first kiss, back in eighth grade, when I was a girly boy and he was a boy-y girl, and we kissed because we knew we were the same thing. We didn't ever kiss again, but he somehow has a say over who I kiss after.

I kind of wish I was a trans man too so I understood him. I know that isn't the kind of thing you say. Though— he's also sort of constantly having a bad time, so maybe I don't want to be a trans guy. I think he feels like he's just waiting to go somewhere else. I am too, I guess.

James texted again: *You: queen. He: slovenly mother-fucker. Fem rights baby.*

I liked that word, *fem*, because him calling me that meant I belonged with him, even though I wasn't trans. I felt sometimes like I wasn't really fem—if I was a girl, nobody would look at the way I dress and call me fem, exactly. But I'm not a girl.

I texted Tristan, *look, i love you, but i need to be real. if you're not ready to come out and own what we're doing, we should break up.*

Two minutes later, Tristan texted back: *ian, you can't pressure me into coming out just because you want me to.*

I looked out the dusty window at the bay, exhaling.

I know. But I can choose to not date someone who isn't out. It sucks. you got stuff to work out, and you can't talk to me at school, and you ghost on me and make me feel like you're embarrassed of me. I don't want that anymore.

I hope you're having fun ruining my life, he said.

I pictured the movie where Tristan was the protagonist. I was not the villain in this movie. I was the inciting event. He had never been happy with me. Now he could grow as a person.

I texted Ian and Opal: *broke up with swimmer boy.*

I put my phone down and let my eyes close, thinking, well, cool. That's it. I did it. I'm done. I'm done.

Then I picked up my phone to take selfies in the bathroom to make myself feel better. I'm cute when the light above the mirror is turned on; I like the way it makes my skin glow, and if I hold my phone at the right angle my shoulders look bigger in a way that makes me feel more like I'm a cute guy, instead of a weird goblin. I'm growing into parts of my body I used to feel were all out of proportion. I used to think I looked totally gross, and now I think I'm pretty hot, even if nobody at my high school is willing to admit it. I can't tell how much of it was ever in my head. I almost like my stomach now, and that's because of Tristan. He'd put his face in my stomach and make a noise in his throat. I like Alice Bag's memoir, where she talks about other punks calling her Gordita, and has a ton of pictures of herself when she was fat and cute in middle school. That made me realize I was cute, too, even though Alice Bag got thin later.

I went downstairs and got one of my mom's yogurt popsicles that she'd just bought out of her box that's marked LUISA'S ONLY IAN STAY OUT. I set up the coffee pot for twelve cups and flicked the switch on. I went to my car and got my art supplies out of the trunk and started making shirts for Rocketpizza. I don't know how to screen print yet, so they're just bleach over stencils that I cut out of the plastic you use to laminate shit. It looks good though. You put a piece of cardboard in the shirt to keep the bleach from leaking through, and paint the bleach over the stencil, and wait for it to take.

While I had the shirts spread out all over my room, I wrote two songs. I knew my band was never going to play them, because they were queer. I played them and hummed to myself on my guitar to figure out how they would go.

It did not feel good, to be done. I wasn't sure I was done.

"Ian, go to bed," my mom called through my door. "Did you drink coffee again? It's gonna keep you up, you idiot. What are you going to do tomorrow when you're a zombie?"

"I'm *going* to bed," I said.

"Hey," she said. "I want you to know, every day I thank God that I only gotta live one more year with this kind of lip from you. I'm just looking out for you."

Starting at about 12 a.m., I found myself listening on

repeat to the one song by Davila 666 that Tristan had said he liked when I played it for him in my car.

El recibió amor
Vidrio, sal y alcohol
Que me cause dolor, dolor

I slept for four hours. I woke up and thought: hey, wow. I'm single. It's Thursday, and I'm single.

When I got to school and saw Opal, they reached their arms out for me.

"The evil has been defeated."

"He's not *evil*," I said. He was kind of dumb and kind of self-absorbed and kind of scared of being gay, and really hot. If I didn't have Opal and James, I probably would have tolerated his not-evilness for a couple more years, and something might have changed. I sort of wanted to keep tolerating it now, if only for the sake of making out on his futon a few more times and getting to see the trail of blond hair that runs down his stomach, past the faint scar where he had his appendix out in the fifth grade. And I liked his dick. It made me feel real.

I managed to wrangle Ken and Devon into agreeing to a rehearsal after school. We used Devon's house. I was wearing my black and white checkered jacket with the fur on the edge and my knee-high boots, because it was cold out and because I was trying to lean into the whole divorcée thing so if Tristan saw me he'd know what he was missing out on.

When I pulled up to Devon's place, which is in the scuzzy part of Lacey, he was vaping in the ditch where his neighborhood meets Sleater-Kinney Road, where his mom can't see him. He looked like an idiot. I showed him a shirt from the back of my car.

"Rocketpizza is dead?" he said. He frowned at me. Devon and I used to be close, but now he acts like he's gotta be tough all the time. "We didn't talk about that."

"It's edgy. Like *The Need is Dead*. It's local." I gesticulated. "I've done tank tops and sweatshirts."

"The Need?"

"Lesbians in the nineties. They had an album called *The Need Is Dead*. Then they went on hiatus for like, two or three decades."

"You aren't a lesbian. We should have paid for real printing," Devon said, and blew his vape steam toward the rhododendrons.

I'd wanted to show Devon my new songs before Ken got there, since I was still trying to win him over to the let-Ian-sing-gay-shit camp. But I could see I'd lost him. Especially with the lyric about sucking balls. He looked bored all the time now. I didn't know what was going on in his head anymore, not like when we were kids. And Ken was somehow five times worse than that. He was stoned out of his gourd and kept making fart jokes. I'd be like, "Hey Ken, can you check the levels on that amp, I can't hear the bass line," and he'd be like, "I can check the *fart* levels," and wouldn't move.

On Friday, Tristan caught me in front of the school before first period.

"Hey Ian," he called, behind me, when I was walking from my car.

I turned. He walked toward me slowly like it was the

easiest thing in the world. The sun was rising to his right, making his face all red-orange-pink like the stained glass in a church. The Pixies, "Here Comes Your Man." Magnetic Fields, "I Don't Want To Get Over You." Borrowing from James, Alison Krauss, "Every Time You Say Goodbye."

"What do you want?" I asked.

"I wanted to say hi," he said. "To say sorry."

"Oh." My heart sank. Did he realize we were broken up? Had I not actually managed to do the thing I thought I'd done? I was wearing my yellow pants and black ROCKET-PIZZA IS DEAD shirt and earrings shaped like stars.

"I'll come to the show Saturday," he said.

"Oh," I said. "I mean, it wasn't really about the show. It was about you coming out."

He winced, but nodded. "I said dumb stuff. I'm just not friends with people like you are. My friends aren't gay. It's tough."

"I know it is," I said. "But it makes me feel really bad when you avoid me."

"I'll stop avoiding you," he said.

I stepped forward and hugged him, and he let me hug him. But my heart kind of sank. I felt like I was caught in a spinning wheel that never slowed down long enough for me to actually think. Part of my brain was like, hey, sometimes stupid things work out. I tried rearranging my expectations of the next few years again. Maybe he could go to Seattle with me for school. Maybe he'd be really into being out, once he was out of high school. Maybe it was fine to date someone you didn't really have anything in common with.

"Tristan is coming to the show," I told Opal. "We made up."

"You do you, baby," Opal said. I tried not to take their obvious moral judgment personally.

Chapter 4

JAMES

After school I wait for Opal by my car. Barb drives them
to school because they hate the accessible school bus and
anyway sometimes it skips their house, but they need a
ride home because Barb works late. She's a therapist, and
most people like to make appointments for after they're
done with their shitty long work or school day. She used to
be my therapist, until Opal moved in with her. After that it
felt weird to tell her stuff about my life, so I stopped going.

Opal climbed down from their chair and then up into
the passenger seat. I had remembered to shove all my
thrift store clothes off of it, for once. I folded their chair
and stuck it in the back on top of the layer of detritus that
my dad was always complaining about.

We smoked in the car again and then stopped by the
King David Diner on the way over to Barb's house so we
could get the big chocolate milkshakes from Goober.
Goober's two years older than us, which makes her cool,
especially because she transitioned when she was a teenager, like us. She's also cool because she plays softball and

rugby and self-identifies as a health goth. She's pretty, with really white-blond hair that goes down to her mid-back, and she has like eight homemade stick-and-poke tattoos over her arms that she did herself. A lot of them are of owls.

Opal has a crush on Goober, but doesn't have the guts to flirt.

"How's it hanging, skank?" Opal yelled as we entered the diner.

"Fucking excellent, little rock," Goober yelled back.

A couple of the older people at David's resent Goober's mouth, but most of the people here are like us and don't bat an eye.

"We'd love some vegan milkshakes."

We take the same table every time. King David Diner has some old arcade games and the table is right next to them, so whenever anyone gets frustrated and quits we can check the slot to see if they forgot any quarters.

Goober came back over and tossed our milkshakes and two vegan chik'n sandwiches down in front of us. "These are free," she said, and left.

"Do you think she's into me?" Opal said quietly as we watched her turn and go into the back.

"I think check back in two years and she'd be down," I said, dumping half a bottle of Tapatio hot sauce on my sandwich.

"God, I hate being in high school," Opal said. "Who the hell do I have sex with?"

"Tell me about it," I said. "Oh well. Think about how hot we'll both be in college. Have you decided what major you're doing at the big fancy city university, Mx. Early Acceptance?"

"Early Acceptance means like, January, not September," Opal said. "I don't know if I'm in."

"Whatever," I said. "You'll get in."

"I'm thinking like, maybe a literal education degree," Opal said. "I hate being a kid. I know it sucks. I'll remember that and be a bomb ass teacher."

"Rad." I looked behind Opal and noticed three punks coming in I had never seen before. Which is rare.

Two of them looked like they were probably lesbians. One had a short buzzcut and the other was covered in tattoos. The third one was a tallish, fat, probably-trans-guy who looked sort of my age but could have been anywhere from one to six years older because of trans babyface. His shoulders were really broad and prickled my dysphoria jealousy brain glitch.

He was kind of hot.

No, really hot.

He had hairy arms and really furry, muscular calves and a cool sharp nose. His body hair was dark, but the hair on his head was bleached with the kind of bad bleach job that made it stand straight up. It was brassy orange. He was wearing a Hawaiian shirt that was printed with images of dolphins and Realtree shorts with zippers on them. Also a tail that came off the side of his shorts, but not like a raver tail in rainbow colors. He looked like he had the potential to be cool. He also looked like he might want to go to a punk show this weekend.

Cogs started turning in my stoned gay brain.

"You're still social work, yeah?" Opal's back was to the group.

"It's all I'm ever going to be cut out for," I shrugged. At the other table, the three punks sat down, and the big guy made eye contact with me. He had a downy mustache. I decided he was definitely a teenager and gave him my best stoned friendly-goth smile. I wasn't sure whether I looked crazy.

But he smiled back.

Opal turned around, and then looked back to me. "Wait, do you know Jukebox?"

"Jukebox?" I really hoped that was not the trans guy's name.

"Jukebox *January*. The lead singer from OVID. The one who looks like a riot grrrl with the chin hairs."

"Oh shit," I said. "No, I didn't know them. I was checking out the dude over there." I hoped I was talking quietly enough that if said dude overheard he would find me tactful and cute.

Opal dropped their fork, turned and looked discreetly/ dramatically as they picked it up, then turned back. "Uh, dude, don't take offense, but that guy is not cute."

"You aren't a gay man," I said. "I like his legs."

"Kinda . . . grimy," Opal said. "Not that I'm complaining, if he'll help you get over Ian."

"Should I hit him up? Or he'll probably be at the show, right?"

"I would guess he will be if he's hanging with OVID." Opal checked their phone. "He could be in one of the other bands, too."

"Cool. That means I don't have to do anything now. I'm too stoned to flirt."

We said goodbye to Goober and took off.

"I don't think I have group in me tonight," Opal said, lighting a cigarette as we went back to my car. "Venus is going to be there. Last time she did this really passive aggressive thing about me not responding to her story when she knew I saw it."

"You think I want to be there?" I asked. But after I dropped them off, I turned my car around, went back downtown, and parked at the library, same as always. Sometimes I think the people who say trans people or gays are all in a cult are maybe right.

Compton's on the fourth floor of an old building in what my dad calls "the bad part of town." It has an elevator that works most of the time, but is so slow that it makes more sense to jog up all the stairs. You arrive on the fourth floor out of breath, and there's the zine library and old copies of *POZ* magazine, and then you turn the corner and grit your teeth.

There were six kids when I got there, sitting on the orange couch and three folding chairs and single pink beanbag. Most were lesbians or something like it; there was a trans girl and a little gay boy. I put the snacks on the table, which Spruce had forgotten to do, and checked the coffee pot.

The first girl, Jenny, who was like, thirteen, was here for the first time. She talked about a Charli XCX show she wanted to go to, and how she had come out to her parents. "They told me I was imagining it, and then they took me to this guy who asked me to think about what it was that was making me think I was gay," she said.

Spruce knew what to do with that kind of share, and told the girl that people were here for her and we cared about her and that we could help her get to group each week if she needed a ride, and we even had fakey "mental health support group" flyers if the parents needed to think the group was something else.

The other kids were pretty boring too, though the little shy gay boy wearing a Panic! At the Disco shirt was apparently having sex with his boyfriend where they both pretended to be fictional characters from a webcomic. He was having trouble because the author had just revealed that the characters were related. I told him where Planned Parenthood was in case he wanted free condoms.

Venus, which is a name a trans girl picks for herself when she's fourteen, was fifteen. We had hung out briefly at an excruciatingly awkward PFLAG event in spring, and Opal and I followed her on Instagram. Last week she'd made an extremely cryptic story that I hadn't bothered to watch all of where she had walked around her neighborhood, filming the sky and talking about betrayal.

"This guy Alex is my boyfriend," Venus said, ignoring the alias rule for talking about people, "and I love him, or I did, but I think I have to break up with him. Maybe not right away, but eventually. We've been dating two months and I feel like he's only using me for sex."

Like Tristan with Ian, I thought. I felt my stomach tensing.

Venus paused. Some people do that in group, looking

for affirmation, but Compton's group doesn't work so great for that because nobody is supposed to say anything during someone else's share.

"Eugh," one of the small lesbians said, nevertheless. She was quiet, so nobody called her out for talking.

"He showed me this blog that's like, trans girls getting dommed, like, porn, and it made me feel weird. And then yesterday I showed him my comics about Harley Quinn and he told me I should draw her naked. Like . . ." She sighed and ate a corn chip from the bowl in the middle of the table. "Like, isn't that kind of *predatory* of him? Or weird. It made me feel weird. I don't know. Like, girls are hot, trans girls are hot, maybe he's just saying I'm hot and doing it in a stupid way. But *then* I found out he's fucking this other trans bitch in Tenino."

She paused again, looking around. She wanted someone to say something.

I felt protective of Venus. I couldn't wait for the designated share back time, even though waiting was the one rule of support group you were never supposed to break.

"One time when I was fourteen, this nineteen-year-old guy, Nolan, creeped on me here at Compton," I said. "He kept sending me emails with weird poems about how I was a hermaphroditic goddess. Then he assaulted me in the bathroom here, like I was gonna be into him just because he wrote me weird poems. Don't do stuff with people who only see you as a fetish thing. Be with someone who gets you. You should dump him."

Spruce sat up straight in her chair. She hadn't worked at Compton when the Nolan thing happened. The guy who was volunteering here then got fired for buying a kid alcohol and hadn't told Spruce or Gemma or Natalie anything about what happened before.

"I don't know if it's *that* bad," Venus said.

"Okay," I said. I sucked air in through my teeth.

"Like he hasn't called me a hermaphori—Uh. I'm sorry that happened to you. That happened here?"

"Yep!" I looked at Spruce meaningfully.

Spruce found her voice. "Let's remember to wait till the feedback portion, James. I appreciate you connecting with Venus and wanting to talk, but we have to wait to hear what kind of support she needs."

"Sure," I said, and got up to leave. My teeth were chattering in what was either rage or a full-on freakout dealio. "Love you, Venus, but I'm gonna step out."

I went to the bathroom for a minute. Sitting on the toilet, I remembered when Nolan had pushed me into a stall in the same bathroom. It was weird, because he genuinely hadn't realized I wasn't into it. That was the worst part. He just wanted to make out with another gay kid, and he thought I was down. If he'd known he was making me feel fucked up, it would have been okay, I could just feel angry, but instead, when I told him to stop, it took a couple times before he seemed to even register I meant it. Then he awkwardly asked if I was okay and apologized, and I told him to go, and he went. I could remember the feeling of his hand on me, inside my pants, digging into my underwear. I wasn't sure if I could call what happened sexual assault, exactly. I'd let him flirt with me and shrugged and hadn't told him no when he asked if he could follow me into the bathroom at the dance. But I hadn't liked it. I wanted it to be his fault, especially now that he'd moved with his army dad somewhere else and my life had gotten so much better.

I took a selfie in the bathroom and posted it to Instagram. I captioned it *support group (death emoji).*

On the way out, I saw Gemma, who looked nervous.

"I heard you shared some heavy stuff in group after Venus's share," she said. "Are you . . . doing okay?" Her eyes went to my legs, like she had X-ray vision and could see my old scars under my jeans.

Goth kid sad! Red alert!

"Yep," I said to her. "Any news about the grant stuff? For next year's programs? Did we get feedback on if we're in the running yet?"

"Not yet," she said with a tight-lipped smile. "But we loved that workshop you and Opal planned for the girls' art camp back in August. We want to do it again soon."

"Totally," I said. "If we don't go belly-up in the meantime, yeah?"

Gemma stared at me with a mixture of confusion and nervousness, opened her mouth, and then closed it again. I raised an eyebrow at her and turned to the door.

I wondered what would take Compton's space when it closed down after the money ran out. My bet was on a weird olive oil store.

I'd miss it.

Chapter 5

IAN

So, skip to Saturday afternoon.

Like maybe 1 p.m., but anyone's guess. We were in Ken's dad's basement. I was wearing my show outfit, which is fishnet arm wraps, a lot of glitter, and Goober's leather miniskirt that she'd worn to Pride in June. It made me feel like Lene Lovich. My wrists were covered in bangles, and I'd drawn Xs on the back of my hands—which is what you do to show people you're straight edge at shows. I'd texted Tristan a pic of my outfit.

You look like a cross-dressing stripper lol, Tristan said. He had missed the concept, which was Gerardo Velasquez on Nervous Gender's debut night. I knew he didn't mean cross-dressing strippers were *bad*, but it was annoying.

"Ken," I said. "This shit isn't working. I don't want to play this song." I turned down the amp.

"Dude, this is our set."

"You said you were gonna play the Dorothy. We did it last week. We talked about it. Please? It's practically the same as 'Fuck You Dad.' And you can still do your thing with the drumroll bang screamy thing."

Ken looked at me with the thousand-yard-stare that I knew meant he had shut off his ears. "It's almost time to load up the truck," he said.

"I want to hear the new song," James said. I tried to focus on James's face. He had his phone up to record me. "Just Ian. You guys can stop and take a break, I just wanna hear it."

Devon shrugged and sat down; Ken rolled his eyes and said he was taking a bathroom break.

"Thanks, James," I said.

I'd been working on the songs for ages, and playing them alone in my room with my amp low, whisper-screaming the lyrics.

Looking at James, I knew that I could play them louder.

James was who I was playing for. People like me and James, who thought it was cool to be weird and screamy and glittery and kind of neurotic and feral and gay.

I let my fingers riff over the first couple chords of "Scum Dorothy," and watched him smile. He grinned like he was at a show and shook his head, and I played the chords again and launched into the lyrics, and Ken and Devon weren't there.

When you scream-play music, you aren't screaming at a person. It's at everything. You feel it deep in your gut and bend over and yell and shake your head and open your mouth, and you shriek. It's like the yell someone makes when they're dying. I'm yelling at all the shitty things in the world, the things that make Tristan the way he is. I'm yelling that I want to understand, and yelling because I don't understand, like a baby. It's a shout for things to feel healed, and a scream because they aren't. That's what music is about to me. My hair stands up on my arms when I do it, and it's the moment when I feel most okay.

James makes me feel like it's great to shriek.

The sun was still on the edge of the horizon when we got to Goat Mansion, but people were already there, milling around. That's how you know Goat Mansion's the best venue—everywhere else, people turn up late. I parked the car two streets away.

"I'm gonna go get some Four Lokos," Ken said, before we'd even unloaded the trunk.

"No you're not," I said, but he was already walking down the block. Devon was following him.

"Just 'cause you're edge doesn't mean we all have to be, Ian."

"Don't call me when you fucking end up dead in a ditch. Is anyone gonna help me with the equipment?" I called after them.

"I can help," James said.

"I'm gonna try to find someone else to lift the heavy stuff," I said. "No offense, but you're tiny."

"Fuck you, Ian, I'm barely smaller than you. You're 5'6" talking like you're a giant."

"I'm the butch here."

I saw the gaggle of people from half a block away. They were sitting on the sidewalk and gathered in a little circle near the fence that divides Goat Mansion space from the edge of the public lands by the train tracks. The teenage goth kids were fraternizing with some crust punks. One of the teenage goth kids had a thing of cheap boxed red wine but had taken the wine bag out of the box and was passing it around to her friends, having everyone chug, shouting "BLOOD BLOOD BLOOD." One of the girls with her let the wine overflow her mouth and run down to soak into her black mesh shirt. I made my way around the house to the back. I knew people would be starting a bonfire.

Bonfires in late summer are hard, because lately there's been a burn ban for longer and longer into the autumn. But Goat Mansion has a rock pit that's pretty big. When I got there, Acorn was piling the logs up and working with a piece of flint to spark it.

"Hey," I said to Acorn. "Seen anyone I know yet?"

Acorn turned. "Oh, hey, Ian," xie said. Xie nodded hir head towards the sliding doors at the back of the house. "You're here way early."

I told hir what was going on.

"Who's buying Ken Four Lokos?" Acorn asked.

"He has a fake. He's so dumb and I hate him." I sat down next to Acorn for a second. I took a deep breath in and a deep breath out, hoping I would calm down. I didn't. I felt my heart speeding up. I turned to Acorn. "Hey, is it okay if I like, cry?"

Acorn looked at me with big soft eyes that said *oh jeez louise*, and put an arm around me. "Oh man. It's going down, huh."

I felt a sob come up in my throat. I put my hand on my forehead. I stood up. "Main thing is, gotta get my gear set up so my stupid drunk bandmates can play this set in front of musicians that are actually good."

Acorn brushed off hir skirt. "Absolutely, baby."

James and Acorn and I pulled the stuff into the back of

the garage where the bands would play, got stuff together as much as we could. After my shit was all there, I didn't really know what else to do. I tuned my guitar a little. James went out into the house, to give me space.

Tristan texted, *hey what's up? I think i'm gonna be late to the show.*

The kids from Quince Quest came in and set up their stuff. They were goth kids from Shelton, and they looked like James, which made me feel safe. Their singer was named Shiori and was one of the kids who had been yelling "BLOOD." Their bassist was named Sophie, a bald, raspy-voiced Asian girl with fishnets and big boots and no hair. She asked me about myself, and I tried to answer without giving too much away: my life is falling apart, my bandmates are straight and getting wasted. She nodded solemnly. I was redrawing the Xs on my hands with Sharpie. I hoped she wouldn't think that was uncool.

I texted Tristan, *how late is late?*

Ken and Devon weren't coming back. I started asking around. Did anyone want to back me up on guitar and drums if they didn't return in time for the set? Sophie asked to see the music for the songs, and I had them in a folder, because I was a band kid. I showed her the new songs, the ones that Devon and Ken didn't want to play. Sophie was like, yeah, I'll do guitar.

We played through one of the new songs together, half-volume because the show wasn't starting yet for another hour or more. A few people poked their heads into the garage. It didn't sound super great, but it was okay. I thought, okay. Okay. It's going to be okay.

"I owe you my life and diner food and gas," I said. I knew I cut a pretty stupid profile, this kid with a band but no band. But Shiori and Sophie acted like it was chill.

Tristan called me.

"Hey," he said. "I got asked to go to this kickback tonight at Gareth's house, and he said he'd pick me up, and so I think I'm gonna go for like, just an hour."

I felt mainly relief. But I realized I also had anger I'd never let go of.

"Why are you telling me?" I asked.

Silence for a second. "I . . . I don't know, I thought you wanted me to come to your show."

"Clearly you have better things to do."

"Ian," Tristan said. "It's just a party. It'll be quick. I wanna get weed from this guy."

"Well, you should go get your weed, then," I said. "I'm dumping you."

"I need you to not be so dramatic. Weed is fucking legal."

"Not the point. Name a time you have hung out with me since the gorge. Not just fucked and then ran home, actually hung out. This is the whole *thing*, Tristan." Surely he could see that it was the whole thing.

"This is so fucking stupid." I could tell he was trying to think of an example of a time we'd hung out. He couldn't.

"Stupid, or gay, Tristan? Is it so fucking gay?"

"Shut up. It's fucking *stupid*. I'm trying." Now he was choking up.

I tried to make my voice level. "I want to be with someone who wants to be seen with me. That's all."

I hung up. I felt tears sting my eyes. I pictured that

Britney photo with the shirt that says *dump him,* and tried to imagine embodying that vibe. I didn't care about Tristan. But I heard the whiny tone in my own voice. *Stupid, or gay?*

Everything was so dumb. I felt sick. He probably was trying. It was just that it didn't work for me, even when he tried, and I didn't understand *why.* We wanted to have sex. Why couldn't we make it work?

James appeared. He was trying to make the drunk goths drink water from a pitcher he'd filled inside. I made eye contact with him and turned away, because I didn't want to talk. But you can't avoid your friends at your own show.

The sun was going down, and more people were arriving. Everyone expected the show to start one to three hours after the posted start time, but everyone turned up at the time on the posters anyway to smoke or catch up with people or drop their backpacks and walk eighteen blocks away to the store to buy beer. The sun slanted through the windows like liquid gold. Someone put a VHS of *Fire Walk with Me* on in the living room, where it already smelled like cigarettes.

A car pulled in by the garage. I saw the person get out on the other side of the car and realized that it was Jukebox January. I sat in the corner as they started to get their equipment out. I was going to look like such an idiot in a second.

Chapter 6

ORSINO

I thought about the feeling I'd gotten looking at the dark-haired trans goth kid at David's Diner down in Olympia this week, the thrill that had gone through me when he made eye contact. I wondered if I'd ever see him again. Maybe he'd be at the show tonight. The thought gave me a fun flutter in my chest.

I thought about what Jukebox had said, about the horrible visions of death or fire not being real, exactly, of them not being the real future.

Their friend Phyllidra died of a fentanyl OD. Three or four people they knew had died in this big fire down in the Bay called Ghost Ship. I wasn't sure what they thought about my dreams, or what they understood about what had happened at my dad's house.

The stuff about Agatha, about me *being* her—I didn't know what they thought of that.

Sometimes they act like I'm their little brother, or their son. They're the first real trans person I ever met offline. They told me about how they'd gotten insurance to cover their top surgery and offered to help me figure it out when I turn eighteen. Which is pretty nice of them. My mom thinks they're a loser, because they've been sitting around not writing their new album for three months.

On the drive down, we stopped at the same Dutch Bros Jukebox always hits between Tacoma and Olympia, just north of the bird sanctuary. They ordered for us and tossed the chocolate chip muffin tops over to us.

We pulled in to the driveway of Jukebox's house on the north side of downtown. I could see their roommate/bandmate Stacey Pham smoking on the porch.

I think Stacey's cool, too, though she isn't trans so doesn't get the ways I'm weird. She calls me *alien boy* a lot, which reminds me of the church kids down in Tenino and how they'd talk about me. She *looks* like a weird Oly punk—but she hasn't lived in Olympia all her life. She moved here from the Bay, and complains a lot about how white Olympia is, which is fair, especially since May, the other Asian girl in OVID, left for Los Angeles. Stacey's Vietnamese. She has kind of a cautious scowl on all the time but also has two premature laugh lines around her mouth. Sometimes Jukebox makes her laugh like crazy and sometimes she freaks the fuck out at them. She plucks her eyebrows real thin and keeps a line of piercings on the right one where the hair should be. She's got short hair with a rat tail down her back.

"Hey, Jukebox!" she shouted. "Come on in, I'm making vegan pizza."

We went into the bright orange living room. Stacey's cats used to be her ex's cats, but when her ex left for Vancouver the ex abandoned them like some kind of psychopath, and now they live here. Stacey loves the cats but isn't really great at picking up after them. The whole room is covered in cat hair and there's cat toys and scratches all over.

I ate three slices of pizza in the orange cat hair room while Stacey and Jukebox talked about how streaming services were ripping them off and destroying the music industry. They'd had like, 300,000 plays on some service in the last year, and they'd only made like $100. I hadn't really eaten anything today, so I just kept going back for more pizza. I didn't talk much. Stacey and Jukebox went over the set list for the show and talked about someone they both hated named Chris who they thought might be there, and whether Chris might want to play with OVID. Robin lay at Jukebox's feet scrolling Insta on her phone. I went in for a fourth slice and Stacey turned around to stare at me.

"You really are just a regular grimy pizza punk boy, Orsino," Stacey said to me, in a way that was clearly her trying to be friendly. "You'd fit right in with all the Evergreen mascs at Le Perv. We gotta find you a little punk girlfriend."

"I'm *gay*," I said through a mouthful of pizza. "So that won't work. Find me a boyfriend."

"Oh, yikes," Stacey said, and rolled her eyes in a way I didn't understand.

"Yikes that I'm gay?"

"It just sucks for you. Boys are bad. You don't want any of the Evergreen mascs, Orsino. They're all total cunts." She looked over to Jukebox. "You know that guy Titus? Or

Lorenzo. God. Both of them just talk over me SO much. They think they're immune from misogyny because they're trans."

Jukebox was eating pizza too. "I think Lorenzo's okay."

"Well, *you* would."

"What does that mean?" Robin asked, in an irritated tone.

"He does like, cocaine."

"Hey, I stopped doing cocaine," Jukebox said.

"It's just obnoxious. I hate that guy. And I feel like every queer guy around here is just like—vibes are off."

At Goat Mansion, it looked like there was already a party—I could see some people I thought I recognized from shows in Tacoma. The sky was a ragged blue that shredded its way through the clouds sometimes.

After I finished unloading the car, Jukebox left me on my own. I went over to a corner to sit and watch someone with a beard in a skirt building a bonfire.

Then, across the yard, I saw the boy from King David's. He was also standing on his own, holding a water pitcher, looking confused. He looked good. He had beautiful round calves, and a line of his stomach showed between his pants and his shirt. His big brown eyes were buried in a heap of eyeliner and purple eyeshadow. I saw him look in my direction and then look away.

I had a little shock in my lower back, where I had fallen earlier.

I went over to him, almost tripping over my feet on the uneven ground. "Hey," I said. "I'm Orsino." I paused, not sure what came next. "You want a cigarette?"

He looked surprised, then happy. My knees got weak. "Cigarettes are bad for you," he said, as he took one and put it in his mouth. Between his lips.

I lit it.

"I've heard that," I said. "You don't have to smoke it if you don't want to. I just wanted to say hi." I felt like I had exhausted the list of things I knew how to say.

"I'm James," he said. "You're here with OVID, right?"

"My sister's dating Jukebox, yeah." I looked around, then saw Robin over by the house. "She's over there. I don't play any instruments or anything."

"Cool," he said. "Me neither. My friend Ian's in this band Rocketpizza that maybe just broke up. I don't know. You know anyone else here?"

"Not really. Stacey's in Jukebox's band, I know her. Maybe this guy from Le Perv."

James turned and looked behind me. "Oh, here's my friend Opal."

"GOTH BRETHREN!"

The person shouting and waving at James had orange hair and a bright green crop top. Their wheelchair rolled fast across the mangled grass. I felt upset but also relieved not to be alone with James.

"Hey, Opal."

"I'm Opal. I use they/them," Opal said, putting their hand in mine. "What's with the tail?"

"Hey, just so you know, Ian is gonna do the show alone with a replacement drummer," James said to Opal, before I could respond.

"What? Who?" Opal's face twisted.

55

"Some kid from the other band. Quince Quest."

"The fuck he is. I'm gonna drum for him. I have to join his band," Opal said.

"Not tonight. He's stressed. Swimmer boy troubles. Drummer troubles. He'll snap at you."

"I know his songs, dude," Opal said. "Even the new ones. A little. I can do it better than a Quince kid. I've been practicing on the drums at Barb's." Opal turned away from us and started wheeling away across the gravel.

"They seem cool," I said to James.

"It's *such* chaotic energy for them to do this now," James said.

We walked over to the house. We stood with our half-burned cigarettes.

"So are you from around here?" James asked me. "Or where?"

"Down south about an hour," I said. "Near Centralia, kind of. But most of the time lately I live up in Tacoma with Robin and Jukebox. You?"

"I'm from here," James said. "I'm in high school."

"Me too. Just online. You go to that Compton House thing?" I asked. "My old therapist was trying to get me to go. I'm trans too," I added. I winced as I said it, but it was the only way James would understand, in case he didn't know.

"Oh, do I *go*," James said, with a tone that made clear he didn't love it. "So hey. What kind of music do you like?"

I was relieved he had another topic. "OVID's good. And I like Dyke Drama and G.L.O.S.S., obviously. And Loone.

And Ragana. And Blood Kennel and Limp Wrist and Dick Binge. And the Pixies. You?"

"I like girl pop country. Dolly Parton. And Marina Diamandis. And goth bands." He smiled.

Word spread slowly through the mass of people that the show was starting. The sun had gone down and I had three mosquito bites. James and I went in the show space together, tripping over the bricks at the door.

The room was dark and ugly and packed. There were lights on the stage and then a tangle of wires near the stage that Jukebox was trying to get some fire safety expert to evaluate at some point after the Ghost Ship fire, but I don't think it ever happened. There were a lot of random piles of shit near the door. The lights that shined down on the tiny little stage were beautiful. I was pressed close to James, and I felt like even when he was inches away from me, I could feel the outline of his whole body against mine.

Ian was a fat pretty gay boy who looked like a girl, with curly brown hair and a way of walking that was like swishing. He was wearing fishnet arm wraps, a lot of glitter, and a leather miniskirt. He looked stressed. His wrists were covered in spiky bangles, and he wore a bandeau top across his chest. His curly dark brown hair was sort of flopping over his face. He was fumbling with a lot of wires onstage. Opal was behind the drums. Behind them was a bald Asian kid on guitar, her leather bracelets clasped around her forearms like armor.

"I haven't actually heard Opal play much before, since they only started on a real drum set after they moved to

Barb's house," James said, screaming close to my ear. I felt a tingle go down my spine when his breath hit my skin. I felt like I could taste him in my mouth.

"ROCKETPIZZA!!!!!" An older woman at the front of the crowd yelled. Some of the goths yelled too. There were suddenly a lot of people around me, and I was worried about my feet getting stepped on by the dudes with the steel toed boots. At least I had my work boots on.

Ian looked into the crowd, squinting. He dropped some wires and stepped up to the mic.

"HEY BITCHES AND BABES AND FAGGOTS," he yelled into the crowd. There was a mix of cheers and uncomfortable muttering. "HOW ARE YOU DOING?"

The two older punks in the front both bellowed at the stage, incoherent jumbled exuberance.

"I'LL TELL YOU HOW I'M DOING," Ian yelled into the mic, which twanged painfully over the speakers. "MY BOYFRIEND AND I JUST BROKE UP AND I SENT MY DRUNK STRAIGHT BANDMATES HOME."

There were some confused boos and apologetic noises. Ian yanked a necklace from his neck and stomped it into the stage.

"BUT THAT IS OKAY," Ian continued. "I LOOK GREAT. OPAL LOOKS GREAT. GIVE IT UP FOR *OPAL*. GIVE IT UP ALSO FOR *SOPHIE* FROM QUINCE QUEST."

James yelled at the top of his lungs, like he was saying a kind of weird ecstatic prayer. The guy with a beard next to me moved away from us in surprise.

"WE ARE A NEW GROUP NOW. OUR NAME IS

MONIQUE FATIGUE AND THE DUSTIES. IT IS A
REFERENCE TO A LESBIAN WRITER WHO WROTE
ABOUT EATING PEOPLE."

Ian was good at riling up a crowd. People were getting
more interested.

"ALSO YOU WILL PROBABLY WITNESS THE
DEATH OF MY VOCAL CHORDS BECAUSE I AM
ABOUT TO SCREAM MY GUTS OUT." Ian shook his
head and smiled.

The drunk baby goths went wild. James whistled through his teeth.

People had been punching and pushing into each other. I got slammed against the wall twice and kept getting shoved into someone's armpit. The electricity came up through my chest, and my eyes went to the ceiling, where the ship was coming down toward us.

You see us. It's time.

The worms' transparent skin exposed their insides. Just over my head, like with the dead frog in the morning. I sank, and watched the shapes of people around me turn into ghosts. Something was unspooling.

Speak to us.

The house went to pieces around me. It became wooden beams and then foundations and then sank apart. Beneath my feet I felt the ancient roots of trees that had been here before the house. I felt Agatha's fur under my hands, then covering my hands, the seat of the truck at my back, even as I was pressed against other bodies—the truck coming toward me, accelerating. I smelled my own BO swelling up toward the ceiling and the heat from us all supercharging the air. I saw a star blasting through the dark of space, hundreds of thousands of bodies moving fast through water.

Gravity now pulled me upwards. I felt like I had already floated away, but when the song ended, the wave broke, and the heat of other people came back. The house sank down around me like it had always been this moment, and never any other.

Ian's glitter was dripping down his chest in waves. My own shirt was soaking with sweat. The crush of bodies and noise and smells had shorted out every sense. I felt shaken. I hung onto James's shoulder to keep track of him, hoping it was okay for me to touch him. We tripped out into the night. The cool night air with the smell of decay and everything hit my skin and my mouth all at the same time.

"I felt . . . Did you *feel* something in there?" James asked me, when we were breathing the cold air. "It was like something was speaking. There were these like . . . creatures."

Had he felt it? He was smiling at me. My spine was a column of flame.

"Yeah," I said. "Actually. Yeah."

"That was incredible." I turned. Jukebox's shirt was torn so people could see one of their nipples through the fabric. I knew they'd done that on purpose.

"Yeah," James said. "It got so hot in here so fast."

"*That set!*" Jukebox exclaimed. "Like, that was phenomenal! So good and raw but also like, they're real! We gotta get this kid a record deal so fast if they want to sell out! They're your friend, right?"

James grinned wider. "Yeah," he said.

"What's going on with the band?" Jukebox asked. Their teeth were all showing in their smile. "Some shuffling stuff? Do you think the current situation will hold together? They literally sounded so so good."

"I literally don't even know," James said. "But he loves you, he loves OVID. Like he and his boyfriend followed you to the Gorge this summer and then down to the Bay when you were on tour. You should talk to him."

I felt deeply proud to be with Jukebox, to be Jukebox's little brother.

Jukebox went back inside to set up for their set. Overhead the trees dropped a few leaves and some of the needles from the scrubby little pine by the house blew over the yard and into the bonfire, sparking. There were at least fifty people at the show. Probably more, inside the house and around in front where they weren't meant to be. We pushed against everyone else as we elbowed our way inside again, because there was nothing to do but go back in. It smelled like sweat. Onstage, Jukebox's muscles bulged and a cord wrapped around their leg, twisting like a snake into their hand. Their voice cut me, broke me down. I felt it happening again: something above me. The lyrics weren't super clear, but I knew them:

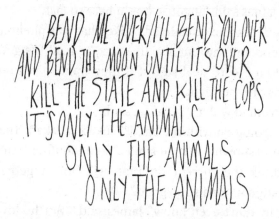

BEND ME OVER/I'LL BEND YOU OVER
AND BEND THE MOON UNTIL IT'S OVER
KILL THE STATE AND KILL THE COPS
IT'S ONLY THE ANIMALS
ONLY THE ANIMALS
ONLY THE ANIMALS

The drums pounded louder, and the screech of the amps hit the walls and made us all rattle. Their voice yanked at something inside me, and I realized that this moment, standing here looking up at their frightening face in its dark makeup, was one of the visions I'd been given before, sometime long ago. I was meant to come here. This was meant to happen.

I saw James dancing, the light on his body red. It was like a shot to the heart.

The ship was coming back again.

Orsino.

What, I said, into the air.

A flash, and I suddenly see every animal that has ever lived on Earth, having sex. It is involuntary—it slides into my brain like something being shoved down my throat, or like my stomach turning.

Zap.

A worm, with undulating loops, floats through the spaceship toward me.

I am Fe 3. I am a Mredi being from the planet you may know as Kepler 186f. Our planet is six hundred light years away.

I stare at it, because they've never been this close.

I am scared. I am annoyed.

We are from one thousand three hundred years in the future. It is a dire future. There is still empire and death. Your people are dead. All humans. All dogs. We need you to bend time, to change the course. You can speak to the past and the future.

Why me? I ask.

Bending time is dangerous. There is an army that wishes to stop us. But the army will not look for you.

I don't think I can help you, I say.

If you change the future to save your planet, you save ours. The future where you avert mass extinction is one where your peoples live to talk to us. Your descendants will help us avoid our own catastrophe.

How do you know that? I ask.

You have the power to see and touch past and future.

I shake my head. Zap.

I was back among the warm bodies.

I wanted to fuck James, I thought, looking over at him.

How did people like him *exist*, who moved in this world so easily even though they were my age? Other trans people *saw* him, and he didn't even freak out about it.

I looked at his arms moving above his head, his eyes closed in the red light. I wanted to pin him down and kiss him and eat something out of him—

We understand desire.

The ship wouldn't go away. A quick flash of heat came through the people around me. I reeled. I heard echoes of music besides the music that was playing, echoes of all the music anyone had ever played in this venue or anywhere in this place. The tremble of earthquakes. I tasted salt and iron in the back of my throat.

We desire your solidarity. We want you to live to care for us.

Jukebox let out a primordial wail. If I had any glass on me, it would have broken. I looked at the sweat streaming down below their scars over their stomach.

A shower of sparks sailed across the audience.

I watched as a tangle of wires sparked and caught on fire.

The mics and audio equipment cut out, and so did the lights. There was a second of absolute silence, and the darkness made all our eyes struggle to readjust. In the dark, for a second, I saw a white light that was a portal to the ship.

We all took a breath in, feeling the opening to that other world, feeling the wind.

The fire spread across the ceiling.

"FIRE!" someone yelled.

Death can come in an instant. You only have to wait and do nothing.

Zap.

Suddenly, me and Jukebox are floating in a dark void.

We dreamed of finding another people, the only other civilization. But you were gone. Your planet had burned. We sought you in the past, with our own psychics. We traveled through time to you because we are opposed to destruction. But our own people wish to kill us.

Jukebox is screaming.

Beings with psychic attunement, between times and species, are loci we can pin our course around. Each time we travel, ripples shake the fabric of time. It is causing parts of your timeline to fracture. You saw the ice.

I nod.

Your planet is experiencing a mass extinction event over the next six hundred years which will destroy all human civilization and kill almost all human and canine life. Your planet tends toward timelines of mass extinction. But there are other timelines.

I fall into a black opening, my eyes burning with a force that feels like a building is falling on top of us.

Here—

I see the past and the present and see the spin and the arc of waves and galaxies. There are beings I don't recognize. I see the rise of the dinosaurs and the comet that hits the earth and makes a huge hole in it. I see birds, lizards, bugs. Great fish and small fish open their gills against cold water. A boat lands; boots dig into the ground. A child screams. I feel my neck stretch, pulled away from my body through a dark abyss with no light. Through a door shaped like an eye there is another stream of blue-black light, spinning away from us. It looks like a long snake. Through this narrow door, there are rivers brimming with red and green salmon, leaping almost onto the banks. Sun spills down onto forests. Plants grow through the cities. The dog's cracked paws don't hit the ground.

It washes over me, too big and frightening to name. Each strand teeters like a needle balancing on its end, thrusting through my body. It feels cold.

Jukebox is there too. I am screaming, and they are screaming. We sound the same. Our screams bleed into each other's. They look at me, and they are crying.

We have only a narrow window to speak to you.

I watch the purple translucent-skinned figure coiling on a rose-colored floor in front of us, slick, its clear skin creased with thin lines. Jukebox is gasping, breathing hard.

Why are you talking to us? I think. My throat is closed up. *Why us?*

Static.

Zap.

I landed back in my body with a jolt. I was outside, standing next to Robin. I was leaning on her. I could smell smoke. I turned around—

The shed we had all been in was on fire.

I had no memory of leaving.

"We have to find Jukebox," Robin said. "I have to see if they're hurt."

My heart beat fast and hard.

Chapter 7

JAMES

We woke up because Ian's mom was calling him.

"Mom?" Ian said into the phone. His mouth was practically in my hair. "Yeah, I'm fine. I texted you. I'm at James's house. I *said* I would be. *Mom.*"

Ian's arm was wrapped around my chest. All of us had fallen asleep on my floor basically the minute we lay down under my purple quilt. I'd had a dream we were all burning alive on a comet shooting toward the sun.

"Yes, Mom, I'm alive, I texted you!" Ian said. "What? Missing? No, that can't be right."

I rolled over and looked at him. *What's up?* I mouthed.

"T—no, that's . . . not where the show was," Ian said. "Not my show. We were . . . at Red House. It changed two days ago because a bigger band was opening for OVID."

Pause. Luisa's voice on the line. Not explosively angry— measured. Which was worse.

"I'm telling you, we weren't at Goat Mansion! We drove by there *early* to say hi to people, but we played Red House!"

I mouthed to Ian to stop talking before he said even more shit, but he wasn't listening.

He bit his lip and shut his eyes. "Yes," he said. "I understand. Mom, I had a huge fight with Devon and Ken."

I tried to hear what was on the other end of the line.

"Mom, I broke up with Tristan, and broke up with my band. I'm really—I'm really upset. Please don't do this. I *need* to be able to play shows. It's my *life*." Pause. "Yes, I'll be home soon," Ian said. "Okay. Yes. I'm sorry for not calling."

If he told his mom he'd broken up with Tristan, they must have really broken up.

Ian ended the call, then tapped furiously at his phone. I saw him pull up the post about the show on his Instagram and delete it. Erasing evidence. But there was a good chance Luisa would have pulled the post up on her computer before she even called him.

"No shows?" I asked.

"She says she is never letting me out of the house to go to a punk show again," Ian said. "I told her we weren't at Goat Mansion."

"Despite the fact that you were."

"Hence me deleting all my posts," Ian muttered, clicking on another.

I opened my phone. My eyes were still bleary, and my body hurt from the pit at the show. I felt like there was still smoke in my lungs. I opened Facebook to see if any of Ian's posts mentioned the show, or if he was tagged in anything. He was *so* dumb.

Then I saw the story from Stacey's feed.

"Shit," I said aloud.

"What is it?" Ian asked.

"Jukebox is missing."

Opal half-sat up. I hadn't realized they were awake.

"What?" they asked. "No way."

"I don't know," I said. I searched *Goat Mansion Fire Olympia* on my phone.

The local news station had covered the fire, and it was front-page news—not that that meant actual front page of the physical paper, since our local paper was an optional insert in the paper from Tacoma now. Above the story about the fire was a short article about two Evergreen students who were sure that the sky had turned bright violet two mornings ago. They had taken a video, which had now gone viral and was being debunked as a hoax.

The online article had a photo of Goat Mansion's smoking rubble with the headline: *Blaze At Punk Concert Leaves Two Injured, One Missing.*

The article interviewed some kids who had been there. Two drunk teenagers from Tacoma had gotten hurt in the stampede. There weren't any photos, but one of them had a broken nose and a cracked rib, probably from an elbow, and the other kid had a black eye and had gotten an asthma attack from the smoke that had triggered some other chronic health issue. That kid had ended up in the ER and was "in stable condition."

The good news was that the fire department hadn't found any human remains in the burned-out show space. All that was there were the ruined remains of Jukebox's amps and guitars.

So where was Jukebox?

"I mean, clearly they're not *dead*," Ian said. "It's a small space. If their . . . like, body was in there, they would have found it, right?"

"They were on stage," Opal said. "Where would they have gone?"

We looked on Facebook and Instagram. Stacey Pham, who I knew had gotten arrested fighting the Proud Boys and who had called out Blood Kennel for being racist last year, had posted this MISSING PERSONS!!! post about Jukebox. Stacey's theory was that Jukebox may have stumbled away from the fire in the crowd but then passed out somewhere, or been triggered somehow into a mental health episode and left without telling anyone. They had friends that had died in a fire a while ago. Jukebox wasn't at their house, though, according to Stacey. That was bad.

"I'm going to make drop biscuits and veggie scramble," I said, getting up. "I can't deal with this right now."

My mom came into the kitchen as we were working on the second pot of coffee. Ian was afraid to go home. The cat was meowing at the back door, but we were all ignoring him.

"What if she already *saved* pictures of the flyers and the timestamp?" Ian asked. He'd had too much coffee and was starting to buzz.

"I mean, also, dude, people might have taken pics and tagged you," Opal said, unhelpfully.

"You already lied," I said. "Lie again."

My mom breezed past us in her paisley bathrobe and opened the cabinet. She took down her *My Favorite Daughter Gave Me This Coffee Mug* mug that I gave her when I was ten. She says that it can contain about 20 ounces of coffee, and therefore is worth keeping even if it's inaccurate.

"What's all this about lying?" she asked nonchalantly. "What deceit lurks in my house?"

"The show we were at burned down," Opal said. "We're all fine, don't worry."

If my mom was another mom, she'd care about something like this. She might even freak out.

"Well, thank god you got out, huh," my mom said. "That kind of stuff can get really bad. One time there was a stampede at a show I went to down in LA when a fuse blew. Christy broke her arm falling off the landing. Some other kid died. At least here everything's one story, huh." She paused. "You guys wore earplugs, right? You're gonna kill your hearing otherwise."

"Yeah, we did," I lied. "And yeah, we're all fine. Ian's mom flipped out though."

"Poor Ian," my mom said, scowling as she added soy to her coffee. She doesn't approve of Luisa's parenting style—the kind where a parent has to know where their kid is all the time. When my mom was seventeen, Grandma Rachel caught Mom smoking reefer and threatened to put bars on her windows. Mom responded by hitchhiking to California and not contacting Grandma Rachel until I was born ten years later. My mom found out I smoked sophomore year when I left a baggie in my backpack; she just asked me how much I'd paid for the bag.

"It's *completely* unreasonable," I said. "Now she says he can't play shows."

"Why wouldn't she let you play shows?" my mom said. "Surely she can't imagine *everywhere* you play will burn down."

"To be fair, punks are not great with fire safety codes," Opal said. "Or accessibility. Last night some dick almost stepped on me while I was trying to get my wheels over the door ledge thing. Had to almost bite someone's leg."

My mother sat down at the table. "Oh honey," she said to Opal. "That sounds terrifying." She turned to me. "Where were *you*? I thought you all stuck together at shows."

I looked guiltily at Opal. "I *should* have been there," I said. "I was chasing some boy."

Where was Orsino, if Jukebox was missing? They'd all come down to the show together.

"I'm fine," Opal said, looking down at the table. "Barb pushed me from behind and we got onto the grass. Just a reminder to carry a fire extinguisher and a taser at all times when Ian and I do shows."

"Okay, do you have a plan for shows? Because we need a plan," Ian said. "She said *no* shows from now on. Even though I said we weren't there."

"You're a good boy, Ian." My mom went to the drawer where she keeps her tobacco and papers and started to roll a cigarette on the table. "But unfortunately, you are a *bad* liar. Your mother absolutely knows where you were." She laughed. "I wouldn't do what she did, but I'm not your mother."

We sat on the couch after breakfast, watching old *Star Trek* episodes. I got out my nail polish and started painting my nails, and then Ian's. Black for me, purple for him.

"I think I'm gonna make prints at the print shop behind Garbage Barge this Thursday," Ian said. "For when I can do shows again. This *has* to blow over. She can't really mean it."

"Printing. Print. Homework," Opal said, suddenly, sitting up straight. "What happens in *Mrs. Dalloway*? I forgot to finish it for my essay."

"Septimus kills himself," I said. "He's the character that I think is gay."

"I buy that." Opal started typing in the notes app on their phone.

"I haven't even started my reading. I haven't even read a book not about music since last year," Ian said.

"Cheer up," I said, lying down next to him, my polished nails held up a little so they didn't smudge. "Did I tell you I made you a playlist? It's songs that remind me of you."

Would he even get it? A lot of the songs *were* romantic. They were what I listened to to process the corny feelings I had that I was too chicken to tell him about. I'd had that playlist for months.

Ian smiled a little and rolled his head against my neck. "That's so nice, James. Is it Marina Diamandis's entire discography?"

"Shut the fuck up."

"Is it?"

"There's *one* Marina Diamandis song."

"Roasted," Opal said from the floor. I could see from their phone screen that they were messaging Jukebox.

"Send it to me," Ian said. He rolled to a sitting position. "James, can I shower and borrow like, a shirt to go home? I'm still all grimy and it's making me feel like a poo slug."

"Let your fingernails dry first," I said. "But yeah." I thought about Ian taking a shower, using my shampoo, soaping his chest and his pits with my oatmeal soap. I wanted to smell his hair. "I think you smell good even when you're grimy, just so you know."

"James, stop being horny," Opal said. "Boy *just* dumped his swamp monster."

"Thanks, James," Ian said. That was all he said. He went to my bedroom.

When I heard the shower start I turned to Opal, who was still looking at their phone. "What the fuck, dude? Don't rat me out like that."

"What, so you can send him fifty more playlists of songs he doesn't like and never say anything?"

"Ugh. You suck," I said. "It's not even like that. Not really."

"Is it a *queerplatonic relationship*?" Opal looked up and waggled their eyebrows.

"No."

"No. You and I know what's going on. You can cut it with a knife, dude. Just say something *direct* to him, and then he can reject you or say he likes you back and we can all get on with our lives." They held up their phone to me. "Now, tell me if Goober likes me."

I squinted at the text from Goober. *Hey little rock, you killed it on drums!* the message said. It was followed by a green heart emoji and a sparkle emoji.

"I mean, she definitely like, *likes* you," I said. "This doesn't give me active flirt vibes. The heart's green."

"I know," Opal said. "Also, I like that she calls me little rock, but here it seems like oochie-coo little baby. *Hate* that." They ran their hand through their hair. "Does everyone just see me as a little cute *munchkin*?"

"Absolutely not," I said. "You're cool and intimidating. It's the opposite problem. Everyone's like, shit, *I* wasn't that cool when I was seventeen."

"What if Goober doesn't like my kind of boi girl gender thing?" Opal asked. "What if she only dates like, high femmes?"

"I know she has a lotta crushes on older women who wear denim, if that's a comfort."

"No! I want her to like *young* people."

I looked at my own phone. I sent the link to the playlist to Ian, after hovering with my finger on the send button too long.

When he came out of my room, my heart fluttered. We're not *quite* the same size, but I wear lots of things a size too big. My Ragana shirt hugged his chest. He looked perfect. "Okay," he said. "Wish me luck with my mom." And then he was gone, to his car and down the rhododendron-lined street.

Opal was right—if I wanted him to know I liked him, I should tell him. But I wasn't sure if I wanted to make it dramatic like that. What if he said no? There was too much going on for him. It wasn't the right time for his friend to come on strong like a load of bricks. And it wasn't like I had a ton to offer him, or his band, beyond what he had already. It would just be me, asking for him to give me something more than he already gave me. Who knew if he wanted to give it?

I thought about Orsino, about the easy way he'd lit a cigarette for me. It had stopped me up short. There I was chasing after Ian as Ian chased after the art he wanted to make and the boys he wanted to be with, and here was someone interested in me, who wanted to do stuff for me on the strength of seeing me once. He was available. He was big and strong and not dating a straight boy, or in an endless cycle of breakups with one, or whatever was happening now. He was mysterious and cool. I liked his legs.

As I heard the cat start scratching at the door again, my phone pinged with a new email notification.

It was from the new principal. Principal Coleman. Weird.

"I just got an email from the school," I said aloud. Opal didn't respond.

Dear James Goldberg, the letter began.

We have received complaints from male students who allege that you have made inappropriate comments toward them while they shared the restroom with you. Noah Daly alleges that you hit him with a door and made a sexual comment to him on our first day of classes this Wednesday. While we have made accommodations for your sex transition and recognize your legal right to use the bathroom associated with your "gender identity." . . .

Evil Noah. The bastard. I forwarded the email to my mom. *This is bullshit*, I said.

Grading environmental science papers rn, my mom texted back. *Will look in a second. Meanwhile—text your dad about Rosh Hashanah, he's bugging me.*

I looked and saw that my dad had in fact texted me. Fancy that. It was the time and day for dinner with him and Kaylin before Rosh Hashanah, and the service times for Yom Kippur next week. Ugh.

I don't really want to go to services this year, I wrote. *I've decided that it's important to me to mark my ambivalence toward God.*

The way we do that is go to shul, my dad wrote. Which is what I would have said to someone else, which made me hate him more. So I did what I usually did: complained to Opal about it.

"He's never done an ounce of reflection since I turned thirteen. Let alone apologized for any of the shit he did where he talked to me about how it was illogical that I was transitioning and going to make my life harder, or where he said he was going to kick me out if I kept wearing boys' clothes. T'shuvah my ass."

Opal shrugged. "Your dad bought you a car."

"It's not my car, it's his. And he's not the only one. You ever think about Abraham abandoning Hagar and Ishmael and everyone just blaming it on Sarah, when it's like, you chose to have a baby with Hagar, dude, you can't just toss him to the wolves even *if* God says it's okay."

"Girl," Opal said. "Chill. I think Abraham is supposed to be a complicated figure. And he's not the only dad in the Bible or the Torah or whatever." They stretched. "You wanna go pick blackberries at the end of the block? We should make cobbler again."

The blackberries in September are the best—fat and purple inside. Opal sat on the side of the road and held the bucket, and I gathered handfuls of blackberries crouching in the ditch where all the vines were, getting scratched. The sun was hot. We took the berries back and baked some of them into the kind of cobbler where you throw. together the vegan butter and sugar and then kinda toss it on top of this mound of berries like you don't give a shit about anything.

Ian texted me while my hands were still dripping with blackberry. *Hey James! The playlist is rlly cute. Thank u.*

No revelations. My heart sank into my stomach.

I had to make a choice: risk chasing him, or chase something new.

I wondered if that guy Orsino would find my Instagram, or if he'd think to look.

Chapter 8

IAN

It is incredible that you can just block someone's phone number, and he can't ever contact you again. Or, he could, if he wasn't a coward, but he was. Tristan had tried calling me two times after the show, and texted more, first angrily, then increasingly desperately, but then? I hit the block button and I simply never saw his shit. And he didn't reach out on Insta or Snapchat or Twitter or Venmo or anything.

I saw him at school, but it wasn't like he wanted anyone to *see* him talking to me. No sir. The couple of times I saw him, he looked unhappy.

Well, I was too.

I sat with Opal on the floor at Compton House, on top of my jean jacket. I was playing music on my phone—Xylitol's 2017 tour tape. *MIND'S A GROTESQUE PIT.*

The younger tweens were gone, so I could play screamy stuff without anyone complaining.

I don't really understand why a space "for ages 12-24" makes sense to anyone.

"I like the ones where they're like *GOBLINS WEARING*

LIPSTICK, DO THE GOBLIN GALLOP," Opal said. "Put that one on next."

"It's a playlist, it's just going," I said.

James had sent me a playlist.

None of the artists were ones I was usually into—it was mostly James's pop crap, except the Xylitol. But it was also deeply compelling. Especially because I was bitter about never being loved again, and all these songs were all about me.

I'd sat listening to it when I first got it, realizing as each track played that it was saying something to me—almost all the songs were about ambitious girls and dreaming of bigger things.

Girls who want bigger things? *That's* me.

Then there were also six songs about wanting a girl who was with someone else.

Which?

Girls who are with someone else? Who is that?

Uh?

Hello?

I was probably just being horny and lonely.

Back at the eighth grade Halloween dance, the one time I'd kissed him, we hadn't been out yet, exactly. We were out in the way that gay kids who can't pass for straight are out. He *had* been telling people that he wanted to go by JD. He had just cut his hair short and had a dumb tuxedo that his mom had bought for his b'nei mitzvah that he wore to the dance with a wolf mask. I kissed him through his wolf mask during "Hey There Delilah." Mostly rubber, a little bit of skin.

During Japanese, I'd kept my earbud in one ear and listened to a whole ass Indigo Girls album. Their voices—I'd told James I didn't like country folksy music, that I was a punk. They sounded like aunts moralizing at you. *But.* I had to admit that everything they sang was so romantic, and the raw smoky sound of their throats made me feel like someone was speaking especially to me.

James didn't look anything like Tristan. He was short and fat-ish, like me. He had floppy curly black hair. He was pretty—he looked like an elf, kind of. Maybe if an elf and a hobbit had a kid.

I thought about James putting his hands up my shirt over my chest, kissing me. A ripple of warm shuddery something.

I thought about him calling me *baby*.

He wouldn't get all macho and push me down to suck his dick because he didn't want to have feelings.

But if he pushed me down to suck his dick—well.

I hadn't really realized that was on the table.

Here's wishing you the bluest sky . . .

It was a Dar Williams cover of The Kinks' "Better Things."

He would let me talk about Limp Wrist's early stuff and show him videos of Gerardo Velazquez performing with Nervous Gender and cry with me about all the music our generation had lost because of AIDS and look at cool album art with me and *get* it.

James made me feel *good* about my music, even when Ken and Devon made me feel awful. And I liked the shape of his wide mouth and his big deep-set eyes. He had always been my kind of person. A kind person. He made me feel easy and good. After he got top surgery, it was like he lit up, and suddenly he was a dynamo in every room he was in, just *moving* more. I felt hopelessly jealous of his body and the way it looked in a way I wasn't sure was okay, because I knew he wanted to be hairier and different looking. But his joy made me feel like mine was possible.

If anyone was down for my level of fat fem faggot in Cow Pie High, it was him. He liked being seen with me.

The only problem was I wasn't sure what I'd *do* with James. Or what he might want with me. I could top, but Tristan hadn't liked it when I did. And I didn't know if James was a top or a bottom. Not to jump straight to sex, but that *was* what was different about being intense gay friends and being something else.

Would he think I was too much of a girl? Would I be able to give him what he wanted out of being a boy?

Something in my brain blipped and shorted out.

That was a weird train of thought.

I was a girl, but in a gay way. It wasn't like I was trans. Except it kind of was. But maybe that was wrong to think.

Natalie and Gemma were there in the office, fighting. There was supposed to be a board meeting happening tonight about the gala, but nobody had shown up for it.

I turned to Opal. "Do you think Sophie will make it? She hasn't texted me." Sophie was maybe officially in our band now. Tonight was the night I'd told my mom I was rehearsing. If we didn't make it happen this time, she might decide to not let me go out another night. *Rehearsing? You were rehearsing the other day*, she'd say. *How about you rehearse your Japanese verbs for that quiz.*

I texted my mom, *hey, we're going to be out until like ten, okay? Opal has to do Compton things first. I'm at Compton.*

"Why are you going through these again?" I asked, pausing at the door, holding the dirty coffee machine. "Shouldn't the like, board or whatever do that?"

Opal smirked, shuffling the resumes. "I'm gonna give them the Speakers' Bureau's recommendations for in-person interviews, and they're gonna feel bad they didn't come to the meeting."

"Hey," I said. "Look what Jukebox posted on Facebook."

CW: FIRE, INJURY AND ALIEN ABDUCTION! I'M BACK MOTHERFUCKERS! It began. At the top of the post was a selfie of Jukebox, taken from just above their head. They had a bruise under their eye that was a purple-green. They were looking up at the camera and grinning. I thought they might also have a scratch on their chin. They weren't wearing a shirt.

Hey all, it's been a scary time. The loss of my favorite PNW venue is shaking me to my core, and since it's only a couple years after losing friends at Ghost Ship, I am counting all my blessings that the world and THEY heralded all my family to safety.

THE FORCES OF EVIL CAN ATTEMPT TO DEFEAT US, BUT WE CAN HEAL INJURY AND LOSS, FAMINE, DROUGHT AND POVERTY, HORROR AND ABUSE. ****THEY**** HAVE COME AND THEY'LL BE BACK.

"What do you think this is about?" I asked Opal. "Is this how they usually are?"

"Oh, nice, they're okay," Opal said. "Thank god. That means we can still hit them up about getting us some more shows."

"*Are* they okay? Like, is this art?"

"They may have some brain stuff. They made that weird

post about being nonbinary meaning they're an angel one time that I think is dumb. But that's just like, part of it."

"What's the other part?"

"I'm talking out my ass. I don't know. They lost people at Ghost Ship. I bet that night felt really bad for them." Opal paused. "I did feel something then, too. I saw things, I felt like. Like, something speaking to us through the music."

I looked back at the photo of Jukebox. "Yeah," I said. "Me too, for a second." I had felt a strange pull in my gut, like a magnet from above me.

Suddenly, I felt like I was being watched. I looked up and saw a dude standing in the doorway, wearing a leather jacket and leopard print pants. He looked sort of familiar.

"Duke!" Opal said. "Hey, dude, what's up?"

Duke had long curly black hair and a beard and a bunch of chains for necklaces. "Just coming to see if you needed a ride home," he said. "Barb told me that the meeting might run late. If there is a meeting."

"There's not," Opal said. Duke looked around, taking in the papers on the floor.

"Do you wanna head on home now?" Duke asked. "I was thinking of getting some Circus Girl pastries and shit before I went to see Barb. I could spot you guys too. I'm gonna make pumpkin soup and watch *The Transfused* with Barb."

Opal was grinning like he was their dad showing up to get them from school.

"Oh, most definitely," they said. "Let me just put this shit back. Nice resume, by the way."

Opal lived in the nook of Barb's living room that had a red curtain drawn across it. They had a record player and a wooden shelf and a mattress and two suitcases and a window where they had a row of succulents. In Barb's living room, outside of Opal's nook, there was a couch and two armchairs and a big TV and a handmade rug and a bunch of old show posters on the wall. In the kitchen, there were a lot of jars of beans.

Opal had met Barb at a show last year, and Barb had started inviting them to readings and taking them out for coffee and breakfast a little bit after that. When Opal's house situation went to shit—their aunt got hospitalized and couldn't take them anywhere and their cousin had parties in the house where people were weird to Opal, and the dogs that lived at the house weren't getting walked or fed and were shitting everywhere—Barb offered Opal a place to stay. I hadn't asked a ton of questions. James lost his therapy because you can't have your friend's new mom be your therapist. Barb had a ramp up to the front door anyway that was ADA accessible, and she could drive Opal to school on her way to do errands. They visited Opal's aunt Jane every month or so. Opal hadn't been asked to pay rent, but was paying about 30 percent of what they made at Compton to Barb to help cover food and stuff. I wasn't sure if Barb knew how much money that was to Opal.

"The house is cold, dude," Opal said.

"I know," Barb said. "It's my menopause. Hey Ian. Your mom says hi. Home for sure by eleven thirty, right?"

I felt myself turn red as Opal and I adjourned down the stairs and went to talk about our songs and practice.

It was cold in the garage, so I was hopping up and down to stay warm. If this was going to be our practice space, I'd need gloves.

"To Play with Me You Need to Stay with Me" was the title of one of the new things we were working on. Which I started to realize was a dumb title.

"To parlay with me you need to bray with me?" Opal suggested.

I was having writer's block, because there were two big fuzzy questions in my head: ARE YOU A GIRL and DOES JAMES LIKE YOU. But I was happy to have Opal do some of the work with me.

We wrote down lyrics on pieces of paper and passed them back and forth and tried to make rhymes or extend ideas. It was fun. It's nice to sit with your friends who are on the same tip and pass thoughts around. It felt like it used to feel with Ken and Devon, when we all got each other.

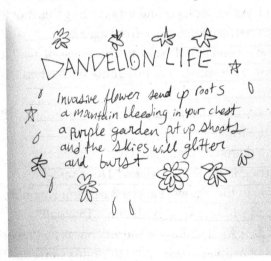

DANDELION LIFE

Invasive flower send up roots
a mountain bleeding in your chest
a purple garden put up shoots
and the skies will glitter
and burst

They tapped at the snare with one hand. "We need a thread running through the song that goes wee-woo-ee-oo. Like wee-oo-ee-oo. Slow like that. I feel like I'm thinking about the feeling of the show, the night the shed caught fire. It felt like that." Their orange hair was falling over their eyes. Opal's smile is like a big flashing neon sign at night. They do music like I do. They feel stuff that I know is the same stuff.

I tried to play the thing they were singing on guitar.

Sophie arrived. She sat like a dude on a stool in the basement, legs spread wide as she played the guitar and put down threads into the thing that was going to be our new song. I liked the way she rocked her bald head back and forth as she played. She was cool. She and Opal talked about wanting the same tattoos.

When we were done, we found Barb and Duke upstairs eating soup with big hunks of bread. Duke had brought out an old-ass VCR player and was starting this movie that was like, a performance piece from ages ago.

"Stay a second," Barb said to the three of us. "It will inspire you. Halcyon days of July 2000. Back when Oly was a real town."

"Grab a drink, too, if you want one," Duke said. "There's beers in the fridge."

"Uh, no thanks," I said. "I'm edge."

"Aw, straight edge? Throwback," Duke said.

"Are you in this show?" I asked Barb, ignoring him.

"I helped with the sets," Barb said. "That's all."

It was dark for a while and the video was just recording the backs of people's heads. Then the lights came up. There was this really big actor in all red who walked out onto the stage through an angular cardboard door and another actor in a red shirt with billowy sleeves that crawled out between their legs. The lyrics swelled. The sound quality wasn't great.

Close your eyes and picture
Paradise
Free of exploitation
Free of lies
I think we know you.

"Wait," I said. "This is The Need!"

"It's their rock opera," Duke said. "*The Transfused*. We were feeling nostalgic about it. We were just babies then."

"Where did you get this recording?" I asked.

"I recorded it," Duke said. "My friend had a camera."

It was so hard to find stuff like this. I had this moment of feeling like, it sucks that I have to tolerate weird older punks to find stuff about what weird older punks were up to when they were cool. That was ungenerous, but like, Duke just didn't seem *nice*. He made fun of being edge. Would I end up like that?

The story was about a bunch of mutant queer-looking animal-human hybrid factory workers in the future who got involved in a revolution, except the revolution was kind of bogus because it was organized by this dude who demanded everyone obey him. There were a lot of guitar riffs and a lot of roller skating across the stage. There was one actor in a wheelchair who kept doing sick spins.

I thought about how many people had to have talked to each other, planned, whittled, built, sewed, in order to make the explosion of color on the stage happen. I felt like there was this enormous bubble of sun in my heart, looking.

My mom texted, *hey, it's getting later. I'm going to bed. Checking in. Are you wrapping up soon? What time are you coming home?*

Fuck.

I texted, *be home in an hour, eating late late dinner at Opal's. Sorry*

In the film, Duke-holding-the-camera panned over to his friend, who was wearing an ACT UP FIGHT BACK FIGHT AIDS shirt. Under those words it said SILENCE IS DEATH.

So maybe Duke had been cool once.

We went downstairs to help haul Sophie's stuff into Opal's room and put her music stuff under a tarp in the car.

When we got back in the house, Barb and Duke had gone to bed. There was music coming from their room.

"I'm going to sleep on the couch," Sophie said.

"I have to go soon," I said.

Back in Opal's nook, Opal wanted to watch a Nelson Sullivan video where Nelson was going home after a party with a drag queen named Dainty Adore. Nelson Sullivan is Opal's latest obsession—some dead guy that used to live with RuPaul in the '80s. I felt myself getting sleepy. I *needed* to go home.

The camera was all zoomed in on Dainty's face. Nelson

and Dainty stopped to pet a cat in a bodega. Dainty was wearing a gold cape with feather trim. They stepped into the street together trying to get a cab, but a lot of cabs passed them before they managed to catch one. "Money talks and bullshit walks," said the queen named Dainty.

"That's so fucking true," Opal said. The video ended, and they sat back on their bed. Their orange hair fanned out on their pillow like spiky flames. The rock salt lamp on their little shelf barely lit up the room with a pink glow. "Money talks and bullshit walks."

"Are you having a thought?" I asked them.

"We should do an art thing to save Compton," Opal said. "Like a concert. Like The Need. Like Nomy Lamm. A fundraiser." They reached out their hand to me on the bed, and I took it.

"That sounds cool," I said.

"You know how the Goat Mansion show felt? Imagine if we could get a bunch of people with *money* to feel like that."

"They'd have to give you money," I said. Compton getting money was Opal getting money, which I supported. And James needed it. I didn't really get it, but then again, I didn't know that many gay people, and that was maybe part of my problem. Not knowing many gay people meant it fucked me up whenever one of them—like Tristan, or Duke—wasn't cool to me.

Compton was important because it meant we knew about each other more, so we didn't need as much from every single gay person we knew.

Right?

"And like, all those ACT UP protest things were so cool and so historic because they were also art," Opal said. "So we should have like, a concert that's also a benefit, and also maybe like, a protest. An action. A movement for power and survival."

"I'd be so into that," I said. "Like, when would we do it? After the gala?"

"I don't think the gala is *happening* anymore," Opal said.

"What the fuck?" I said. "But it's so important, right? And there's already people signed up to volunteer." I felt my heart speeding up just looking at their face.

Opal rolled their eyes and covered their face with their arms. They looked more wobbly than I had seen them in a long time, like they were gonna cry. I knew that shit was rough for them all the time, but I didn't see them ever break down. I lay down next to them on the bed, watching for clues about what I should do. We sat there in silence a minute.

They rolled over and put their face in the pillow.

"James is just avoidant about it. He knows it's fucked up but I think he doesn't know what else to do."

I reached over and stroked their shoulder through their bright yellow sweater. "So we would do the concert to substitute the money we won't make in the gala," I said. "To save Compton." I thought about it. I had seen James plan a bunch of events with Opal and people. It couldn't be that hard. We could do it.

"I bet we could get other people to help," Opal said, sounding like they were trying not to be nihilistic. They looked to me for affirmation. "I bet we could get like . . . punks to help."

"Punks love shows," I said.

"Yeah. They do," Opal said.

"I bet we could do like, a big marathon punk show." I was already thinking of people we could ask. "We could do like teen bands and then maybe two featured bands that are big. We could get someone, right?"

"A rock musical," Opal said. "It *has* to be a rock musical."

Chapter 9

ORSINO

"We're gonna change the world, we're gonna change the world," Jukebox sang. They were piling sweatshirts into a bag. They'd decided to move back down to Olympia more full time to record their next album with OVID. Until last week, I knew, the album had been mostly just an idea, but Jukebox said they'd written the last eight songs all in a row on Sunday and Monday, start to finish, all the music and the lyrics. They hadn't slept for those two days—they filled a notebook with the songs and recorded demos over and over on their laptop's shitty audio using just Robin's guitar. They'd left coffee grounds all over my mom's counter. Now it was Wednesday, and they were talking with their friend Fish at Lone Popper Records about when they could get time in with Stacey and Dogman to record the tracks in a studio space. That meant they couldn't keep staying up at my mom's house in Tacoma.

"It makes sense," my mom said, kind of drily, when Jukebox explained that they'd be going back down. "You do pay rent down there, not here." That was a dig, but

Jukebox didn't catch it. I could tell she was relieved. I wasn't sure how I felt. I didn't want to stay here with just Mom. I waited until Robin and Jukebox were in Robin's room to ask. I stood at the end of the kitchen table, leaning on it.

"Could I go stay with Jukebox while they record the album?"

My mom looked up from her homework at me and raised her eyebrows. "You know, I was thinking about suggesting that. I think it's a *great* idea."

I stared at her.

"I actually found you a therapist in Olympia, so if you wanted to go spend time down there every week around your therapy day long term, that might help me a lot with the driving back and forth."

"A new therapist." I hadn't heard about any new therapist. Shouldn't she have asked me?

"She's named Barb Reisman, she has her own practice. First appointment's in a week. Don't give me that robot face. I'm swamped with school, I'm never around. Therapy's good for you, so's Robin. You've been doing better lately, and maybe it's just having some other people around like you. God knows I don't really know what you need. Just do your homework." She gestured to her biology textbooks, which were all over the table. "We both gotta pass biology. And don't put more than like fifty a week on the credit card, or our bank account's gonna zero out."

"I think it's just going to be a couple weeks," I said. I felt the lurch in my gut that I'd felt before. It was stupid, since I had just asked for something and she'd said yes. But I wanted her to say something else—ask me questions, tell me it wasn't appropriate, anything.

"Sure. But your life and Robin's life is all about those Olympia shows anyway. And you can sell your cartoon animal art online from anywhere, right?" Mom tapped the edge of her mouth with a pencil and went back to the homework she'd been working on. Numbers and stuff I didn't know anything about. Chemistry that she needed to pass the nursing exam. She scowls when she's thinking the exact same way Robin does.

I went to the tiny kitchen, where Jukebox had left the eggs, cheese and milk after making breakfast, and started to put stuff away. I wiped the counter down, then started to get my shoes on to check on my skulls in the bucket outside.

"Gonna check the skulls and dump the scum," I said. I didn't look up from my laces. I wanted to be outside. I wanted to feel animal bones in my hands, and think about how small we all were in the universe.

"Oh, that reminds me, while you're down south, you need to go by the property and grab whatever else of your stuff is still at your dad's house," Mom said. "He says he's gonna start throwing stuff out. I know some of your art is still down there."

"What the fuck," I said. I wondered if he was just saying that to get us to come back one more time. Then he'd drag us to the basement and put us in an icebox.

"Language."

"*He* hung the skulls in the barn. Thought he liked it."

"I know." Mom scribbled something out with her pencil

and picked up her calculator. "You only have to be there long enough to get your stuff. You can take Jukebox if you go down, just to be sure. He won't embarrass himself in front of someone outside the family."

I wouldn't have counted on that, but I didn't say anything.

I use a toothbrush to scrub off my collection when they're done in the bucket and have been in peroxide a few days. I go in little circles over the bones, trying to be gentle. There's a thrum from them that's not like the thrum from the ship, but it's like they're on the same frequency. *You are between species . . .* I felt the ghost of the animal. I felt the patter of feet over the ground and the hot breath like it was coming from my own mouth. The show had been a weird moment. It felt like I'd pushed my visions through to other people for the first time. But I had no idea what to do with that.

"Here's your possum skull," I said to Jukebox. It was an older one; I'd put it into a clear Tupperware with some cloth around for cushioning.

Jukebox had one backpack over their shoulder and another bag under their arm. "Oh, sweet, dude," they said, grinning as they peered into the Tupperware. "This is the *best*. Aw, she's beautiful."

"Hey, weird question. Can I live with you?" I asked. "For like, a couple weeks, I mean. While you make the album."

Their face went blank for a second, their eyes wide. I swallowed. Then they smiled even bigger. "Oh, shit yeah," they said. "I *need* you, man. We have to combine powers to spread the ship's message. Duh. I thought you knew that."

"Sure," I said, exhaling. "I mean, you know. Just checking."

I helped them haul the rest of their shit to the car; Robin was only taking a couple bags, though I had a feeling that was because she was mostly wearing Jukebox's clothes these days. Mom stood at the door in her bathrobe as we drove away, crossing her arms, barefoot, like a woman in a country song. The sky was gray again.

"So," Robin said as we hit the interstate. "I thought about it last night, and I realized that Stacey and you haven't really talked about the fire and what happened."

Jukebox rolled their eyes. "She's not gonna get it."

"Well, right." Robin pursed her lips. "She's worried that you're acting kind of like last year. I think you guys should talk about it."

"She's been like, telling people I need a doctor. Fuck that shit. Like I need the psychowhatever complex because I can *write* for a change."

"Fuck that," I said.

Robin shot me a glare.

"You should talk about what it means for your art, is what I'm saying," she said. "I texted her a little." She sounded careful. "She's just thinking it's a mania thing. She said it sounded a little like what you were feeling last year after you got back from Missoula. She's just worried." She looked back over her shoulder at me and made eye contact.

Jukebox was silent, and I was kind of scared for a second, since their hands went rigid on the wheel. The car passed two billboards in a row advertising legal weed. "Yeah," they said slowly after a second, breathing out. "I do get that she sees it that way. But I feel like I've been visited, like, not to sound crazy, but in a life changing way. The music that night gave me this vision. And Orsino was with me."

"Orsino has visions, but those are all tied up in shit with our dad killing Agatha," Robin said. "Jukebox, it's *not* aliens."

"Robin, please don't speak for me," I said. She looked surprised. I never talked back to her. "It *might* be aliens. Like, it's weird we had the same vision."

Jukebox nodded. "I don't know if it's from another dimension, or the future, or what. It's bonkers, right? But. I saw all that shit. Someone's sending a message, you know?"

"Sure," Robin said. "I mean, I'm definitely not opposed to the idea that the universe sent you a message. I don't think Stacey's *totally* right."

"Those visions of the future world. That's meant for us to do something with. Us. Me and Orsino. And the aliens are gonna help."

"Yeah," I said. I tried to remember when the aliens had offered to help.

"You guys know the Bible, right?" Jukebox asked. "Maybe it's like Moses and Aaron, you know? Maybe you're the prophet, and I'm the mouthpiece." They laughed.

I couldn't hide that them saying that made me feel kind of good.

Stacey was obviously pissed off at Jukebox—for vanishing after the show, for dipping to live at Robin's, for expecting her to jump for joy about the album that they'd all been trying to work on together and that Jukebox now said was done, without anyone's help—but she helped us get all our stuff inside. Jukebox was talking to her the whole time about the album, just on and on, even as we were climbing the steps to their room and while Stacey made space for Robin's bags in the hall. When we had our stuff inside, Stacey picked up her bags and tried to leave, but Jukebox sat on the couch with their legs out blocking her path, talking about the chord patterns and vocal effects that they wanted in the song. Finally, Stacey let out a hard breath.

"Look, Jukebox, I wanna play through this with you, I'm excited too, but you have to relax a minute," she said. "I have to go to work right now." Stacey had an apprenticeship at an acupuncture studio.

"Let's play through stuff when you get back tonight," Jukebox called, as she went down the steps outside.

I went to make lunch, and when I turned back from putting the hummus in the fridge, I saw Jukebox leaning on the counter, staring at me.

"Orsino," they said.

"Yeah," I said, shoving bread in my face.

"You know how the aliens said that we have to break the timeline?" Jukebox took down a piece of paper and a pencil, and started drawing. I could tell that it was one of the worms.

I chewed. "I'm not really sure what they meant by that, but yeah."

"I think we should try that," Jukebox said. "I think we both need to. We're really similar, you and me. At the show—I think other people felt the other timelines there too, the past and futures and stuff pulling on them. I'm thinking music could maybe trigger it. But I also think it's about you being there, with me, that gave us the visions. It's like I'm with a past version of myself. Like we're linked. And you have the ability to do something I couldn't do, and I have the ability to put it into the world, which you can't yet."

"Huh," I said. I liked the idea of being linked to them.

"You mainly get nightmares," Jukebox said thoughtfully. "I do too. But the ship. They changed something. Because we were together. My past is your future, but it doesn't have to be. We can make it something else."

"It felt like something opened up," I said, because that was true and I didn't know what else they were talking about.

They took a piece of bread from the bag I opened. "You heard the aliens. We have to share the vision, and then like, inhabit it. And then time will change."

"Maybe," I said.

Jukebox was smiling. "When everyone sees what could happen, how the world could be transformed, and we all know each other—that's when revolution starts."

Robin stuck her head in from the next room. "Hey," she said. "Jukebox. Mom says we should drive Orsino down tonight to get his art out of Dad's house. You down?"

"Long ass drive," Jukebox said. "But sure, gimme a bit. I still gotta do laundry. And then—" they reached out and drew Robin into a long, messy kiss. Their other arm snaked around her waist.

I put on my sweatshirt and went out to walk around Olympia.

You can walk from one end of downtown Olympia to the other in maybe twenty minutes—it's antique stores, tattoo parlors, the bus station, Vietnamese food, the witch store, four bookstores, a comics store, a big ugly condo block, and then all the cafes. Up the hill above the lake there are the state buildings and more houses. I like the small old one-story buildings best. Then there's the port, where one side is all timber and the other side is where the timber used to be before I guess the bay got too shallow. I walked to the water and smoked one of Jukebox's cigarettes there, looking down into the mud.

Jukebox seemed crazy, but also so full of love for me and everyone else. I pulled out shells and tried to feel the life from them like I could with bones. I wanted to do what Jukebox asked me to. I thought I felt something, but it could have been my imagination—just kind of the wash, the back-and-forth pull of the tides. I could have been imagining it. Some of the animals grew on the shells of the dead ones, down in the silt, I knew. They were really old. They'd been growing on each other's bones back to the beginning of shells.

Jukebox had shaken me. I didn't know if their thing was real or not, but they'd seen the ship too. And now they wanted me to *do* something.

Maybe I didn't have to do anything dramatic to break into the better future for our planet. Maybe I could just recycle and be kind of decent, and things would work out.

Jukebox would not agree with that, probably.

I walked from the docks to the diner with the orange walls, went inside, and ordered a coffee and an egg sandwich. The waiter looked gay, but I couldn't tell for sure.

Lots of people sort of tapped into nature or whatever without seeing a spaceship. Lots of people tapped into it by talking about angels, or gods, or ancestors. I had aliens.

Maybe everything was just in my head and Jukebox's head, and there weren't any aliens at all. But then I had different problems.

The bell to the diner jangled.

"Hey," a voice said. "What's up?" I looked up.

It was Goth James, from the show. He was wearing a dark purple sweater that went to his knees and the same spiky collar. He blinked his big dark maple syrup Bambi eyes and every thought I had that wasn't immediately related to being gay evaporated out of my head. I looked down at my ripped-up camo shorts and back up at him.

"Hey," I said. "Your outfit's sick." I could have hit myself.

"Aw, shucks," he said. His voice was nice. It was high and nasal and had kind of a raspy sound.

"Yeah," I said. I heard my voice and hated it. I hesitated, looking at his chest instead of his eyes. I wanted to talk to him. I had to talk to him. I couldn't miss it. I had to look at his eyes. I looked up. "Hey, can I give you my number?"

"Oh, hell yeah," he said. He was smiling. At me. "I meant to ask before things caught on fire. You wanna add me on Instagram too?"

"Sure," I said. I handed him my phone. He added his name to my contacts as JAMES SAYS TEXT HIM XOXO.

Was this it? Was I doing it?

"You in town because of something going on tonight?" he asked.

"My sister's been spending the day with Jukebox. Up on the west side. I came down because my mom wants me to get my stuff from my dad's house and Jukebox is gonna drive me. You know about what happened to Jukebox at the show?"

He sat down across from me. "I saw their post. Seems kind of trippy."

I wasn't sure how much to say, but he looked at me and his eyes were so big and dark and pretty. I knew he liked Jukebox's music. He would want to know what was happening with them. "They've written like, a whole new album since the fire," I said.

James raised his eyebrows, then looked over and waved at the gay-looking waiter. She walked over to us, her hands in her apron pockets, her shiny black flat top haircut reflecting the yellow ceiling lights. "Hey Morwen," James said. "Could I have a blackberry milkshake?"

"You need a Lactaid with that?"

"I got 'em in my bag."

"Okay, hon." She looked at James warmly, glanced at me and nodded, and walked off.

James looked back at me. "She thinks I'm a baby lesbian," he said confidingly.

"Huh," I said. I didn't think James looked like a lesbian at all.

"With Jukebox. The post on Facebook. You think that stuff was a joke or an art thing? Or what?" He put his chin on his fists.

"I don't think it was a joke or an art thing," I said. "They had an abduction experience. They're making drawings of it and writing about it." And trying to get me to use my psychic powers to save the world, I didn't add.

"Like, real aliens."

"Yeah," I said. I wondered if he would laugh that off or get worried, like Stacey.

"Cool," James said. "How long are you in Oly? Where are you hanging out?" His pink mouth on the straw, cheeks drawing in. A strange shock eating at my stomach, down to my dick. "If you're not doing anything, do you wanna walk around and look at stuff downtown with me? I don't wanna do my homework. I can show you the bookstore."

"Yeah," I said.

James was short, but he stood up super straight. I walked behind him, looking at the way his hair curled behind his ears. Even with his thick calves and baggy shirts and his stompy Doc Martens, the words I thought looking at him were *graceful* and *flouncy*. He'd probably never been in a fight. Probably, he didn't even know how to hold his fist. I felt protective.

The bookstore was a few blocks away, and was open until ten. It was staffed by a lot of middle-aged people who tried to ignore us. James told me there was a cat who lived there who was named Janx. We found him in the back, curled on a chair. I stroked him, and he let out a noise that could have been a growl or a purr.

James brought a book over to me while I was trying to pet Janx. It was called *To Survive on This Shore*.

"Have you seen this? I love this one. It's a photo book of old trans people." He opened it like he'd looked at it before and showed me pages: a picture of an old black man leaning on a swing, a white woman with huge glasses grinning out at me.

"None of them are that old," I said. "That's pretty sad, huh."

"Look at *this* one," James said. There was a page with two old fat trans men on it, bearded and hairy and shirtless, holding each other. Their chest scars were almost invisible under their gray chest hair, and their bellies hung down over their jeans. They looked like truckers, solid like trees. On the other page, one of them sat with his legs hanging out of a red truck.

I felt something looking at them—the opening in the sky. It wasn't that I'd never seen pictures of old trans people before. But these two men, holding each other.

"Oh word," I said. I wondered if James liked them or was making fun of them. "*They're* definitely fucking."

"Yeah. Imagine how *beautiful* they are in bed together," James said, his voice low. I realized he wasn't making fun of them.

"I wonder when they transitioned," I said. "You think they were lesbians and stayed together?" Had they had other boyfriends before they met each other, found their double?

"I *love* these pictures. I think they're married." He looked back at the men, grinning, moving his lips slightly like he was going to say something else, but he didn't say anything.

I reached out and touched the back of his hand. There was an electric shock.

I saw a man with a dark beard touching an older version of my body. I felt the weight of the tides, water changing the shape of rocks, the stars shooting past. I saw the spherical ship, and another great ship straining toward it as if through gauze. A warship.

"Woah," James said, as my fingers slipped off his wrist. "What was that?"

I thought of Jukebox, and what they'd said about the show, and about me sending my visions to them. "I don't know," I said. "I got a flash. What did you see?"

"Um." He shook his head. "Hey, you wanna go to the goth coffee shop?"

I looked at my phone. "I haven't gotten an update from Jukebox or my sister," I said. "So, sure."

Le Perv served coffee and stuff in front and beer in the show space in back. Stacey's friend Neon worked there two nights a week. This was one of the nights. Neon wouldn't give me beer when I had asked last week, so I didn't try again. James and I both got coffee and sat down in one of the sticky booths.

"You believe in aliens then? You're both like, alien people," he said. He gestured to my sweatshirt, which I realized was the one that said ROSWELL on it.

"I've been having dreams about aliens for a few years," I said. Here we go. "The shirt's just a joke."

"Huh. What are the dream aliens like?" James asked, chin on hands. That was nice.

"Most of the alien stuff online is bullshit, it's about being afraid of the government or foreign invaders or spies or whatever," I said. "But my dreams aren't any of the green people anal probe stories or that shit. It's like, lights in the sky, and these beings with worm bodies talking about changing the future. It feels so real. And then, the show. Well. Something happened there too."

"I felt something at the show too," James said. "Kind of a contact high thing."

"No." How could I explain that I knew it was real? "There *was* a ship." I stopped and drank coffee. "Uh. Sorry. How's your life?"

I hoped he thought I was the good kind of freak.

"My life's boring. My friends are cooler than me. My deal is just my asshole dad trying to make me think he loves me after ignoring me for years, and my school telling me I can't pee places." He smiled, kind of shyly. "And like, going to shows to see boys."

I laughed, feeling my stomach turn over. "Am I boys?"

James blushed and looked down at the table. "I don't do this much," he said. "I've been getting over this weird . . . you know, weird stuff. But I thought you were cute the first time I saw you. I told my friend Opal."

"I thought you looked cool too," I said. Yikes. I looked down at the table, down at the floor. Back at him.

James reached across the sticky table and rubbed his thumb over the back of my hand, almost experimentally. It was like touching an outlet. I felt him in my head again. I don't know how I knew it was him, or that he was in there. It wasn't a physical presence. I felt things coming from him, like streams out of the side of a glacier.

I was watching a big ocean, from just above the ocean, from inside the ocean. It wasn't a place I had ever seen before. It was, I knew suddenly, a world from before there were any animals, or any plants. Just water, stretching forever. Billions of years ago. In my head, my body melted down into the gray ocean under a gray sky, into the salty black water. I felt a sense of purpose and peace, slipping under the waves. The purpose was just to disperse, merge and part and merge again. I felt the millions of bacteria around me, combining and growing, becoming something bigger and more complicated. I didn't understand it.

My phone buzzed. I pulled my hand back.

"Sorry," I said. James looked like I felt. My head was spinning, mirror fragments of the images and feelings circling the drain.

Hey bro, gotta convince stacey to play new songs with me, Jukebox's text said. *Gonna make some alien visions come true. Can't drive u to ur dads, sorry. Come home tho we have dinner.*

"Fuck," I said. "Jukebox isn't driving me down to my dad's anymore. They have band shit."

"Sounds legit," James said. He drank the rest of his coffee fast, like it would steady him.

"I have to get my art back. I hate when they change plans like this," I said. I stood up, feeling large and miserable and dry-mouthed. I had no idea what James thought was happening right now, or if he'd seen the same things I had, or what they meant. That was two in one day. What was happening?

"Oh. I can drive you," James said. "I have a car."

"It's like a forty minute drive, dude," I said. I rolled up the sleeves of my sweatshirt, trying not to look at him.

He grabbed my arm through my sweatshirt. His grip was surprisingly strong. I turned around and found myself looking into his big, dark eyes.

"Hey," he said. "I don't want to do my homework."

Out in the street, there was a wash of water flooding the sidewalks and road like there had been a heavy rainstorm, swirling down the sewer drains. It smelled like salt. It was only a few inches deep. People were wading through it, looking surprised and confused. I looked down and saw a shell that didn't look like anything I had seen before. By the time we got to James's car, the water was gone, like a flood had receded, but there was a crunch as he pulled out, like another shell was caught under the tires.

Chapter 10

JAMES

I had never driven this far south before on my own, and definitely not in the dark. I was glad it wasn't raining.

The wide beige fields we had driven by earlier were gone, and I was back to feeling like the night sky had swallowed us whole. My car's lights lit up the road for a few yards in front of us, but no further. I didn't want to turn on the brights because the road was so curvy. The trees on either side of the car were thick and dark except for little clearings where there would be a single house or mobile home breaking up the foliage for a second before disappearing back into the woods. Orsino looked like he was asleep in the seat next to me, and I was worried he had drifted off again. The map was going to tell me where to turn, but the little roads here were not very visible at night.

"Hey," I said. "Can you tell me where the turn is? We're getting close I think but it's too dark."

"It's a little ways," he said, his eyes still closed. "You pass a church with a sign out front that usually says something ominous, and then you pass a field with a barn with a busted roof and a Trump 2016 endorsement painted on the side, and then it's trees for a bit, like two minutes, and then the next field is the farm."

"Can you open your eyes and stay awake so you can help me?"

"I'm awake," he said, but he sat up and adjusted the back of his seat so he was no longer reclining, and stretched. I glanced sideways at his big arms and stomach as his shirt slid up. He had a narrow trail of fur cutting down in a vertical line through his belly button toward the top button of his jeans.

"Should I turn up the music so you can't fall asleep?" I turned the volume up, and Suzanne Vega's breathy voice swelled inside the car.

You seem to me like a man on the verge of burning . . .

"Okay, here's the church," Orsino said. The church's sign said JESUS SEES YOUR SIN AND SUFFERS.

"Rad," I said.

"We used to go there when I was a kid," Orsino said. "The church moms didn't like me because I was weird."

"What did you do?"

"I played warrior cats with their kids and scratched people. Their kids were into it, it was fine, but the moms would tell my mom to take me to doctors."

"How long ago did you guys leave the church?"

"A few years ago. Around when I came out and my sister ran away. Mom still believes in God but she's kind of fed up with organized religion now."

"Sounds bad," I said.

"You have no idea," Orsino said. "Here's the barn." We passed a field with a dark shape in the middle.

"Has your dad been running the farm since you were born?" I asked.

"My parents got married when my mom was eighteen and they've lived here since. But except for the land, my dad doesn't own anything so we're fucked if he ever violates his contract." Orsino paused. "Or actually I guess *he's* fucked. My mom is divorcing him. I'm not talking to him."

"Mood." I wondered how it was gonna be for Orsino at the house if he wasn't talking to his dad. I wondered if they fought. The picture I was getting was kind of grim. "I hate my dad too."

"I don't know if you know anything about chicken farming," Orsino said. "He signed on to be a franchise whatever with Tapper Chicken, so he doesn't get to keep most of the profits from the chickens he raises and he has to buy all this equipment and he isn't allowed to keep them in nondisgusting conditions because of the company guidelines. He's basically trapped in chicken poverty hell forever."

I wrenched the steering wheel to turn in the narrow drive Orsino gestured to. "Thanks," I said. My car's wheels crackled over the driveway.

"You wanna come in?"

"Is your dad here?" I didn't want to see a fight. "I gotta go back soon."

"He might be home. Unless he's out with Reese. But you drove all the way. I can like, show you art."

"Sure." I liked the tone I heard in his voice. The worry I had was leaving.

The house was a low, rambling farmhouse. There was a motion sensitive light at the end of the driveway that blinked on as we passed it. As we drove up past a shed and a fenced-in yard, towards the front of the garage, a muddy yellow dog dashed abruptly across my headlights. I let out a little shriek and slammed on the brakes.

"Oh, that's Ranger," Orsino said. "He's our outside dog. Big goof. Don't worry, he knows not to get hit." Orsino unclipped his seatbelt. I shrugged and turned off the engine. We were about twenty yards from the house. He started to open the car door, then stopped. I thought he was looking toward the light on inside the house.

We walked down to the edge of the driveway and crossed over the road to the other side. There were no cars coming; it was late.

"There's two barns—the shed for the tractor and the other equipment, and then the chicken barn, where the Tapper chickens live until they're big enough to go get slaughtered," Orsino said. I could smell something hanging in the air—faint and rotten and dead. I wondered if it was the chickens. On the edge of the field, there was a line of dark black-blue trees against the black-blue sky. I could hear birds in the woods. We were really in the middle of nowhere.

Inside the barn there were a few painted deer skulls, plus a lot of unpainted bones glowing white in the dark. I shuddered. Orsino turned on the dim, buzzing fluorescent bulbs. The high white light at the top of the barn didn't give the best lighting, but I could see now that the skulls bore detailed images. Oil paints—paintings of mice and detailed flowers and birds.

"That's Rose Deer," Orsino said. He pointed to the deer

nearest me. The skull was covered in red glass beads and small cloth roses. On the deer's nose there were blue wet-looking leaves, dripping on a yellow background. "She died of a broken leg, we think. We found her in the woods 'cause she stank so bad. I made her pretty. She would have been beautiful when she was alive." He took down the skull and looked at it. "I don't know what I'm going to do with these, up at Robin's. Jukebox says I should sell them on Etsy, but I don't think they'd like that."

"Who? Jukebox?"

Orsino laughed. "No. I mean the deer."

I looked up and around again. Orsino's art was beautiful. I tried to picture what his life had been like down here, when he made it.

We walked back to my car. I unlocked the door, and Orsino stood there, watching me.

"Thanks again for the ride," he said. "You didn't have to do that."

"Oh. Yeah, no problem." I felt an odd mixture of disappointment and confusion.

"Can I kiss you?" Orsino's face was not very visible in the dark. "It's okay if not. Just wanted to ask."

I swallowed. My throat felt dry. "Oh, sure, dude."

He came around the hood of the car and stood in front of me. My stomach twisted tight. I shut my car door and leaned against it. He leaned forward and put his hand on my stomach and put his other hand in my hair and pressed his lips against mine, harder than I had expected.

His hands were bigger than mine and really warm. His chapped lips tasted like iron and when I put my tongue between his lips, his mouth tasted a little sour from the coffee he'd had earlier. He smelled like sweat. It was good. I felt like I was on a roller coaster shooting down from the peak.

"Dude, I'm so gay," I said into his neck. I reached up and put my hands in his hair. It was dry and fluffy, like it looked, but I liked touching his head. He shivered as I ran my hand over the back of his skull.

He put his tongue in my mouth. His downy stubble brushed my cheek. When he pulled back, finally, I felt off-kilter, like there was something steadying me that had disappeared.

"You're really beautiful," he said, his voice so low it was mostly a rasp. "I want to go on a date with you. A real one."

I grinned. "You *would* be the first boy who takes me on a date." His hair splaying out weirdly, his sharp lopsided nose and weird, bright stare.

"What's that supposed to mean?" Orsino asked.

"No—no. Sorry. This is—just cool. You're beautiful."

Thank god I was trans, I thought. Thank god the people like me were like this.

It was better because he was so country-boy, all ruddy and blond under his bright bleach job, with big arms and big legs and a big, broad stomach. I could feel his binder under his sweatshirt, feel the heat of him rub into me. I suddenly understood why people were into jocks, though Orsino wasn't a jock. Difference was intoxicating. *Why* were we so different? When we had to be so much the same?

I kissed his neck. I had wanted to kiss a boy's neck for years, and he was the right height for it to actually work. There was a zap when my mouth made contact with his jaw. I felt the thrill he was feeling bounce back into me and my hair prickled all up and down my arms with it.

He gasped.

A painful shock chattered my teeth.

I saw a big flower opening and opening, taking up the whole field of my vision with red and pink light. There were great dragonflies around it. Then: Oceans, the stars at night. A pig and a child walking. Worms. A great bird-like creature, running.

A huge jolt of lightning went through us both, and we shook together.

"Oh," I said. I reached out and grabbed his shoulders, and kissed him. Why did everything feel like this? Everything was painfully bright, electric, hard.

I was standing in a window, looking out over a hill of brush, a cloudy sky and gray sea. I was older; my hands were wrinkled. I had a dark beard, was wearing a heavy sweater. On one of my fingers was a silver ring with a blue stone. I turned to look at the mirror that hung on the wall of the place where I was, in the house on the hill by the sea. My face was wrinkled too, a deep vertical line in the middle of my forehead, more around my mouth. The walls of the place were painted blue. The yellow curtains blew into the room with the smell of salt spray. A baby cried, and I turned at the sound, away from the window, and walked into another room with a sink and a clay stove and shelves of plants on the cobbled wall, where a small wooden cradle sat in the corner. I reached into the cradle, picked up the baby that lay there on a cotton mattress, held it to my chest. The baby was mine.

I let go of Orsino, screaming. I was falling over.

"Fucking holy shit," I said. I turned to him again, grabbed him, gasped into his chest.

There was a cry from a large animal, not far off. It sounded like a raven, throaty and sharp and atonal.

I glanced in the direction of the sound, and froze.

There in the sodium light against the house, a tall feathered creature stood on two legs, stooping toward the ground with small clawed arms. It was over seven feet tall. The light reflected off its head; its claws made marks in the dirt among goat hoofprints. I stopped breathing, tried to make sense of its size and color. Its feathers were blue. It did not look like any bird I knew.

Ranger, the dog, barked. He was tied to a line on the tree and he stretched his cord as he angled out toward the intruder. The creature stood rigid, looking toward him. I thought of *Jurassic Park*, of the velociraptors' teeth. But this creature seemed nervous. It turned and ran, leaping over the fence and toward the black line of woods.

"Did you see that?" I asked Orsino.

"It's not real," he said. "I know it looks real, but it's from long ago. It's not here, now." But he sounded uncertain.

I was kneeling on something velvety and wet and soft. I looked down. We were crouching on bright red flower petals the size of baby blankets. They were scattered all down the driveway.

"Are you okay?" he asked.

"The ocean," I said. "It was me. That was me. It was my face, but older. That was me. It was the future."

He knelt next to me. "It's freaky. I thought that man looked like you."

"Do you like, make those up?" I asked. "The images?"

He stroked my shoulder. His hand was big and steady. "No," he said. "They're of like... possibilities. I think. And things from the past. Times in the past when things might have changed. But I've never had anything like this happen before."

I pressed back against his hand. "That was intense. And weird."

We held each other on the flower petals, gravel digging through to hurt our knees.

The drive back was all weird and hazy. I thought of the heavy blue feathered creature, wondered if it was in the woods somewhere. The flowers had seemed real.

I should have known, I thought, that there was something big around the corner.

Thursday I turned in the bullshit paper on the Constitution and impeachment, took a test in physics, and got stopped in the hallway by Mr. Coleman.

"James," he said. "I trust you got my email."

"Yep. I'm allowed to use the bathroom *corresponding to my identity* according to state law and the school district. It got added to your school district policy two years ago."

He stared at me, frowning. "Okay. So, what I heard was that you slammed a door into Noah Ford's chest, and told him to do something obscene."

"Check your facts," I said. I tried to walk past him. "He was harassing me."

Mr. Coleman stepped to try to stop me. "That's just very different than the story I heard. And frankly, James, given your behavioral record . . ."

"I'm making a Title IX complaint." I stared up at him. I knew he was looking at my shirt, which said GOTH BITCH.

He breathed out through his nose.

"Okay. So there's two sides of the story here. We can talk about it. But James, you have to understand that your behavior only makes things worse. You're confrontational. Forgive me, but you can be a little bit too much. And you've made classmates very uncomfortable. Until this matter is settled, I am *suggesting* that you use the gender-neutral bathroom in the nurse's office, like you did last year."

I didn't use the bathroom at all for the rest of the day.

I drove Opal home and ran into their bathroom and then pissed really long into the toilet, thinking about how I wanted to destroy Mr. Coleman.

Opal wanted to nap for an hour, so I told them I'd meet them downtown. Barb could drive them or they could take a bus.

Ian met me at the back of Garbage Barge, at the door to the studio space. He told me that we were all going to organize a drag show concert fundraiser to save Compton House.

"This is 'cause the gala's shot, huh," I said. "This is Opal's idea."

I'd been at the board meeting. I knew nobody wanted to admit that by January we couldn't make rent. I leaned against one of the big wooden art counters, checking to see if there was wet ink on it before I hopped up on the edge. The art space behind Garbage Barge is messy. It has low ceilings and exposed bulbs and a bunch of wooden counters all over the place.

"Yeah," Ian said. "But it would also be a great place to showcase teen bands. Especially if we can get a big show space that isn't dangerous. I've been thinking about it. There should be way more overlap between your guys' shit and then like, normal people who like having fun."

"We have bowling club and card game nights."

He looked at me seriously. "That's what I mean."

Goober came over and clapped me on the back.

"Dude," she said, and gave me a fist bump. "Where's Opal?"

"They're coming," Ian said, and Goober looked relieved.

She took the stuff Ian was holding and put it down on a table. "You guys have transparencies you wanna use?"

"Yes," Ian said, dropping his bag on the floor. He dug out sheets that I guessed he'd prepped ahead of time. They said MONIQUE FATIGUE AND THE DUSTIES and had a picture of a fish in a wig. Goober made me a cleared off space on one of the tables and gave me a permanent marker and some construction paper.

"If you wanna make your own design, use this. You can cut shapes out of this and tape them to the transparency," she said.

We had to stretch the screens, which meant Goober

held the frame and I pulled the screen down really tight while she stapled it with a staple gun that had been on the other side of the room in a pile of dirty paintbrushes. Then she went to go set up the darkroom lights.

I got an idea.

"Hey," I said to Ian. "So, Mr. Coleman told me I couldn't use the boys' bathroom."

Ian looked up at me. "Shit, James. Why wasn't that the first thing you said?"

"A lot's gone on," I said, which was true. "But yeah. Maybe we can do a campaign of posters at the school about how it's transphobic. It'll tick them off more, but then everyone else will know it's happening."

Ian looked nervous. "Like, posters where?"

I pulled the transparency over and Sharpied some backwards words on it, hard, so the ink was thick and you couldn't see through it. Ian stood behind me, watching as I sketched it out. My handwriting has always been pretty good. He put a hand on my shoulder, and I felt a ripple of calm warmth wash down my back. His hand was different from Orsino's, his touch lighter.

FREE TO PEE PEE POO POO FOR ME ME YOU YOU, the transparency read when I finished a minute later. END TRANSPHOBIC BATHROOM POLICING AND LET KIDS PEE IN PEACE. The last part was a little crowded, but it was legible.

"I was thinking maybe like, this, but all up and down all the hallways."

"Bravo," Ian said, sounding uncertain.

I checked my phone and realized Opal was waiting outside.

James where are you open the fucking door, the most recent text said.

"James, what the hell, I've been texting," they said when I opened the side door to the street. It was getting dark out, and I could tell why they didn't want to wait. Bike punks and people like to hang out right on the corner by Garbage Barge at night, and there was already a group out there smoking. Opal knows some people, but not everyone.

"I'm so so sorry," I said. "We had to do the emulsifier thing on the screens and I didn't see my phone."

"Let-me-see. Let-me-see," Opal chanted, wheeling inside. They looked at Ian's screens and then mine.

"Is this about the bathroom shit?"

"Yeah," I said.

Goober was on her phone. "We should leave the screens alone for a bit," she said. "Do you guys wanna go into Garbage Barge next door and try on clothes and stuff for a bit to wait?"

We did.

You don't buy clothes at Garbage Barge; you just go try them on and laugh and take pictures. Not a lot of it is stuff I would actually wear to school, but it's good dream material. There's a leather jacket rack, a rack with dresses from the 1940s to the 1990s, a bolo tie display, a scarf display, and a Big Boots shelf in the back. The people who run it now got rid of the 1$ bin and the Free Bin. Opal says now that it's expensive it's okay to steal.

I went to the dress rack with Ian and Opal and we started spinning it, faster and faster. The colors blurred together. We let go then each stuck a hand in to see where we landed. It's like *Wheel of Fortune.*

"What's the thing you wanna do for Compton, Opal?" I asked them. I'd landed on a 1970s pink and orange floral dress with a really high collar and long skirt. I pulled it out and held it up to myself and turned to Ian.

"Very sister wives," he said. He had a tiny silver dress. "Wanna swap with me?"

We switched dresses. Ian pulled on the floral dress over his clothes and walked over to look at himself in the mirror, lifting the skirt to dig in his pocket for his phone. He took a selfie posing with one hand reaching toward the purple plastic light fixture.

"So, Ian and I were talking about it," Opal said. "We just have like, a really cool band now, and Compton needs money, and the gala's canceled. So we can put it together. We can make a show and raise money. It can be a youth-written drag show. Ian's mom has to be okay with him playing *that*." They held up their dress, which was fake snakeskin. "Also, look, I'm a crocodile."

"That would be such a good show outfit," I said. I looked over at the counter, to see if the mean girl with white dreads was watching us. She was folding clothes. Really fast, I ducked down and took my shirt off and threw it on the floor. I pulled the silver dress on over my jeans. It was too tight, and the collar went down almost to my navel. "Have you talked to the board yet? I think they'd love the youth doing this. Especially since it means they don't have to do work."

Opal grabbed a leather hat that was hanging off a bust sitting on a tiny table and put it on. "Not yet," they said. "I was actually thinking of writing to Jukebox to see if they wanted to get involved and get some of the bands in town in on stuff. And then we can script like, a scene, and then go to the board. I'm moving on it, though."

"That's very smart," I said. I handed them a boa. "Also, I went on a date with Jukebox's girlfriend's brother last night. Maybe that's an in. He's part-time staying with them down here."

"What?" Ian asked, turning around.

"I know, right? I have a boyfriend," I said. "Maybe. He has alien telepathic powers, also."

"What?" Ian asked, again.

"I think that's great," Opal said. They wheeled over to the mirror next to Ian and grabbed a pair of heart-shaped sunglasses out of a basket. "I think Jukebox is our ticket. Also, JAMES! Do you know about The Need's rock opera back in 2000? We can do like, a new version of it. A political drag extravaganza. With teens."

"A political drag extravaganza with teens is the best thing I've heard all day," I said.

"We will do it super cheap and we will promote local businesses who support us."

"We'll get *so* much money," I said sarcastically.

"We gotta believe we will get so much money," Opal said.

I looked at the leather jacket rack, trying to find the right one. "Enough to pay for two salary positions without any grant funding." I was beginning to picture it. You'd have amateur drag acts, and then really metal punk band numbers, with some homemade props and a lot of really earnest gay teens. And a lot of glitter.

"I think Duke may know people at the film society, too," Opal said. "So, like, long shot, but we might be able to get that space. Maybe even for no money."

"That sounds like a long shot," I said.

"We're LGBT *teens*," Opal said. They looked at me and pulled the sunglasses down on their nose. "I'm housing *unstable*." They gestured to their chair. "I'll go tell them I depend on Compton to live and that the elevator there is busted."

"Let's go back to *boyfriend* and *telepathic powers*," Ian said. He was taking off the floral dress. The white dreadlock woman was looking over at us now. She looked annoyed.

"I went on like, a weird date," I said. "By accident. I ran into that trans boy Orsino last night as I was going home, and we hung out. He kissed me and I think we're gonna go on another date maybe. And he has telepathic powers that aliens maybe gave him. A giant flower showed up in my head and then it was real. And a bird."

Ian cocked his head to the side and wet his lips with his tongue. I looked at him and wondered what he was thinking. "Okay," he said.

"Ian, trans people are all weirdos," Opal said. "Have you not realized that yet? We all do alien something. As our cis ally, you should understand." They were putting bangles on their wrists up to their elbows.

Goober appeared next to us. She pulled out a purple crushed velvet gown from the rack. "My mom had something like this in the 1980s," she said. She looked at me. "James, you look great in that. You should get it."

I thumbed for the price tag, which was safety-pinned to

the collar. "It's sixty-eight dollars," I said. "That's more than a month of testosterone without insurance. That's more than sixteen bags of Trader Joes frozen mangoes."

"That's more than I have in my bank account," Opal said.

"Do you guys need any help over there?" the white dreads lady yelled.

Ian pulled a plaid cape on over his shoulders and did a turn. "We're good, madam," he said. He strutted away from me down the length of the store, then turned and looked directly at me before dropping to his knees and letting the cape fall over his head. He started crawling toward us again on the floor, throwing his head up so the cape came back up. His curly hair was all messed up, and I couldn't help cackling. He kept crawling. I could feel Opal looking at the cashier to see when in this performance she would come over. She looked like she was wondering the same thing. Ian reached my feet and grasped my shoes, fake-kissing them. I felt a tingle in my stomach again. I couldn't stop laughing.

"I should be a really dramatic space prince," he said. "In the show. With a cape."

"I wanna be a space anarchist," I said.

"No," Opal said. "You *have* to be the cow that gets abducted." They tossed me a cow-patterned fur coat. "The space prince teaches you about peace and love and you go back to try to teach Earth and then you get murdered and served as a burger."

The cashier, finally, had had enough. She came over, her tall wooden heels clicking on the cement floor. "Hey, can I hold anything for you all at the counter?" she said, menacingly.

"We're good," I said.

She looked at me. "You need to put that back on the rack if you're not going to buy it."

Opal wrote an email to the board that night.

I'd made eighteen perfect screen prints of my PEE PEE design in bright yellow-orange ink on a black background and ordered pizza for us and Goober. We hung the prints up to let them dry and then sat around Opal as they typed on their phone. Goober packed up her equipment and took off. We had to be out of the room by ten. The studio lights were dim, and I felt kind of high, hanging out with my two ride or dies. I almost forgot that I was mad that the principal had nearly given me a UTI.

The subject line was: *Alternate Proposal for Winter Gala Funding From Speakers Bureau Members.*

To The Board, it began.

"Hold on," Opal said. "I gotta get in the space to actually type this."

While Opal typed the email, me and Ian started writing a rock musical script. We knew we were going to have to ask other people to work with us on it, eventually, but if we came with a bunch of good stuff people couldn't say no.

"Can they be big glowy worms?" Ian asked. "We could get like, those kid tunnels made of cloth and hoops and cut them up and put lights inside. Then people could dance in those. Even if they suck it would look cool. There could be an alien mating dance."

"Yeah," I said, making a note that said *horny worm aliens.*

"We could use it to dissect gender and patriarchy and racism and capitalism," Opal said, still looking at their phone, thumbs poised. The screen was reflected in their eyes. "Like, the aliens don't have any of that, and they start a revolution by abducting James the cow and teaching him and then returning him to earth and then James spreads the gospel of worm."

"The gospel of worm!" Ian said.

I couldn't get over him. What was I gonna do if I liked him *and* Orsino?

I wrote THE GOSPEL OF WORM down on a piece of paper.

When we finished working, an hour later, we had a professional email and five pages of scribbly notes and drawings that me and Ian had done about the plot arc, pacing, and number of songs that the musical was going to have. We stopped, finally, not because anyone showed up to kick us out, but because Opal looked down at their phone and said, "Oh!"

"What?" I asked.

"Duke's making seitan tacos," they said. "Barb's gonna pick me up."

Ian and I looked at each other, and I knew we were thinking the same thing. *That guy.* Thank G-d for Ian.

"Is Duke like, moving in?" I asked.

"I don't know," Opal said, looking up. "It might be sick if he did. He gets shit. About having weird family shit, about everything. He's been around."

"I guess that's good," I said. "I just *hate* straight guys."

"He's not straight," Opal said.

Ian walked me to my car, since it was dark. I carried my box of posters under one arm. As we passed Circus Girl bakery, I reached out and took his hand. I'd missed holding his hand. We used to do it a lot more, and then we did it less and less as Tristan got more serious over the last year. Ian held my hand, but he seemed a little nervous. As we walked up the hill to the library parking lot, he put his hand in his pocket. I put my hands in my pockets too.

"Sorry," I said, not sure if I was supposed to be.

"So you like, are maybe dating this guy Orsino," he said. He avoided my eyes.

"Oh," I said. "I mean, maybe. Not yet. But he's hot and trans and like. I don't know. It's so funny how tough he is."

"Yeah," Ian said. "I saw him at the show. He's tough."

"That doesn't mean I can't hold your hand. Does it?"

Ian looked at me, and I tried to understand the expression he had. "No," he said. "I'm sorry. I'm being dumb." He sighed. "Tristan would get jealous about stuff like that. It's why I stopped. One time we fought because I held your hand at school."

I didn't know what to say to that. Hot Tristan was jealous of *me*?

"You're not dating Tristan," I said. "You can do what you want."

Ian stopped walking, and looked at me. "I think . . . yeah," he said. He took my hand out of my pocket and held it. "Okay. Yeah. I've missed holding your hand." His hand in mine was dry and warm and it felt . . . *really* good.

"So what do we think of Duke?" I asked. I wanted to

change the subject so we wouldn't overthink the hand-holding thing.

"Hate him," Ian said.

I cackled. "Thank FUCK," I said, too loud. "Me too."

"It's fucked up to be all hetero and act like you're more queer than like, people gay dating."

"He's from Oly and he's old and trans and he thinks that means he runs this town," I said. "He thinks he's like, our fuckin' ancestor."

Ian squeezed my hand. We walked through the bushes around the edge of the library parking lot. Mine was the only car still there.

"He is smart, though," Ian said. "To give him credit. And nice. I hung out with him when we rehearsed. And he can cook."

I nodded. "Seitan tacos."

"Opal was all down on him and then fourteen seconds later it's like they think he's their dad. I think that a lot of it is them wanting something stable."

"Yeah," I said. I felt my heart sink, thinking about Opal's excitement when here we were talking shit. "I think I'm just worried he's gonna turn out to be bad. Because dads are all bad."

"Just *most* of them," Ian said. He switched the hand that was holding mine and raised my arm up in a solidarity handshake. His fingers gripped mine. One time he told me his dad hit him when he was a kid. He'd stopped when Ian got "old enough to remember," but Ian remembered.

I leaned forward and hugged him, maybe too hard. He

hugged me back. We broke out of it and looked at each other, holding each other's sleeves.

He kissed me on the cheek.

"Do you ever think," I said, and then stopped. I didn't actually know the end of my sentence. *Do you ever think it's okay to want more than one boy at once? Do you ever think you'd date me? Do you ever think maybe you'll become a famous punk star and I'll be your weird social worker boyfriend who you come home to between tours who has a bunch of foster corgis?* What was I going to say?

"What?" Ian asked.

I thought: *I like the shape of his face. It's round and his cheekbones are so high and he looks like a really beautiful fairy. I think he looks like a romantic hero. I would think that even if I just saw him at the mall and didn't know him.*

"Do you ever think maybe aliens will come down and fix everything?" I asked. "Like, bleep bloop, zoop, full communism?"

He looked down and let out a weird snort. "It would be easier than having to actually do anything. It would be nice."

Chapter 11

IAN

Don't count your chickens is a good motto.

He'd held my hand. He blushed when I kissed him.

The way I felt about him was how Leslie Feinberg says it is when you're a butch having feelings about femmes, like I just wanted to make his life easier and take him places and show him off and protect him. And I didn't understand him in some ways, but I did love him. We weren't lesbians, but that was what queerness was about. We all had a shared history.

And we were planning a big, amazing show that would save Compton House.

I felt his cheek against my mouth when I shut my eyes.

Whatever! Whatever.

James had his stupid poster graffiti plan, and he needed my help, and I'm an amazing friend, so I was helping. I got up early to meet him in the school parking lot at 5:45 a.m. That would give us fifteen minutes before someone in the band room would notice I wasn't there. I was always at school first after Mr. Farro for jazz band, to set up and tune the double bass that three other people used.

No Indigo Girls nonsense in the car on the way, full Davila 666. They have slow beats, but I like the jangly guitar and lo-fi sound and rough choruses.

The sky was a strange purple, and I kept thinking I saw mountains of ice towering over me that turned out to be hazy gray formations of fog.

The parking lot in the morning stank of cow manure from the farm next door and the fields down the road. I could see James's car as I pulled in, parked by the portables. He was standing by the trunk, illuminated by the weak yellow glow of the car light. He was wearing a purple leopard print shirt.

"Sup, conspirator," James said, hauling the posters out of his car in a stack. "Mayhem time, yeah?"

"What's that?" I asked, pointing to a suspicious tomato sauce jar of white goop in James's hand.

"Wheat paste," he said. "They're not going to get these babies off the wall without a fight."

"What if you get expelled?"

"Then I sue," James said simply. "And then I go learn to be a mountain man in British Columbia."

"Oh, yeah, you'll be great at that," I said.

Nobody else was around in the parking lot, and there were no cars except for Mr. Farro's SUV, parked down at the end of the teacher lot; the sky just had the barest tint of red over the horizon. You could see cars pass on the country road, their brights on.

"So," I said as we walked toward the doors. "My role is to be a distraction, yes?"

"Not even," James said. "Make sure the band guys don't

see me and do a quick walkthrough of the halls to scout for janitors before your band starts. I'll do the rest. This is my hill to die on."

"Not *just* yours," I said, but he didn't ask what I meant. I wasn't sure I'd be able to say it if he did.

I let him in through the band room with my key. Mr. Farro was sitting under a big poster that read MUSIC IS A LANGUAGE THE WHOLE WORLD SPEAKS. WHINING ISN'T. that a senior clarinetist had made him last year. Every time I see it I'm reminded why I don't hang out with band kids at school.

"Morning, Mr. Farro," I said. "Can I go to my locker in a second? I think I left some pages from 'East St. Louis Too-dle-oo' in there, and my tuner."

Mr. Farro is a small bald man with a mustache who sleeps probably two hours each day. He directs symphonic band, concert band, jazz band, and marching band for our high school *and* the one on the other side of town. If James was worried he was going to stop the plan, he didn't need to bother. The Farro was staring at his phone when I asked him. He looked at me for less than a second with red eyes over his triple espresso latte.

"No problem, Ian," he mumbled.

I got the school double bass out and verified that it was in fact out of tune again, because of Jennifer, the freshman who had used it yesterday. Well, I could deal with that in a minute. I tore down the hall after James. The school was creepy quiet this early in the morning. Not even the janitor was there yet. The EXIT signs gleamed like evil eyes above every door. Most of the overhead lights were still off, though the lights in the science lab and computer lab were on. I craned my ears for any sign of life. Down the first floor hall, I could hear the sound of a wet paintbrush slapping plaster. I followed the noise.

James had gotten six posters up already. They shone with the wheat paste mixture against the walls, stuck like flies in egg white. He started when I came down the hall toward him, then grinned at me.

I looked at his work. PEE PEE POO POO FOR ME ME YOU YOU: END TRANSPHOBIC BATHROOM POLICING AND LET KIDS PEE IN PEACE gleamed in yellow letters from black posters perfectly spaced six feet apart all the way down the hall. I wasn't really sure who would even get his message. Most people at this school didn't know what *transphobia* meant.

"This looks sick," I said. I felt kind of creeped out by the gleam in James's eye. I've wanted to stick it to the shitty school admin a few times, but I'm too conflict-avoidant for that. I'd never gotten in trouble for anything at school besides dress code violations. What would they do to him?

"I'm gonna do this hall and then the cafeteria and then the bathroom doors and the principal's office door," he said. "Forty posters total."

"I think you should do the office and cafeteria first," I said. "I can keep the band kids from going through the cafeteria for a minute, but when they open the main doors, you're on your own. Good luck. Love you." I went down the hall a little ways to my locker, to grab a music folder and make it look like I'd actually done something.

"Love you too," James said behind me, quietly. I turned

around but he was looking away from me again, at the wall. He glanced over at me, met my eye, and then looked down at his sticky wheat-covered hands.

I went and barred the door that went from the outer courtyard into the cafeteria before I went back to band.

"Janitor says he needs to keep people out of the cafeteria," I said when I got back, loud enough that Jared the alto saxophonist looked up from talking to Morgan the first trumpet. "Something about mopping with disinfectant out there. He's gonna lock the outside door."

"Thanks, Ian," Mr. Farro said. Then we launched into Duke Ellington, and as usual I was the kingpin keeping it all together. Even though jazz isn't really my thing. You can't have a band without a bass line, and especially not when the trumpets are half asleep at their stands.

My heart sped up as the hour neared its end. Would I come out and see James being led away by school security officers? As soon as the bell for the end of jazz band rang I practically knocked myself over putting my music away and hauling ass to get out and find James.

In the cafeteria, it looked . . . normal. Kids were sitting around talking, even as the big yellow-print posters stood around them, dripping from the walls. Someone had put up wet floor signs in front of them, though there was no wet floor. There were a couple clusters of people in front of some of them. I saw Opal coming in through the front doors and ran over.

"Seen James yet?" I asked.

"No," they said. "I saw the posters though. This is legendary. We gotta get pics to post before the school tears them down." They paused and took a picture of the nearest sign, which was the one on the principal's door. One corner was bent a little, as if someone had tried to pull it off with their hands. But the paste was already dry. The poster, for now, was stuck.

It was at that moment that the door opened, and the red face of Principal Coleman thrust out of the door and looked left and right, like a marten emerging from a tree. His eyebrows were drawn into a knot over his eyes and his mouth was turned down so far that it must have hurt his face. Opal and I watched in silence as he hurried in the direction of the hall with the lockers.

I felt my stomach plummet. I heard Opal stifling their laughter next to me.

"Ian, don't look so sad," they said, barely able to talk for laughing. "This is totally epic."

"James is going to be in so much trouble," I said. "And I helped. What if they kick him out of the *school*?"

"Dial the anxiety back." Opal rolled their eyes.

James wasn't at lunch, and he wasn't in English class that afternoon. At lunch I texted him, and he didn't reply. Opal didn't get a response either. Finally, he texted just as sixth period let out and my manager at McDonald's messaged our Slack to make sure I was coming in, since two people had called out. I told her I was, and then I opened the text from James.

Real life criminal over here, babie, James said. *Suspended for a week. Went to grab celebratory coffee and hit the record store. Meet me there?*

My shift started at five, which didn't leave a lot of time

between school and work. I went and spent three minutes trying to start my stupid car and then hightailed it downtown, through the rain. There was a check engine light on again on the dashboard. I made a mental note to ask my mom about it. On the way there, I listened to "Extraordinary Girl" from James's me-playlist. The only thing he could mean by that was that he thought I was an extraordinary girl, right?

James was parked at the library, and I parked there too before fast-walking down the hill to Cloudy Evening. *On my way,* I sent.

Cloudy Evening's been around since forever; they sell postcards, vintage comics, stickers, wall scrolls and old VCRs as much as they do cassettes, CDs or records. But it's a good place to browse, and they've got a Local Artist section. That was where Opal and I first found OVID's self-titled back in sophomore year.

Speaking of.

Standing next to the counter, talking to the red-haired girl working the cash register, was Jukebox January. They were laughing; so was the girl. The girl was taking a big printout poster from Jukebox and taping it up in the window. I looked around for James; he wasn't here yet. I stood, frozen, wondering whether I dared talk to Jukebox. They'd said nice things at the show, but that was the show. I didn't know if they thought of me as a little kid, or a shitty chaotic punk boy, or what, when we weren't in the same lineup. I glanced to my right, where there was a tower of old Archie comics, and pretended to be interested in looking at the covers, while I made up my mind.

"Monique Fatigue!" Jukebox said, coming over to me and throwing a hand around my shoulder. "I didn't know you liked Archie."

"H-hi," I said. "Oh gosh. I saw you there and wasn't sure if you were busy. How are you?"

"I'm great," Jukebox said. "I know that show was pretty messed up, but I guess I've pulled around to the place where scary experiences come with a side of total transformation. Of course, we have to get money to replace our equipment that got fucked."

"Oh man," I said. "I didn't even think about that." I thought of what had been on the stage when the fire caught. Amps, at least. The drum set. I remembered the shriek and the electric crackle that had felt like the whole place was splitting open, and how I hadn't known what was happening at first. All their shit must have gone. That was thousands of dollars.

"We're doing okay on the online fundraiser," Jukebox said, "but we're holding a benefit show this weekend at Red House anyway, for us and Goat Mansion, to rebuild and whatever. The Goat Mansion people use some of the show money to pay their slumlord, you know, and now they can't."

"That's awful," I heard myself saying, looking at Jukebox's silver buckles on their leather vest, the bright orange sweatshirt underneath, the wolf tattoo on their forearm and the ghost tattoo on their neck. They were so cool. Did they really see me as someone in their world? Less than a month ago I'd been in a band with two straight boys called *Rocketpizza*.

"Yeah. You want in?" Jukebox said. "You can get on the lineup, if you want, as an opener. You guys ruled. I don't have time to put it on the posters I've already put around town, but I'll add you to the Insta and throw it in Sharpie on these, if you want."

"Are you serious?"

They grinned. I found myself looking at their slightly crooked canine teeth and thinking about wolves. "Of course. You're what's up and coming. Hey, I meant to say, I wanted to talk to you about Lone Popper Records. I think they're looking for new artists right now. It's not the greatest or anything, like you won't get rich, but I could have my friend talk to you this weekend."

"T-that would be amazing," I said. Then I remembered my mom's ban on shows.

"Saturday at ten," Jukebox said. They shoved a poster into my hands. "Post it online and I'll message you the details on Insta. I have your drummer's info."

It was at that moment that the door of Cloudy Evening opened, the bell ringing. James walked in and saw me. His eyebrows shot up and he grinned.

"Hey, Ian," he said. "Hey Jukebox."

Seeing him reminded me. Space cow. The Compton thing. Opal wanted Jukebox to be a part of it. It felt awful to ask something of Jukebox, when they were giving me and the Dusties so much without even expecting a favor back, but I had to, or Opal would be mad I hadn't. "Jukebox," I said. "James is involved in Compton, the queer kid group. I was . . . we were wondering if you'd be interested in participating in this big show that Opal and I want to do for

Compton House in a couple months. We want to do like, a rock opera revue with local bands. The directors quit at the same time and the regular fundraiser they do isn't happening and the org will be out of money."

"A rock opera?" Jukebox said. "That sounds a little high stakes." They looked at James. "Who's writing it?"

"Opal," James said. "Ian's new drummer. It's about aliens bringing messages of peace and anticapitalism and queer love and saving the world."

There was a sudden fire in Jukebox's eyes. "Wow," they said. "Wait, did I tell you about my next album at the show? I forget."

"No," I said.

"That's what my new album's *about*, practically. I had *visions* about that, dude." They looked back to me. "It's in the air. Hey, this is awesome. I'm totally in. Talk this Saturday, yeah? This actually is gonna make my day. Awesome. Save the world, man. You're doing it. You're just a kid, and you're already doing it. They better look out."

They held up their hand for a high-five.

I high-fived them. As I did so, I felt something hit me—a little shock, carrying with it images of a great storm swallowing a wooden boat, a beaked and feathered creature opening its mouth to eat a strange plant, blood running down someone's chin, and beautiful tall women in leather, a kiss with bad breath, and the drumbeats of transformation, or . . .

I felt like an enormous wind had swept through me and left something inside me scraped up in its wake.

The bell tinkled as Jukebox dashed out the door with

their pile of posters. I looked down at the sheet in my hand, which was photocopied in black and white. I recognized the art—it was the same art that had advertised the first OVID show I'd gone to at the beginning of last school year. Jukebox must draw the pictures. Curving creatures in black brush pen spit water droplets this way and that around the words DIRE NEED BENEFIT TO SAVE GOAT MANSION. Underneath, there was a photo of the old show space, with flames drawn in ballpoint around the edges.

"Look at you, getting stuff done," James said. "How fortuitous that I asked that you be here, huh? And me only a deadbeat."

"You got *suspended*," I said. "I feel awful."

"I mean, duh. I was asking for it. I'm meeting with the principal next week with my mom," James said. "My mom's probably gonna ask for in-school suspension so I can still do work and catch up on homework. Lucky me. No idea what my dad will say. I'm avoiding his calls."

"What else can he do to you?" I asked.

"He could take away my car keys."

I had no idea what my mom would do if she found out I'd vandalized anything. Though I guessed I'd better start learning to break the rules if I wanted to make music.

How was I going to make this show Saturday?

"I have no idea how I'm gonna do this show without my mom finding out," I said. "I guess I need to ask her. But then if she says no, I'm fucked."

"Tell her you're working," James said. "You work late Saturdays."

My mom had shown up for my shifts before, to order something and tell me how proud she was of me saving money. Also probably to check on me. But that didn't mean she would *this* weekend, right?

James filled me in on what the principal had told him, and how he hadn't peed all day again. Everyone would just keep having to fight the same fight again and again.

"I shouldn't complain," James said. "I'm happy I did the posters. There's statistically at least one other trans kid at Cow Pie who isn't out yet, and they'll remember this day. I shall be their hero." The phone in his pocket started to buzz and he pulled it out and made a face. "Ugh, it's my dad again."

"Don't answer it," I said.

"Bye bye, daddy," he said, hitting the red phone on his screen. He looked up at me. "So hey, I've told you about this boy, right?"

"No," I said. I wasn't sure I wanted to hear this.

"I'm not sure I want to hear this," said Opal.

"I need *advice*," I said.

"And we need three songs minimum for the show tonight."

"Stop being mean," I said. I pouted and kicked my feet petulantly in the air towards the low yellow sodium light hanging from a wire. I was slumped upside down over the torn-up office chair where I sit to play bass in Barb's basement. Opal and Sophie and I were having an emergency jam session to get at least two more songs together for the show. We were really doing this by the seat of our pants. I had called out of work sick, and I knew my manager was mad, but since everyone else had just been sick, I had plausible deniability. Mom thought I was working. Sophie was sitting there, with a freshly shaved head, studying me, chin on hand.

"In my opinion," Sophie said. "This sounds fucked up."

That threw me for a loop. "Why fucked up?" I asked.

"He's like, *messing* with you," Sophie said. She paused and scratched her bald head. "Or he's just stupid. My last girlfriend was like that. Like a goldfish. You disappear for a second and it was like you stopped existing." She pulled at the sleeves of her *Exorcist* sweatshirt.

I pouted more at Opal, hoping they'd interject. They didn't—just looked down at their drumsticks.

James wasn't messing with me. I knew that much. And he was smarter than a goldfish. Probably.

"Say something," I said to Opal. "What do you know? Does he like me or not?"

"I plead the *fucking* fifth, Ian," Opal said. "If you guys want to do friend incest, you do it on your own time."

"Ew," I said. "Don't call it that."

"Look, talk to James if you're confused," Opal said. "I do know that at one time he had a crush on you. He told me not to tell you because he didn't want to fuck up your friendship. But I don't know what's going on right now any more than you do. There's the new boy. I don't know."

Sophie looked back at the music. "Okay, so, break over, yeah? I didn't drive down here to be a therapist." She bit her nail, squinting at the page. "I like what we're doing here with the G chord riff. Maybe let's go again with that and Opal can get more smashy on drums. I liked the cymbal last go."

I wasn't sure if this was any better than Ken and Devon, emotionally. But we were making way better music.

The first three songs Opal and I had been writing were all about flowers. Sophie liked them too—she said they reminded her of Songs For Moms, a Bandcamp mid-2000s girl band she liked from the Bay. She'd added some fast, twangy country-type chords to them, which I was okay with. Pansy Division had done it first. We called the songs "Oleander," "Dandelion Life," and "Hyacinth Bloodlust."

"I think it's possible for you to do the screamy thing, if you want to," Opal said casually, after we laid out the first sixteen bars of "Hyacinth Bloodlust." I wasn't sure if that was a suggestion or a passive aggressive way of saying I should. I'd been trying to do some of the vocal training things I'd looked up online and not totally destroy my vocal chords. I thought what I'd been doing sounded good.

"I like the way I sound *clear* on that first line," I said, panting a little. "I can scream later in the song. If I scream all the time, I'm gonna blow my voice out."

"Can I scream?" Opal asked. "I think what I'm saying is I need to scream."

They rolled their head back and looked at the ceiling, their green glittery eyeshadow gleaming in the half-light, their mouth so wide I could see their cavities. "Like—" Opal let out a sound like a dinosaur destroying a prehistoric shark.

"Hot," Sophie said. She had a deadpan kind of face on.

She squared her hips and put one leg up on the table covered with our notes and music, looking intently toward Opal. "I mean that. Go again."

Opal howled like a wolf.

"*That's* how we're gonna get famous," Sophie said, turning to me. "No offense, Ian. But that's dynamite."

Red House has a real shitty basement. It's maybe fourteen feet by ten feet, and the stage is just some boards someone built up. It's too small to play to huge crowds, and the ceiling is low, so the sound sucks. But it's made of cement, which isn't flammable, and it has a fire extinguisher, and the people who live upstairs put in some surge protector things, so the cable situation isn't as bad as it used to be. I thought that if my mom knew I was here, she wouldn't be that mad.

Which meant I probably should have told her. I could picture her telling me that she wasn't mad at me for playing shows, she was mad at me for lying. Mad, she would add, for lying *badly*.

I hoped she wouldn't want McDonald's tonight.

Sophie and Opal and I pulled up at nine. Sophie, who hadn't been in Olympia except for shows at Goat Mansion and Clown Barn, made a face when I turned off the car.

"Are you sure this is the place?" she asked. "This just looks like a house." She had a point. It sat along one of the un-sidewalked neighborhood streets on the East Side, with some scraggly trees and a Little Free Library in front. The only way you knew it was a punk show house was the falling-down couch on the porch and the Halloween skeleton wearing a silk robe balanced on the roof. And it was red.

"It's *Red* House," I said. "It's the place. It's just early." I looked over at her, worrying that she was reconsidering this whole venture. I was too, and if both of us were, it would be harder. She was pulling at her sleeves. I vowed not to gossip about boys to her again. "I promise this will be good. At least as a network thing."

"I love to network, baby," Opal said. "I've been messaging Jukebox about the show. We're putting together a spiel for the board to sell the Compton rock musical. I think we can get more people on board tonight if we go do the really earnest queer teen thing."

"I hate being earnest," Sophie said, rolling open the window and squinting out at Red House.

I knew nobody would really be there 'til eleven, which meant that only the other bands would see our show, if that. I wasn't sure how to break this news to Sophie. But James had said he would be there, and that was good. And Jukebox's friend was supposed to be there, and if we could get some studio time . . . not even a deal, I told myself. Studio time is what's more important.

I thought of the money I was losing tonight from McDonald's.

Maybe we'd make something on merch. Each shirt had cost about $7 to make, and so if we could sell them for $20 . . .

"Hey," I said, skipping up to the person setting up the table for tickets at the door. "I'm Ian. I'm with Monique Fatigue and the Dusties. We're opening tonight?"

The person, a fat Black butch masc with red hair and a

faded G.L.O.S.S. shirt, looked up at me mildly. I could see them assessing my age and maybe my gender. They looked at the poster on the table. I saw that *Moniqe Fateeg + the Dusties* had been scribbled in in Sharpie above the other bands' names.

"Hey, okay," they said. "It's a bit till we start. Craig's not even down here yet."

Our sound in the low room was not what it should have been. Opal said it was going to be okay once we had the echo setting on the mic. The stage didn't have a ramp, which meant we had to lift Opal's chair up; they ended up getting out and climbing up onto the stage on their knees and then getting back in their chair once we'd put it up there.

"Fuck bullshit punk ableism," I said.

They grunted. I wasn't sure if it was a *not the time* grunt or a *you poseur, pretending you give a shit* grunt.

We tried to figure out the echo setting for ten minutes before giving up and just going through our set really fast with the amps low. The lights were wrong, I thought, and the room was too small. Everything sounded flat. My heart was beating fast, and I was nervous that I wouldn't chill out before the show. Last time, when stuff had gone so well, it was 90% adrenaline. Now was the actual test.

"Your hands are shaking," Sophie said.

I looked down and realized they were. "Oh," I said. "Whoops."

"I think we're okay," Opal said.

That wasn't comforting. Especially because there wasn't anyone there yet. It was 9:30 now. I kept glancing out into the little side room and the yard.

At 9:45, Jukebox stuck their head around the door into the show space.

"Damn, this is smaller than I remember," Jukebox said. "Tiny box vibes. No wonder I never come here." They laughed. Tonight they were just wearing a leather harness and no shirt, even though it was cold out. Ripped jeans. They went up to Opal and Sophie. "Hey, guys," they said. "I'm so glad you could make it."

"Can we show you the newest song?" Sophie said, loudly. "Before people get here?"

"Hell yeah," Jukebox said. "I was gonna spray paint that one lyric on the wall in here before you started. It works so good for the whole vibe. You cool with that?"

I looked at Opal. I had no idea Jukebox had read our lyrics.

"I sent them some recordings of us earlier," Opal said. They turned to Jukebox. "What are you spray painting?"

"I love that one line—*weeds springing up in the open cracks with seeds to spread*," Jukebox said. "It matches the theme of the night. Rebuilding, you know? I thought I could spray paint it in this glow in the dark paint I got behind you, we could get some pics to share."

Sophie and I exchanged glances. I didn't really feel—but Jukebox was already painting behind us. The smell of paint filled the air, and we moved outside to stop our band stuff from getting it.

When the whole little show space was filled with paint

fumes, Jukebox stood back and admired their writing. They'd added a little flower at the end of the line. "Now play," they said.

We did. Opal's drums rolled like rocks rattling down the side of a hill, and I found my voice enough to start screaming the way we'd tried before. We all screamed together—

It was too flat.

"I like that," Jukebox said anyway. "Dogman's gonna love it, too. Look, I know people are coming, they're just late and running on Oly time. You guys want popcorn?"

We set down our instruments and went outside to the stairs at the bottom of the green-lit porch to sit with Jukebox and Stacey and Lorenzo and two other people we didn't know yet, who gave us popcorn. Stacey was wearing white Dickies and went up the steps to sit on the ratty couch for a second before springing up shrieking and turning around to show us her now-grubby ass.

"These are new pants," she cried, as Jukebox cracked up.

"That's the cursed couch," Lorenzo laughed. "You don't sit on that."

"Don't worry. Dirt looks hot on those," Sophie said, tossing a handful of popcorn in her mouth. I could see the hunger in her eyes as she looked at Stacey.

At ten thirty, bikes started rolling up. People left them in kind of a pile against one tree. A couple cars arrived. One was James's.

"Hey," he said, hopping out and scampering over. He was wearing a mesh tank top under his denim jacket. He looked windswept and excited. "Did I miss the set?"

"Nah, we haven't started yet," I said. "All the smokers are

smoking and the ten people who are gonna be here aren't here."

"I knew it," James said. "No offense. Nothing starts on time."

But as soon as James was there, it seemed like everyone was. Suddenly the air smelled like cigarettes and weed. Jukebox came over with a guy in a yellow tie-dye shirt and long hair, who was Dogman. He smiled and shook my hand, then Sophie's. He started to lean over to Opal, which they hate, so they reached up preemptively and punched his hand.

"I'm Opal," they said. "I'm the brains. I need you to get everyone on your label to commit to playing a song for a Compton House Queer Youth fundraiser."

Dogman looked taken aback. "What?" he said.

"It's that rock musical thing I was telling you about," Jukebox said. "We're gonna make it happen. Save the support groups, and the gay music camp, and the craft nights and bowling nights for the gay kids. We can put it on the website." They laid an arm around his shoulder. "I know JetPig said yes, and Sandy Thong."

Dogman nodded, scowling. "I couldn't understand everything you said in your voicemail. This is on a pretty tight timeline, right?"

"December," Jukebox said. "But we can do it. We pulled *this* together. We just need to show support. It's about mutual *aid*." They punched his shoulder. Dogman, who for all his grubbiness seemed kind of delicate, looked even more taken aback at having two body parts punched in succession. "But hey, that's for later. I'm talking with

Compton Monday night." They turned to me and Sophie.
"You guys are *on* now."

I felt so sick.

HYACINTH BLOODLUST
Oh my blood my blood
 hits the roof of my mouth
oh my blood my blood
hits the roof of your mouth
   go South   oh
Gone forever down the drain
      Diseased blood
Wish I cold taste your blood again
   Hyacinth
   wash the water in your hands
   Hyacinth
make me a better man
   show me yours
   show me yours
   break my bones again
   On the street outside your house
   Pull my heart out of my mouth
   → EVERYONE
      SCREEAM←

I looked up at the end of the song, sweat in my eyes, not sure how I was going to do this again. It sounded way too flat. James was looking at me failing at this. Jukebox was on some shit about us being good that felt weird, because we *weren't* good.

A camera flashed.

I felt like I was going to throw up. Like, actual bile coming—I set down my bass, then picked it up again, then swallowed hard. There were ten people in the room, and all of them were just standing with their arms crossed, looking at me. Did they think I looked stupid?

I felt suddenly sure that my body was completely wrong. The other ten people at the show were outside. They hadn't even come in.

But I looked at James.

Opal counted off again—"ONETWOTHREEFOURAH-HHHH."

James looked at me encouragingly. He even danced, when nobody else was dancing. He threw himself around as if there were invisible people moshing with him.

"FATAL WRECK!" Sophie yelled at the end of "Dandelion Life." Her hand went out and smacked me in the face.

"Ouch," I said. Someone in the audience who I didn't know laughed, and the misery that had been under the surface the whole time was suddenly all over me. I felt like a pimply, oily, crusty, stupid kid. Nobody took us seriously. It would have been better if I had just stayed with Ken and Devon playing shitty straight metal shows where everyone was wasted, and never had to realize it.

I staggered into James as I went offstage. He'd come up to the side without me noticing. He was holding two beers.

"Hey," he said. "You're amazing."

"I don't want beer," I said, barely conscious outside of the anxiety buzzing through my arms. "No beer. Move."

"They're both for me." James moved, and I bumped through the door to the outside. There's only one show room in Red House. You're inside with too many people, or outside with too many people. The ten people who didn't deign to come listen to us turned around as I rounded the house quickly, still carrying my bass. James followed me with the beer. I sat down on a curb behind a rhododendron, feeling my throat trying to swell up and escape my mouth.

"Hey hey," he said. "Come on. That was great."

"No it was not," I said. "James, just get out of my face for a second, okay?"

He looked deeply wounded. "Come on, Ian," he said. "Not every show is a blockbuster. People will talk about this one though. These ten people each know ten more."

I felt the bile coming again, so I didn't say anything. I put my head in my hands, thinking about lying to my mom for this.

James started chugging the beer. I could tell he was doing it for my benefit. Or to annoy me, whatever, same thing.

"Stop," I said. Something came over me, and I grabbed his empty beer bottle from his hand and tossed it against the back wall of Red House. It shattered.

He stiffened, crossed his arms. "Woah, there, Miss Edge. Chill out."

"I'm *serious*. My mom had a friend who died drunk driving when she was eighteen," I said. "She's had dreams about her ever since. I'm driving you home."

James nodded and belched. "Well," he said. "If that makes you feel better. Sorry for fucking up the vibe by being substance-dependent."

Looking at the shattered glass, I knelt down. I had just remembered—

"I told my mom I was working," I said. "That's how *I'm* gonna die. And for what? They looked at us like we were an infomercial."

He nodded. "They're Oly people. I'm sorry, Ian."

I felt tears coming up in my eyes.

"God. I don't know. Jesus. I'm sorry for throwing the beer bottle."

"It's okay," James said, though he didn't sound completely okay. "You have beliefs. I *am* going to drink this other beer. That way you absolutely gotta drive me, and I can make sure you're okay. Friends stick together, right?"

I thought about how I'd left Opal and Sophie in the show room with all the gear and felt guilty. I stood up. "It's stupid for me to expect every show to be different now. Sorry. I just had a minute there where it felt awful."

"You barely had a week," James called, as I headed back toward the door. "It's amazing you don't sound like a chorus of lobsters."

The audience had filtered back out to smoke, and the show room was empty. The painted lyrics gleamed on the wall. Jukebox and Dogman were talking with Sophie and Opal. Jukebox was squatting on the edge of the stage. Opal and Sophie looked like they had been caught by surprise. Dogman turned to me.

"So," he said, "Monique. Good to see you all play."

It felt funny to get called Monique, but not bad. Really not bad.

"He likes it," Opal said. They turned to him. "We're really open to feedback."

Dogman smirked. "Yeah, I mean, you sound pretty awesome for a band that's only been together a week. I really love the uh, harsh vocals. You're obviously music nerds. And the visuals of all of you are great—Ian's so fem, and Opal's so like, rocker dyke butch, and Sophie's somewhere over in alien territory. I love the rough pop punk sound you're trying for—it's like early RVIVR."

Opal seemed irritated at the *trying for*, or maybe at the word *dyke*, and Sophie was prickling too, but I made eye contact and they both let it slide.

"So, we're gonna definitely get signed with Lone Popper," Sophie said, grinning like it was a joke.

Dogman shot Jukebox a sharp, worried look, and then looked at Sophie carefully and pulled at his mullet. "You're pretty new? But I like what you played today."

"Totally," Opal said.

Dogman looked nervously at Opal's phone, which was open to the voice recorder app. "I know Jukebox really cares about this show you all are planning, and you know I'm all about queer youth. Compton does great stuff. The, uh, support groups, the dances, the sex ed."

"This is more than just saving Compton," Jukebox said. "This is an opportunity to heal whole communities and get us to talk to each other. We can open each other up to visions of a better world. We can elevate the entire community's consciousness. That's what art's *for*."

"Sure," Dogman said, uneasily. "Well, superficially, it's to raise money, and I agree with Opal that we can probably help with that."

"Nice," Opal said. "Now, who do I talk to to get these Red House idiots to put a ramp in here?"

Jukebox's smile faded a little. "Oh shit, little dude," they said. "I didn't think about that."

Opal raised an eyebrow.

"Cool, let's go out and smoke or some shit, yeah?"

I hung out with James for the rest of the show, mostly to make sure he didn't drive home drunk and didn't have too much more to drink. He seemed done after the second beer, though. We danced, and I kept looking at the way he was moving, and trying to copy it—his arms went out, and mine did too. Once during Jukebox's set, we wove our fingers together. There was an image in my head of a bright planet spinning through space that wasn't Earth. A great warship orbited it, shaped like a crystal and flecked with silver armaments. Then there was a picture in my mind of a woman sinking into steaming water, outdoors, rain falling around her. For a second I felt like I was underwater.

At the merch table, after, three people bought shirts.

Sophie kept raising her eyebrows at me whenever James touched my shoulder or held my hand.

I did have to get home soon. I wanted to talk to Jukebox

more, but I couldn't. I already had a missed call from my mom. I texted her, *staying late to clean. Barf in the bathroom.*

I drove Sophie and Opal to Barb's, and then James and I went to the other McDonald's, across town, to pick up food to make it look like I'd been to work. If there were McDonald's leftovers, Mom wouldn't ask questions. Then back to James's house, to drop him off.

James was smoking his vape pen sitting on the ground in front of his house as he ate his Oreo McFlurry with the spoon.

"So," he said. "Starting tomorrow, Dad's taking away my car keys for three months. I'm grounded." He sounded flippant. "He thinks I'm going to his tonight, but I'm *so* ditching and staying at Mom's or Opal's. And he can go get the car from in front of Red House if he wants it so bad."

Shit. "I'm so sorry," I said.

"What?"

"It was dumb of me not to stop you, with the posters. And to make you leave your car there. We should have got your mom—"

He laughed. "You think I care? Mainly I'm sad I can't go to your shows all the time, without the car."

I wasn't going to be able to play another show like that without James there to egg me on.

"You *gotta* come to my shows," I said.

"Even if I drink beer?"

"Yeah."

I couldn't tell what the expression on his face was. I felt my eyes traveling down below his collar to his mesh shirt under his denim jacket, and to the hair on his stomach I could see through his shirt.

"Ian," he said, "do you wanna make out?"

I looked back up at his face in the yellow light of the porch. "What?"

James stuck the spoon in his mouth, not meeting my eyes. "I don't know. Maybe I'm just . . . feeling slutty, but I made out with that boy Orsino the other day, and I think making out is really *fun*. And I've never done that with you. And now you're single, so we can. If you want to."

I felt a shiver go through my arms and down in my stomach. His eyes were looking at me now, so intensely. "Uh, sure. Yeah. Fuck," I said.

From his face, I wasn't sure if that was the right thing to say, but he laughed nervously and hopped up, and then grabbed my hand and hauled me up too, so we were standing with our noses nearly touching.

"Cool."

We got back into my car. We crawled into the back seat, both struck with the same high nervous giggles. I felt my heart pounding the inside of my ribcage. His breath was warm. James was about the same size as me, and we were both too big for the narrow backseat crowded with band gear and merch. My knee was in the T-shirt box, and the box buckled under me, so I lurched forward. James started to lean back in anticipation of being kissed, and then I tried to move and my head hit the window. But then he grabbed the front of my shirt, and even though my back was in a weird position, I stopped moving so I could kiss him.

James kissed harder than Tristan, and bit at my lip. As

soon as our lips met his hand was on the back of my head, too. Tristan never did that. James petted my hair, hard, and pressed his fingers into the back of my neck. It was like everything suddenly lined up.

The box of T-shirts fell to the floor of the car.

I put my hand up under his shirt, thinking about how he'd worn a binder until just this summer. His skin was warm. I felt a weird pang. I wished I could have touched him when he was still wearing the binder. Was that bad? I wanted part of his past that I didn't get to have. I pushed my hand up along his stomach and felt the raised line of his scar. I stopped. I was *not* sure if I should touch him there. He shivered and smiled against my mouth.

"That's . . . really nice."

I wanted to have scars like that.

I definitely couldn't say that to him.

I wanted—

Then his tongue was in my mouth. I could taste his ice cream, which would have probably grossed me out, except it was James. He was kissing me hard, his hand reaching to clutch me. I felt out of breath, but when I gasped for air I wanted to kiss him again as soon as our faces came apart. I felt myself getting hard in my pants before I could stop to think about what exactly was happening, or how things would change because I'd said yes to this, or what would have happened if I'd said no. He was kissing my neck. He bit me. I yelped.

He stopped.

"Is that okay?" he asked.

I felt weak and dizzy. I didn't want him to *ask*. I didn't

want to think about what I wanted. I didn't know what was okay because I didn't know what the implications of any of this were. I had no idea what was happening in his head.

I nodded, and he bit me more. That'll leave a mark, I thought, and imagined my mom seeing it and rolling her eyes. He came down on top of me, his weight on my stomach and across my lap. Our mouths met again, and his hair was in my eye.

I moved so I could hold him in both arms, and then I heard the noise of a truck shifting on the highway, and everything hit me at once.

"What are we *doing*?" I asked him. I felt a hot poker thrust of fear from my gut up through the roof of my mouth. I realized we might not think we were doing the same thing.

I could feel him stop breathing for a second.

"Just . . . two guys being dudes?" His voice was carefully jokey.

"Oh," I said. My voice dropped and cracked.

God, why was I such a drama queen?

James laughed nervously. "Ian, you're my friend, this can be whatever, but you're *really* hot. It's fun to kiss you."

I meant to calm down, but I couldn't control the panic rising in my chest. I felt the earth falling out from under my car, and us falling into weird oblivion. I felt shivery, suddenly, which I hadn't felt before, even though it was cold outside. My teeth started chattering. How could this be happening? How could this be happening with *James*?

"I think I'm a girl," I said.

"What?" James asked.

The panic rose into a tide, and whatever was in my mouth was no longer in my mouth.

"It's like, the middle of the night," I said, and I tried to sit up, but couldn't, because he was on top of me. My heart rate sped up again. "I'm *so* stupid."

He pushed himself up on his elbows over me. "Are you okay?"

I wasn't sure. No, I wasn't okay. I couldn't look at him. "Yeah," I said. "Totally. Totally, totally. Just, this was . . . random." I tried to take a deep breath.

He frowned seriously and started to sit up, which was hard, because we were crammed between my bass and my backpack and my knee was scrunched up on top of the T-shirt box. "I'm sorry," he said. "This is weird for you. I'm sorry. I should have checked in more."

"Yes," I said, then felt bad for saying it. His big puppy dog eyes were staring at me. "I just have . . . I didn't expect it."

"Sure," James said. He looked upset.

I was still hard. This was confusing.

And—I looked at my phone. 1:23 a.m.

There were three missed calls from my mom. Shit. Shit-shitshitshit.

"My mom is going to freak out. I was gone way too late. I'm sorry, I just can't . . ." I felt my voice start to get hysterical. My face was flushed and hot. "I'm sorry, James, I shouldn't be like this, this shouldn't . . . it's a million other things."

His face crumpled. "I didn't think about the time. Your mom. Totally. You should get home. Here, I'll get out. Go, go. Good night." He scrambled out the door, tripping over his feet and slamming the latch shut on his side too hard.

I sat at my weird angle on the T-shirts, staring at the gray carpeted ceiling over the backseat, trying to catch my breath. *What was happening?*

I heard the screen door and front door rattle and slam.

Was he really going? Without talking at *all*? I fell down into the gap between the backseat and the front seats and fumbled my way out the other door. He was already inside.

"James," I yelled. "Stop, stop a second."

He couldn't hear me or something.

I turned around and saw that his McFlurry was still on the ground by my car.

I got home, and Mom's light was out. That was a relief. Depending on when she'd gone to bed. But then, after I had locked the front door as quietly as I could and crept quietly down the hall to brush my teeth, I heard the floor creak outside her door.

"Ian?"

"Yesh," I said through my toothpaste. Shiiiit.

She stuck her head around the door. Her hair was pulled back under the scarf she wears at night. She had on her "worried" expression, which is the thing that comes before a bunch of her other more frightening expressions.

"Ian," she said. "Party went off the rails, huh? It's *late*."

I spit out my toothpaste. I was still wearing my show clothes. I wasn't sure if she was registering that. "There was this *horrible* mess in the bathroom at work," I said. "You don't even wanna know all what. Barf and stuff, and blood, and *teeth*, and someone left their trash in there, and someone had knocked it all over the floor. We had to stay late cleaning."

Mom folded her arms. "For three hours past your shift? Why would Sidney do that to you? She knows you're in high school. You want me to call her? She's violating the Washington state labor laws."

I could come clean or I could keep digging. If I thought on my feet fast enough she might let me go to bed, even if she didn't totally believe me.

"I was the only one who could clean it because Rachel's terrified of bodily fluids. I said I was fine with it. But then I just sat in my car for a while after, I was so tired," I said. That was not a very good story. Mom raised her eyebrow. "What?" I asked. "You tell me not to drive tired."

"Okay, try again," she said. "Ian, *did you go to work tonight?*"

"Yes," I said, indignantly. "I told you."

She pursed her lips. "Ian, look at you. You've got glitter and a crop top on. You expect me to believe that you were at work, and cleaned someone's barf, and *teeth*, and then sat in your car and got dressed nice and did your makeup, and then somehow smeared that shit on your lips over the rest of your face while you were driving home?"

I reached for a washcloth to wipe my face off. James had smeared my lipstick over the edges of my mouth. I avoided her eyes.

"Don't you dare use one of my white washcloths to wipe off black lipstick, Ian," Mom said. She pointed to her cabinet. "Use a makeup wipe and then use one of the brown washcloths."

Without saying anything, I went to the cabinet and got out her makeup wipe.

"Keep going," Mom said. "I wanna hear this. What happened after work?"

"Look, I'm really upset lately," I said. "After Tristan, I've been a mess."

Mom made a hum in the back of her throat and cocked her head. "So that's why your bass is not in your room and is in the hall, right?"

I felt like stomping my feet. I may have flapped my hands a little bit, in frustration. "Fine! I went out! I played a show! Can you just give me a minute to wash my face," I said. Too loud.

"I know you are not talking back to me at two in the morning on Sunday," Mom said. "And what I don't understand." She paused, for emphasis. I kept scrubbing my face, trying to get the makeup off. "What I don't understand is you clearly made this plan, right, and you did all this stuff, and you got home three hours late, but you did not make a plan to lie about it."

The lipstick wasn't coming off.

"You don't understand," I said. "Music is *part* of my future. I need to do shows. This came up really last minute, and you would have said no."

"Yeah. Because you went to a show a bit ago and there was a *fire that burned the place down*."

"I was opening for a band I love. I *had* to do it. You told me I couldn't go to shows anymore, and that's like—like cutting off my legs."

"Nobody's cutting anything, Ian. I can't believe you'd

say that. You're friends with Opal. How do you think they would feel if they heard you say that?"

"Opal has *legs*, Mom. *And* they get to go to shows."

"Oh, so maybe you can just go live at Opal's house then, with the weirdo lesbian."

"What was I supposed to do? Ask? You would have said no."

She made the humming noise again and shook her head. "You lied to me. Look, did you do drugs tonight?"

"No," I said.

"Again," she said.

"No," I said, miserably. "I *don't drink*. Mom, I talk about this all the time. That's what the Xs on my hands are for. That's what they mean, I don't believe in that stuff. You would know that, if you *listened* to me at all. The only thing I do is music."

She squinted at me. "You lied to me about one thing. Now I don't know what else you're lying about. So, I have no choice. *You* can't use the car anymore. No sleepovers for the foreseeable future, and no more driving alone. You're grounded, *except* for activities that are *safe* and *educational*, during the *day*, that I know about and drive you to. That can be music. Okay? I'm reasonable. But I gotta know, and I gotta approve. No more lying. It's a bad look. What would your grandmother say?"

In one way or another, the weekend just kept getting worse.

Chapter 12

ORSINO

I wondered if I was doing it. Was I bending time, yanking another future closer?

The men in my dream wore black gas masks. Dog-me knew that the men wanted to eat me because they had not eaten for weeks. They had been traveling through the fire. Dog-me tried to bite them, but they wore gloves and stuck a knife into my side—not even my throat. These men did not know how to kill dogs. But it didn't matter. I was going to die anyway.

There is a moment in the past which, if changed, might have prevented this.

I saw the pink orb like a second moon, saw the face-not-face of the being who had spoken to me. Behind it, the sharp-edged shape of the warship.

We cannot stay at these coordinates. We will need to relocate soon to avoid battle with the imperial military. But you are not who they are pursuing. You can continue. You, and others. Continue opening to the visions. Share them.

It was 5:23 a.m. My phone was on 23% because I'd forgotten

to plug it in. I scrambled and stuck the charger into the wall, but it took a minute for my phone to recognize it because it was an unsupported accessory. If you get it in at just the right angle, it works.

I saw on my lock screen that James had texted me. I took a shower before I checked the text, because I knew I couldn't handle it before my heart calmed down. I put my head under the shower head, on the coldest setting. I felt like one big keloid scar. When I'd chilled for a second, I turned it up to almost boiling until I was warm again. My hair was bristly and stuck out in all directions as I put the towel over it. I threw on my sweatshirt and jeans from yesterday, stumbled back to my room, locked the door, and let myself flop on the floor and look at my phone.

James' text said: *hey orisno ! hope ur good. You're cute and i'm looking forward to seeing u when ur back at oly! I got suspended and lost my car for doing the stupidest shit ever. I'll send you a pic.* There was a little emoji of a devil. Attached was an image. On my dad's Wi-Fi, it took a second to download. Finally it did. PEE PEE POO POO FOR ME ME YOU YOU, the sign said in bright orange-yellow letters. END TRANSPHOBIC BATHROOM POLICING AND LET KIDS PEE IN PEACE.

I grinned and hugged my phone to my chest for a second. I felt like I'd won something.

Then I texted Jukebox, again. *Hey, I know you were out late last night, but can you please come get me from my dad's? I'm gonna die out here.*

I hoped my dad didn't come back in the house.

I'd been stuck here for days now, and every day I'd tried

to get Jukebox down to drive me back. I hadn't seen the feathered creatures running through the woods again, after the first night with James. But the nightmares were more vivid than usual. I should have waited to come here until Jukebox could drive me both ways, I realized, but I'd thought that they would for sure be able to make the trip before their show. No go. They were all excited about the show and getting money back for their equipment. So I was stuck here.

The first night I was here, I'd sent my dad a text after I kissed James in the car. *Here to pick up stuff,* it said. Dad had left it on read. The next morning, around eleven, he'd come in for lunch as I was sitting on the couch, going through my old sketchbooks in the living room. He made his sandwich without looking at me, and I'd felt all my old reflexes kick in as I stayed quietly rooted to my seat, unable to move. There was a rule with my dad that you didn't make a sound until he did, or he could explode.

"Almost burned all that shit," he said finally. His voice was more gravelly than I remembered it.

"Well, thanks for not doing that," I said, not looking up. "I'll take it."

He grunted and turned, carrying his turkey sandwich out of the house, back to work. He was out the rest of the day; after he finished the farm tasks, his truck drove off down the road, and he hadn't come back that night. The truck came back the next afternoon, but I didn't see him, because I went and walked in the woods on the edge of the property until it was dark.

Right now, I could see that the door for the chicken barn

was open, which meant my dad or one of his seasonal guys was over there.

The cows had moved so that they were under the big tree in the field outside the barn. I thought about how one of those cows was the one whose calf had wandered away and died in the woods last winter. We'd found her calf half-eaten by coyotes. The calf's skull was with my other stuff in cardboard boxes, now. It was the biggest skull in there.

I went out to feed the goats. I stood in the middle of all of them, in the shed, and they nuzzled my hands. The goat-smell got all in my nose. Their noses were warm. I stroked Mama Fattie's head. She's the oldest goat, and starting in September we always put a little blanket on her to keep her warm. We have a heater in the shed for really cold days, but it wasn't quite cold enough to turn it on, because of how expensive it is. I looked at my phone again.

Jukebox had texted: *Hell yeah little buddy. Sorry about yesterday. On my way in an hour.*

I looked out the window again, towards the tree by the road.

I remembered my dream.

Suddenly I knew what I needed to do. I felt awful that I hadn't thought of it before. It was the only time I'd be able to do it.

I had to dig up Agatha, before I left.

I threw on my dad's jeans from the hamper and his plaid work coat, so I wouldn't get my only clothes muddy in the rain. I grabbed his gardening gloves from the box in the garage. The shovels were already outside, leaning against the wall of the house. I took the biggest one.

I've shoveled dirt and shit and other stuff my whole life. Your hands get calluses after a while, even in gloves. Your muscles adapt. But I'd been living in Tacoma. As the blade of the shovel cut into the dark mud and I jumped on the edge to get purchase, I wondered how long this job would take. It had been a while since I'd needed to dig anything up, or put anything under.

Thuk. The shovel went into the mud.

Agatha was about three feet down. If I dug fast, I could get her up before Jukebox got here. If my dad was working, and didn't come back until lunchtime, he wouldn't be able to stop me from digging her up or taking her back with me, to where she belonged.

I'd gotten Agatha when she was one year old. I was ten. She was traumatized from her former home, where there was either dogfighting or just serious abuse; the shelter didn't know. My mom had been nervous about her being in the house, because the first day she had pressed her head into my leg and then barfed into the couch cushions. I've never felt so close with anyone in my whole life. I trained her really good.

Thuk.

When I'd go on walks at night, she went with me. She could understand me, and she could even jump in and out of my first floor window at night, if she needed to go out and smell something or pee. She was agile, beautiful, intelligent. She knew me like nobody else did, because I didn't have to explain the way I was to her. We would wrestle in the yard.

I didn't know how far decomposed she would be, if there would be anything left but bones or if maybe somehow there would be a miraculous preservation, and she wouldn't have changed at all. I thought of her sweet black fur and the gray around her muzzle. The crackle and hum of the shadows started as I got deeper down into the dirt.

Thuk.

I hit her spine, first. The rattling electric shocks got stronger the more dirt I pushed away. Agatha wasn't wrapped up at all, and she was in soil that was neither dry nor clay. But she wasn't just bones and teeth, the way some websites had told me to expect. Parts of her hide and fur were still covering her bones.

I laid her out on the ground in front of me and felt the tears coming and the snot rising in my throat as the cold mud seeped through the knees of my pants.

Her ribs were crushed from the car, where my dad had run over her. Her skull was dirty, with one bullet hole in the middle where my dad had shot her, after, when she was crying in the road.

My dad had backed me into the pantry and told me he knew that Robin had made me think I was gay and was making me bind my chest. He said I thought I was gay because I was retarded and thought everything that bull-dyke Robin did was normal. I told him he was the retard, which made him hit me, and Mom screamed, and then I hit him, which made him raise his hands dramatically and say he wouldn't ever raise a hand against his daughter. Then Agatha died. My dad's not like me. He knows how to kill something, when he wants to.

I wondered if the bullet was somewhere in the dirt, but I didn't look. I thought about her eyes and her tongue and got a flash of fire in my head.

I felt her last thought: *where is the Boy? The Boy isn't here. He doesn't love me.*

I started to panic. The electricity under my knees start seeping harder into me. There was nothing I could say to her.

I couldn't leave her here.

I backed away and sat down in the mud, looking away from Agatha and breathing deep. I tried to sense the rain and the cold sky above me, but I could hear the fire crackle.

Then I sat, for too long, listening to the birds, feeling my paws burning.

Flash.

"Orsino!" Jukebox yelled, brightly.

I looked over. Jukebox's car was parked in the drive, the edge of it almost touching the house. The lights were on, shining into the goat pen, and the goats were yelling. Ranger was barking from behind the fence. Jukebox was waving, leaning out of the driver's seat.

I couldn't answer. I waved. Jukebox squinted at me, and I heard the car door slam. They walked over, their swagger out of place against the backdrop of the place I grew up. They had on their big black sweatshirt, the hood pulled over their hair.

"Hey, little bro," they said. "Sorry I'm late. What's—oh, shit."

I was covered in mud, and Agatha's body lay, rotten and long and black-red-yellow-brown-deeper-brown, across the ground in front of me. Jukebox's nose didn't wrinkle. They looked steadily down at the year-old dead dog, then at me.

"Agatha, right?" they asked.

I nodded.

"Robin told me. About your dad. That guy's a monster." They knelt down next to me, and I could feel in the rain that they were crackling with light and fire inside, just like me. The hair on my arms and my head started to stand on end, and my bones started to shake.

"I have to . . . to move her," I said. "She's still with my dad, and she's afraid." I didn't know if that made any sense. Obviously—super obviously—the dog was dead. But she was inside me, the same way she'd always been. We understood each other. My dad had killed her, the way he would have eventually killed me if I'd stayed. And she was stuck here, unless I stole her back.

Jukebox, to my relief, nodded.

"I think what you're doing is smart. You think about her a lot."

"I dream," I said. "In the bad visions of the future, I'm a dog. It's like I *am* her. Like it's her ghost in me."

Jukebox put a hand on my arm, which felt awful. I didn't want to be touched. But their touch still sent a wave of feeling into me anyway. Cold, hard wind from distant mountains. The water that fell on my face was the river a million years ago and a million years in the future. I was grateful. I looked at them, trying to smile and not sure if I was smiling, and their eyes looked back into me, weird and deep and gray-silver.

"We're not gonna be in the bad futures, Orsino. I'm gonna find like, a box or something, to put her in. Where should I look?" I'd never heard them speak so gently. I started to open my mouth to say that there might be something in the garage.

Then I saw my dad.

He was coming up the drive in his black shit-covered work boots, his red raincoat pulled up around his neck and the hood pulled low, and he was walking fast. He was carrying an empty plastic bag, the kind we use for feed. He must have been coming back to the house for lunch. He had seen us. He was walking toward us.

"Hey," he called, in his dangerous voice. "What the *fuck* are you doing?"

We couldn't answer, because we would have had to shout. Jukebox stood up first. I scrambled to my feet. I was worried that Jukebox would say something and my dad would get the gun. I realized we weren't gonna get any of my shit into the car after all. The most we could do was get the fuck out of here. I turned to Jukebox, to say this, but they were glaring at my dad and kind of grinning at the same time, and then a gust of wind came, and I saw that all the hair on their head was standing straight up.

Flash.

Lightning crackled through me on its way to them. Not real lightning—there wasn't thunder, there wasn't a storm, just the drizzle that had been going all morning. But I felt a buzz of energy pass through me like I'd just stuck my hand against an exposed telephone wire.

"Who the fuck are you?" my dad demanded. He turned

to me. "Jess. Who the fuck is this? What the fuck are you doing? What kind of sick fucked-up shit is this? Put the fucking dog back in the ground. It's *dead*."

"Hey, man. I'm Jukebox," said Jukebox. Their voice was lower, more gravelly than I'd heard it before. They held themselves upright and rigid. They stared my dad in the eyes. "I'm here to drive him. We're getting his stuff and we're going. We'll be out of here in an hour."

"The fuck kind of a name is that," my dad said. "If you're not off my property in five minutes, I'm within my rights to shoot you dead, son."

"*He's* your son," Jukebox said, pointing to me. "I'm not your anything, man. I'm just helping him move his shit."

"Dad," I said. "I need to take Agatha with me. I need to get my art. That's it. Then we're gone."

"I don't know what the fuck you're up to, but it's nothing that belongs here. Not on my property. You wanna go do your shit, you do your shit, but you can't bring it back here. This is my house, understand? It's my house, and my land, and you can't come back here and dig shit up, tear up the yard. Are you *both* retarded?"

I looked at my dad, and felt the old frozen feeling come back, the one that used to drive me under my bed. All the anger I'd ever contained, rushing through my stomach and pushing up into my neck and my tonsils. I felt the nightmares bubbling up, with the tar around my feet and the comets rushing down and the van sinking under the water and the bile and blood and knives shoved into me. His fist in the wall. His voice, echoing after Robin as she ran. I felt the horror of animals burning, and the horror I'd felt when my dad had braked hard in the car, sending me into the seat in front of me, and the ripple of the earth's crust sending devastating earthquakes to crush cities.

I wanted to hit him. I wanted to split his skull with the shovel. I could also sort of *see* the anger my dad felt, hovering around him like a shuddering, red mass. I knew he wanted to hurt me too.

Jukebox was laughing.

I wasn't sure if I heard them right at first, but their high, hyena cackle got louder against the wind as the seconds passed. They grinned at my dad, their crooked teeth white-yellow against their red mouth. Their hair was still standing straight up on their head, waving in the wind. The wind was more intense now.

"Something funny?" my dad asked.

Jukebox turned to me. "You feel it, right? The rush. All the bad things. Everything bad that's ever been done, everything bad they could do, or that could happen. Running through you."

I couldn't speak. I nodded.

Jukebox smiled. "And you've given James images. Visions. By touching him, right?"

"You're going to fucking regret coming here, Juicebox," my dad said.

"Yes," I said. I felt the red blood running out from my dog-mouth against the pavement, the tires over my ribs.

"Then on three," Jukebox said. "Just hold his hand. And let him see it. You're stronger than him. He can't handle it."

"What?"

"One. Two."

"Jukebox!"

"Three."

They lurched at my dad, arms raised. He raised his hand to strike them on the head at the same time—a side hit, with the flat of his hand, but he would have hit their ear and knocked them over, he was so much taller. Shit. I threw myself between them, catching my dad's hand in mine, grabbing it tight. It was hard and calloused and red, and he tried to grab my hand, bend my fingers back and throw me to the ground. But I braced against him, and tensed my shoulders, and felt the rush of things I felt and saw it collide with his red, horrible anger—

Flash.

I let the rush of things flow into him, and Jukebox grabbed him from the other side, both hands clutching his wrist. The buzz ran through all of us, from the hole in the sky, from the place beyond the world. Jukebox and I saw everything as it moved, but it didn't stay with us—we were a channel, funneling the images and feelings and pain like a rapid waterfall. All my nightmares were made real. Disease ripped into our stomachs with acid ulcers. Blisters rose on our skin as we were sprayed with sour, bitter chemicals. Creatures choked on unbreathable air. We were Agatha's bones crunching under his tires. We were four-legged, thin and sick, walking up the ramp to a slaughterhouse, and the sound of the electric shock hitting the pigs in front of us sent us into a panic. The panic passed out of me into my dad. I could feel it in him: the hiss and pop of his body breaking and being cut, the feeling of powerless-ness and fear and torment, the unending slide, the rising tides of fire, the bleached bones of his friends, the boats and houses overwhelmed by waves and unstoppable gale winds. People screamed as the sound of gunfire echoed. I had seen it before, but it was new to my dad. Black oil smothered our mouths. He was the one who was stuck in it, with no comprehension, no way out, only the sensation of being trapped, overrun, frozen like a deer in headlights. We were just the channel.

I wondered if I was stretching time thin so these images, past and possible, sluiced backwards from the future at us like rainwater off a roof, or if these visions were just us, feeling something that had always been here to feel.

My dad stared at me in horror, eyes wide with red rims, mouth slack. His eyes rolled back in his head. Suddenly, I felt scared; I felt him. I *was* him. I was inside him. His stomach turned and his bile rose and his lungs contracted. I felt the uncomfortable pressure in his bladder. I could taste his cigarette breath.

I dropped his hand, breathing hard. Jukebox let go at the same time, and he sank to the ground. His eyes fluttered shut and he lay on his back in the mud. I could feel that I was shaking, trembling, unable to stop.

"He's pissed himself," Jukebox said. Sure enough, I could see a dark stain creeping down from the crotch of my dad's jeans. I was unable to open my mouth to speak. I wasn't sure what I would say. I backed away from him, turned to Agatha, and bent to hold her. Her cold, horrible body was the wrong size against me. She should have been bigger, and breathing. My hands sunk into her.

"He's just unconscious," Jukebox said, behind me. I

hadn't thought to wonder if he could be anything else. "Better get that box, and your other stuff."

Terror in every organ. "Then we'll get out of here, yeah?"

I went and got the boxes from inside. Jukebox stood by the car, smoking, looking at the inert figure of my dad on the ground in the mud. It took me three trips to carry everything. Jukebox didn't try to help, and didn't try to go into the house. I was fine with that.

"That was incredible, you know, Orsino," they said to me as I put the last box in the trunk. "I can't believe what we just did."

I couldn't believe it either. I wanted to leave.

I carried Agatha over to the car, and wrapped her in a tarp that had been just inside the garage. I emptied a plastic bin of camping and hunting gear next to the door of the house and threw it all into the garage, where it was dry. Then I put Agatha in the plastic bin and snapped the lid on. I wasn't sure how much it would stink up the car, but I'd render her body for bones or rebury her later.

We pulled out of the drive, Jukebox looking back over their shoulder. My dad still wasn't moving, but I got out to look again and saw that he was breathing. His eyelids fluttered and he mumbled something, and I backed away. We pulled the car around him, down onto the country road.

"Roll the windows down," Jukebox said. "Agatha loves you, but she's gonna stink."

They hit the gas. The wheels scraped the road, and the chicken barn moved past their window and faded away. Ranger's barks subsided. I wasn't gonna see him again, I thought. But my dad liked Ranger. He'd be fine.

I thought of the feathered creature in the woods. Was it going to be fine?

But I couldn't go back for everything.

"Thank you for back there," I said.

Jukebox grinned, and reached out and grabbed my hand, tight. "Hey man, any time. I'm sorry I didn't come back sooner. But I'm glad you fucked him up. And now we know what your powers are, right? You can do that to *anyone* evil."

I didn't feel sure about that. "I don't know if it would work like that," I said.

Jukebox and Robin and I parked outside Compton at sunset that night. The building was one I'd passed a couple times before. It was ugly as sin, as my mom would say.

"I'm gonna go get a drink," Robin said. "Meet me after." She seemed irritated. She went into the building next door with a rainbow flag hanging on its window.

The bubbles appeared on the screen and James texted back: *on my way!*

A minute later, I heard a door slam at the end of a hall, and the door we were standing in front of burst open. James was panting a little, and grinned at me. He was wearing the same shirt as in the selfie he'd sent me earlier.

"Hey," I said. It felt so fun to see his face after such a short time, smiling.

"Sup," he said. "Come on up. We're just starting, there's snacks." He stuck his hand out to Jukebox. "Super glad you could make it. We'll talk about what we're doing when we get upstairs."

We followed James inside. The hallway was gray and dingy, and I thought the ceiling looked like there was mildew in it somewhere—the brown on the edges of those little square panels.

At the top of the building, where all the heat seemed to have gathered, there was a big room full of bulletin boards. I recognized James's friend Ian from the show, and his friend Opal. There were a couple other kids there too. On a whiteboard on one side of the room, Ian was writing THE WORM ALIEN ROCK OPERA: A PLAN.

"Hi," one of the older adults said. She stood up and shook my hand, then Jukebox's. "I'm Spruce."

"I'm Natalie," said the one who was drinking a coffee. The sides of her head were shaved.

"I'm Gemma," another one said. "Jukebox, thanks for coming."

Jukebox smiled like they knew everyone already. "Oh yeah," they said. "It's so sick."

"I think everyone's here now," Opal said. "Jukebox, thank you so so so much for being here."

"No problem, bro," Jukebox said.

I went and sat next to James, who was eating carrots and hummus on an orange couch in the corner. "What's going on?" I asked.

"We're trying to do like, a fundraiser, and we need punk bands to help us. We gotta butter Jukebox up cuz they know people." He said this in a low whisper that made the hair on the back of my arms stand up.

I nodded. I could see how that could be a thing.

Ian came over from the whiteboard and sat on the arm

of the couch on James's other side. James was looking at Ian. Ian wasn't looking at James. It was like they were magnets, but I wasn't sure whether they were getting pushed away from each other or towards each other.

At the front of the room, Opal had gotten their chair up to the head of the table and was passing around something that looked like a book report, stapled on one side. Each of the older queers looked at it in turn and reacted with raised eyebrows.

"So look," Opal said.

"Yeah, let's start," James echoed. He went and stood up next to Opal and clapped his hands. Opal looked up at him with what I thought might be annoyance.

"Look," Opal said. "We're in emergency mode. We have to do a fundraiser. I know this. You know this. There aren't any grants."

"We still have the Pell-Whitman-Duff grant," a woman at the table said. "But that's just for houseless youth."

Opal stared at the women angrily.

"Well. I was watching *The Transfused* at Barb's house, a couple days ago, and realized like, we need to do something like *that*." They paused for a second, and took a deep breath. "A rock musical."

The adults in the room were staring at Opal with a measure of respect, careful empathetic smiles, and fear.

"As representatives of the now-defunct Speakers' Bureau," Opal said, "we want to make sure that we get this rolling. We'd like to ask for the Board's support. To start, we need to spend the remaining programming fund for supplies. I know we only have like $200. The main support we need is social. We need cheap scrap lumber from someone's yard. We need to promo this to every school GSA in the county. We need rehearsal space and performance space. We need musicians."

One of the adults opened their mouth and shut it again.

"Opal," one of the board members said. "This is a great idea. That's why we're here. But it's maybe not the right *year* to do it. We're stretched thin right now."

"That's the *point*," Opal said. "We're stretched thin, but that's why we need this now. We can't afford *not* to do this. I need a place to come every week. I need this for my resume. But lots of kids depend on Compton's programming to feel like they have any community at all. We have to make sure it's funded. We need to remind the community that it's up to them to make sure places like this stay around."

"A show could also bring in new people," Ian said. "I never come to Compton stuff because I don't like support groups."

"It can be just like Gay Music Camp," Opal said. "We admit it's an emergency, and we rally people. Jukebox knows everyone. If they put the word out, talk to friends, make an announcement at every show in the next week and a half, we can get this going."

Jukebox had a sudden fire in their eyes. They were grinning their crooked grin right at Opal.

"So," Jukebox said. "It's like a big festival of social justice punk. To raise money?"

"Yeah," Opal said. "A *rock opera* of punk."

"We haven't had the best luck with all-ages shows, in

terms of PFLAG support," Natalie said quietly. "There's a lot of questions about substance use and safety for youth, especially after the incidents in August with the kombucha turning out to be alcoholic."

"For teens," Jukebox said. "And we'll get a big audience." They smiled, chin in hands, and turned their septum piercing with two fingers, like they did when they were excited and thinking. "Cute. Cute cute cute cute *cute*. Remind me. The show is like, already written, right?"

James had this one. He held up some sheets of notebook paper. "We have a plotline—it's about some worm aliens that come to earth to teach people peace and love. They abduct a cow and then the cow tries to spread the word but it gets turned into a burger but then everyone who eats the burger has a kind of revelation about capitalism and homophobia."

And I could tell that was it. Jukebox stood up and practically jumped on their chair. "Yes, yes yes yes yes."

I felt scared.

Everyone's eyes, including mine, were on Jukebox. Their dark eyeliner and their birdlike mullet. They looked like a comet.

Jukebox went over to the board with the summary. "Bands. You want to get Dirt Mama, we gotta get RIND and Emu Union. I know Jenny and Dogman and Rex, those are no problem, they don't go on tour until February."

The board members sat there, looking more and more like those little dolls in antique shops that look like they could be alive but aren't. Jukebox walked around the room, making plans, talking just to Opal.

"I think that the Metroplex Vintage Theater would let us use space toward the end of December if we didn't bump any of the mini horror film fests out of the way," Opal was saying.

I realized Jukebox was the main show here. James was looking at Jukebox. James didn't necessarily want me sitting next to him at all. Maybe it had just been about Jukebox the whole time. I felt kind of sick, thinking that.

"I'm going out for a smoke," I said to James, who was taking notes to build a timeline of when they were going to be calling which people about using what space. James nodded, then looked at me and stuck his tongue out and rolled his eyes a little and smiled.

"I'll come out in a bit," he said. "I wanna hang with you after this, don't disappear, okay?"

I nodded. I looked at Ian, who was now sitting at James's feet, with a laptop open, working on a spreadsheet. I looked between Ian and James, and wondered what the deal was with them.

I went out into the parking lot. It was cold for September, but it felt good to sit in the cold and shiver a little. There weren't any cars. I dug out my cigarettes and sat down on one of the cement blocks that marked the parking spaces. The stars were coming out overhead, and the moon was rising over behind the trees on the east side. I watched some cars drive by, and listened to their music booming a little through their windows.

The moon rising over the edge of the city looked pink to me. I thought about Agatha, and how I would clean her bones, what bucket I could use. I wondered if my dad had woken up yet. What if I had really hurt him? But his eyelids had fluttered.

I wondered if this rock opera was what was supposed to be happening. Were we doing it right? Could Jukebox cut a hole in time with music, somehow cut back to whatever point we were meant to locate in the past and reroute us like a train shifting tracks?

When James came downstairs, I heard the sound of his steps a few seconds before the door swung open. He walked up and I felt his hand on my shoulder.

"Want a cigarette?" I asked him, holding out my pack. I looked at him again. He was so pretty in the weird streetlight. I didn't like that I thought he was so pretty. What if I couldn't be with him the way I wanted to?

"Yeah," he said. He took one. "I've been trying to vape but, eh. Light it for me?"

I lit it.

"What was this whole deal about?" I asked him.

"It's insane," James said, which wasn't an explanation. He sucked on the cigarette. "They're not like, happy, but they're letting us move forward."

I finished my cigarette and stamped it out, stood up. I wanted to touch him, but didn't know if that was the vibe.

"Why are you here, if it sucks?"

James's face went funny. He looked at the ground, frowned. He stuck out his tongue. "The support groups here are dumb, but they saved my life when I was younger. I used to self-harm and was super lonely and lived my whole life on the internet. I got here and finally had a group of people. And they're annoying, but they made me less crazy."

"That's cool," I said. "That you had that." I felt jealous. Deeply jealous. I felt sick.

"It's just like, there are so many things wrong with it and they're broke all the time. I'm kind of ready to let it go to hell, but Opal doesn't want it to. Which is more ethical. So I want to make this fundraiser thing go off." He shrugged. "Also I'm here so I don't have to give my dad my car keys, which he's taking away because I'm suspended. I hid out at Opal's last night so I could keep my car one more day."

He sat down where I had been sitting.

"Is this based on what I said about the aliens?" I asked.

"Not really," James said. "Not originally. It's more so we could get Jukebox. Since they had an alien vision too."

His arm went around my waist. I shivered in spite of myself. I tried to focus on the feeling of it. I just wanted him to touch me.

"Okay. Hey," I said. "What's the deal with you and Ian? Your friend."

"What?" James asked.

"You were looking at him. And he was avoiding looking at you."

James looked embarrassed. "Oh," he said. "That's—this weekend we had a weird moment after his show where we made out for fun, and it was weird and we both feel weird about it, so it's like, we're recalibrating from that."

I knew what the look James was giving Ian meant. It was the same one he'd given me.

"Oh," I said. "Cool. Yeah, I was just wondering. Gotta find out what I'm getting myself into and everything."

"Just so you know, I'm maybe a slut," James said. "I didn't realize it before, but I think I am. Making out with you felt good and gave me weird visions and made me want to make out with more people, and . . . well. I'm dumb, I guess. Sexuality activated, or something."

"That's cool," I said.

"But I didn't get visions with Ian. It was nice, but really awkward . . ."

"Sure," I said, uncertainly. "Just trying to know whether I can make out with you again, or what's going on." I paused. "I'd like to."

James blushed. He took a drag off the cigarette and tucked one of his longer strands of hair behind his ear. "Yeah," he said. "I like you. I'm supposed to be home to talk to my dad about the suspension stuff, but let's go make out somewhere first."

We went to James' car, which was parked at the library. There were no other cars in that lot, either. He had to turn the key twice in the ignition before the car turned on. The windshield wipers went back and forth across the glass.

"We could just . . . in the car," I said.

"No, I know where to take you," he said. "I can lend you a coat, if you want. There's a couple on the floor in the back."

"Where are we going?" I asked. I texted Robin, *impromptu date with goth boy. Text you in an hour.*

You have to bury Agatha or do something with the body when you get home, Robin texted back. *Stacey is freaking out.*

"There's this park," James said. "With waterfalls. You can see the waterfall and the whole lake from the bottom of the trail, and there's this place off to the side that's like, kind of magic."

That sounded good.

James drove for just a little way. He didn't put music on—the only noise was the whir of the defrost going on the windshield glass to keep it from fogging up. I watched the dark trees and the moon from the car window. We pulled down a hill and into a parking lot. There was a gate locked in front of us. James pulled off to the side, one wheel of his car in a ditch.

"Now we walk," he said.

We had to walk around another closed gate in order to get to the trail.

"We're not supposed to be here," James said. He looked giddy.

I could hear the rushing water from a ways off. It was dark—there weren't any lights except on the paved sections of the trail that looked over the river. I watched James move in front of me.

"There's salmon ladders here," he said. "They're super scary to look down at. Look. Look." He got out his phone and turned on the flashlight function. He grabbed my hand and pulled me forward, toward the fence at the edge of the river. The river hit this cliff and went over in a series of white, noisy falls, and the pavement around the edges of the river had these metal grates. James shone the light down into the cavern under the grates, and I watched the white, churning water bubble around the steep mossy salmon ladders in the dark.

"Wow," I said. "That would suck to fall into."

"My stepmom is always talking about writing a murder mystery that's set here," James said. "Come on, let's go down the trail. You're gonna like this I think. You can see stars. And you're an alien, right? So that works for you."

"*I'm* not an alien," I said.

"No," James agreed. His hand on my hand.

The trail was muddy and went around the edge of the river. Wooden banisters on the edges stopped you from falling in. James turned the flashlight on his phone off so our eyes could adjust to the trail. The highway crossed over the river, and as we went under it you could feel the rumble of the cars overhead.

We crossed a footbridge that in the dark really did make me feel like I could fall off and die in the rushing water. James didn't pause, dragging me by the hand, his warm palm on my palm.

"Okay, here we go," he said. He pointed to a set of steep, wet stairs that dovetailed off the main trail. I could barely see the shapes of wet leaves crisscrossing the stairs that went down into darkness.

I followed him.

The bottom of the stairs was just this square of cement, but when we got there I could see the view James had talked about. The road and downtown were across the lake from us, lights shining. Little islands stuck up here and there. The biggest waterfall was behind us, thundering in the dark. I was cold and could feel the mist from the falls on my skin.

"This is where we make out?" I asked. "It's kind of wet."

"This is secret place number one," James said. "There's number two over this way." He pointed to the side of the cement square that went up against the hill. I looked. "Follow me."

We went up a little footpath between two rhododendron bushes, James using his phone flashlight to light the way. The hill broke down into a rocky incline and a stream ran off the main river between the rocks into a pool that trickled down into the lake on one end. It was like a little cove. The streetlights on the highway above us shone down through the leaves on the trees, which hadn't all fallen yet.

"*This* is where we make out," James said.

I couldn't really see his face, but I saw his teeth flash white in the dark.

I grabbed him by the waist and kissed him. His lips were fuller than I'd remembered from a couple days ago, and felt hot, and his mouth opened against my face. His sweatshirt was too bulky. I wanted to feel him against me. I couldn't believe he'd brought me here. It was dumb, and also sweet, and dramatic. That meant something good, I could tell.

I put my hands under his shirt and felt the sparks coming, reaching up. His chest was bare and his skin was hot. I didn't know if I'd be able to stop myself from having visions. I thought of Jukebox, telling me to channel the good visions. What if we both disappeared here, got pulled up into the ship?

"Did you have top surgery already?" I asked him.

"Yeah," he said into my neck. "Last summer."

"How the fuck did you swing that?" I asked. I paused.

I really didn't want to hear. Whatever it was, it would be about how his mom was cooler, or richer, or something about Medicaid that I already knew but hadn't been able to make work because I lived in three different places and didn't understand doctors and didn't have a car and my mom worked all the time. "Never mind. Can I touch your chest?"

"Yeah," James said. "Yeah. Here, let's sit down."

He sat down hard on the leaves and pulled me onto his lap so I was straddling him. I felt my knees getting wet on the ground and knew James's butt must be wet too. I felt his skin and felt myself buzz against him. I liked the beaded-up feeling of the scars on his chest.

"I'm sorry you got suspended," I said, unzipping his jacket a little.

"It'll be fine," James said.

"I mean, you were sort of guessing that you were going to get busted," I said.

"Yeah," James said, without much feeling. He was staring at me. "I can't believe how much chin hair you have." He touched my chin. "How long have you been on T?"

"Just under a year," I said. "I was kind of hairy before, too."

The noises of the night around us—the water, and the leaves—seemed like they got more intense. I kissed him harder, and he gasped into my mouth. He put his hands in my hair and pulled me on top of him, hard. I felt my hands in the muddy leaves on the ground, heard the spring trickling down the rocks behind him. I felt my dick get hard in my pants and felt my belly get hot. This was the first time I'd ever done something like this, but it felt right. I liked that he had a place he wanted to take me. I grabbed his wrists in my dirty hands, kissing his jaw, and he bucked his hips against me.

"You bring boys here a lot?" I asked. I wasn't trying to sound jealous.

"No," James said. "Once I smoked weed here with my mom."

"You have a totally different life than me," I laughed.

"I know," James said. "But there's also so much that I feel like we already know about each other."

"Hmm," I said. I let the sparks in me dance down my hands into his wrists. We both gasped, mouth on mouth and belly on belly.

Electric shock. James pulled his hand out from my hand and moved it up my shirt. A spark moved from his hand to my chest. I could *see* it. I felt dizzy.

"That's okay, right?" he asked.

"Yeah."

I kissed him again.

Many eyes, one mouth, fused; worms crawling over one another. A scrolling concave wall of crystal spires, each flashing with different mirror images of my family's farm, my sister's face, my dog, a city where the houses were woven from plants.

We were both one seal in a river flush with salmon. Maybe it was this river, a long time ago, before the salmon ladders. Maybe it was the future, after the ladders were gone. The sky was stormy. We were big and dark gray and fat and hungry and strong, with teeth that could take a salmon easily and eat it easily. Our jaw ached from hunting. Our nostrils flared above the water. Other warm seal bodies and cold salmon bodies brushed against us in the river. There was no dam and no brewery and there were no distant highway lights. Our muscles burned, one animal.

James was clutching me, his hands on my back and my ass. He was breathing hard. I could feel he had his right hand down his pants, touching himself. His face in the night was shadowy and I couldn't see all of it but he was so, so handsome. Had I ever thought about what boys I would kiss would actually look like? Had I thought about kissing another trans boy, and how he would be so so handsome? And how it would feel for him to want me, maybe *because* I was trans? I lowered my hand from his chest, touched his soft stomach, which was kind of cold. I felt the hair around his belly button. He shivered, and I felt how small he was. I kissed his mouth more, then bit his ear. I wanted to bite hard, but he yelped. I wondered if the moon above us looked pink again. I felt like it should be pink. I put my tongue as far into his mouth as it would go and James moaned, so loud that if there had been someone out on the wet cement viewing deck by the waterfall they would have heard him. I shivered, and it felt really good. The earth was shaking under me. I rubbed the mud off my hand on my jeans, then put my hand down his pants. I could feel the elastic waistband of his mall goth black jeans stretch over my wrist.

"Is this okay?" I asked.

"God, yes. God, yes," James said, into my neck. "You don't even know."

Spark.

We heard a noise in the water on the other side of the bushes, in the lake facing the fall, a rush of sudden movement that swelled and sounded like something frantically swimming, leaping, sinking, leaping. Or many, many things. Salmon, I suddenly thought. So thick that you could walk on their backs.

"Fish," James said weakly.

I was a seal. The fish were everywhere. I was also over James, hands down his jeans. I felt his dick through his underwear. It was stiff and warm in the palm of my hand through the soft cotton, the size of the last half of my thumb. I knew I wanted to suck his dick. Maybe I wanted him to suck my dick. I wanted to know how he tasted. I wished I had a bigger dick so he could feel it hard against him through my jeans. I thought about taking off his shirt. His hands were in my hair, pulling kind of harder than I wanted him to, but it also felt good to have him pull that much. His eyes were open so wide, and he was smiling. I didn't know how to touch his dick, from this angle, or if I should be trying or just trying to go slow. But when I looked at James, and felt him breathing harder and harder, I knew I wasn't doing it that wrong.

"You're *really* hot," James said. "I so needed this. Exactly this. You."

He stumbled up against me as we walked back.

We turned toward the water before climbing the wet stairs and saw the impossible glint of hundreds of fins, thousands of moonlit scales emerging and disappearing beneath the black water. Alive. They filled the churning pool beneath the falls, so that every part of the water seemed to be wriggling and tossing. Like a body made of thousands of bodies.

"That's more fish than I've ever seen," I said. "So much for declining salmon runs."

"They go further, too," James said, pointing. I looked; I could see that there were more fish approaching through the water from a distance. I had never seen that many of any kind of animal. It was a flood of salmon. If it had been daytime I would have see their red backs, their green beaks; in the night only their huge shapes seemed real. I felt a chill of unease, the sparks dancing in my hands where I had touched James.

The salmon leapt towards the ladders, up to where they would die.

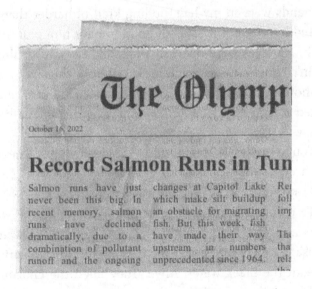

The Olymp

October 16, 2022

Record Salmon Runs in Tun

Salmon runs have just never been this big. In recent memory, salmon runs have declined dramatically, due to a combination of pollutant runoff and the ongoing changes at Capitol Lake which make silt buildup an obstacle for migrating fish. But this week, fish have made their way upstream in numbers unprecedented since 1964.

COMPTON Youth ROCKS!

OUTLINE FOR "GOTHPEL of WORM" YOUTH DRAG EXTRAVAGANZA

first song— WYRM WEDDING WALTZ with RAGAMA

Cow descends — cops attempt to make burger

cops defeated

Worm dance worm girl dance

SONGS—
QUIET PEACE   MAGIC BURGER

Cops suck
cops suck again
★ Light hope ★
Revisit visions of good future
Revolution
begins!

...NOVEMBER
(six weeks later)

Chapter 13

MONIQUE

The theater we got to let us rehearse in and perform in—the Metroplex—was run by some old volunteers. I'd only been there once, when James had dragged me and Opal to see a weird anime about a medieval witch who had too much sex. Barb had gotten the theater for us, because her best friend was the head of the board of volunteers. Everything inside smelled of old cigarette smoke and stale popcorn, and there was a "ladies' powder room" on the second floor that had splendid old mirrors but toilets that didn't flush. The elevator looked like it was probably held up by a system of hundred-year-old pulleys.

Everything in downtown Olympia smelled like dead salmon. Whenever we opened a door, their essence was there. They were dying on the banks of the lake as well as farther upstream. Cleaning crews had been designated to gather and compost them, and seals had swum in from outside the city and been eating salmon under the bridge for weeks, but there had been hundreds of thousands, and they'd filled the lake and the estuary.

The set pieces we had already built were based on Opal's ideas about the original *Transfused* pieces, put together by a bunch of Compton's more enthusiastic fourteen-year-olds and some of the weirder volunteers at the Metroplex, built from scrap wood someone had in their garage. We had a big plywood board that was kind of the shape of a house, a big circle we were going to paint silver that would be the ship, and then different angular pillars covered in feathers and bright purple paint. Painting them had been fun, and when the stage was first set up, I had thought it looked insane and cool, if totally amateur.

I glanced at where Jukebox was crouched in the corner on their phone, then looked at the blister on my finger that I'd gotten from hot oil at work. It hurt more for playing so long. I pressed the middle of it, winced, and sat heavily back down on my amp. My ass was sore from sitting on the floor and dancing. My bass felt heavy and my gut kept turning like a bicycle wheel inside me. I looked back at the handwritten sheet music photocopied and taped to my music stand.

SCENE SIX—ACTIONCOW, the title at the top of the page read.

I wished I'd never agreed to this.

"Five minutes," Opal yelled from the back of the dim theater. "Everyone get ready to get places. Everyone go pee."

Half our cast was spread out on the stage on their stomachs, drinking donated kombucha and eating stale bagels that Jukebox's friend Raz had brought over from a cafe. Picture a garden bed strewn with slugs, only it was gay teens on a black box stage. Barb was sitting in the audience, looking attentive and friendly to all the teens, waiting for my and Opal's part to be over so she could drive Opal home. I could tell that everyone else felt the same mix of dehydrated and anxious and bleary-eyed that I did. I had eaten too much salt today, and I felt like crying. When Opal yelled, though, everyone started scooting different directions, getting ready for our next run-through. Including me.

I kind of wished we were all talking to each other more. There was a lot we could talk about. We were all gay teens, and we all had some kind of idea about art. Venus had good ideas. But instead we were here, waiting to be told what to do.

The show was this Saturday. Three weeks ago, when we'd started rehearsals, I'd felt optimistic about everything, despite the way James had stumbled out of my car and how I was grounded and how I could tell that James and Orsino had done something.

Mom had said it was fine for me to be part of an all-ages show.

"See," she said. "I think *this* idea is amazing. Your music can contribute to something important. Working with other people to make this, that's great. You don't have to play in basements to make art."

I didn't tell her that a lot of the people involved were the same ones that played the shows she thought were dangerous to go to. Mom still hadn't given me permission to use the car, but she dropped me off at the Metroplex after school two times a week so I could rehearse with everyone else, and let me do one weekend rehearsal with Opal and Sophie per week, as long as I showed her my grades online every Friday.

And the first week at the Metroplex had been good. James had put the word out to all the GSAs about the show, and a ton of kids showed up, geeky and bright-eyed and ready to hang out with other gay kids. James had brought all his warm-up activities from drama class and sex-ed workshops and we played name games, and Jukebox had brought in bands and let them choose what songs of theirs they thought went with the scene. We'd all worked together to finalize a script and paint the sets bright pink and vivid orange and toxic green, with help from Metroplex volunteers.

Two weeks ago, Opal and Sophie and I had recorded our three songs and released a mini-album on Bandcamp, and we'd gotten 1,452 downloads since then, thanks to Jukebox posting about us. It hadn't made much money, since only about 80 people had paid for it, but that was okay. We'd been distracted, trying to fit in practice times around my abridged grounded-kid schedule. I thought that maybe after we dropped our recording, I'd have room to focus, and then I could talk to James.

But then James had posted a picture of himself lying shirtless against Orsino on the couch in Jukebox's house, with the caption FTM ALIEN BOYFRIENDZ FOREVER.

Opal pulled up next to me onstage, the lights catching the buttons on their vest. "Nobody touched my kombucha, right?"

"No," I said.

"Good," Opal said, and wheeled their chair behind the drums, jostling the cymbals. I felt like I could see the vein in their head popping.

"Where's Sophie?" I asked.

Opal pulled their sticks out of their vest pocket and tapped the drums lightly, sounding out the first bars of "Actioncow." "Smoking and venting with Stacey and Goober and Jennifer out back, probably." They sighed.

Sophie and Jukebox had fought about the key change in our song twenty-five minutes ago. Also the lyrics, which Sophie said should be simpler.

I felt confused. In the moments where Jukebox was annoyed, it was like all the things they'd said before about us being prodigies and a great band just disappeared. They said I was dropping a beat when I knew I wasn't. But maybe I was. I wasn't that good.

Part of me felt like we should just be having fun, instead of trying to make it good.

At the same time, though, it was obvious that Jukebox thought what we were doing was almost cosmically important. And I didn't not agree. I liked being around so many other weird gay kids. It was important for us to make a thing together.

This is the best I've ever felt, they'd said just the other day after we finished a run of OVID's number in the show. They'd been panting and sweating so much that you could see the shape of their tattoos through their white shirt. *We're making art, but we're also going to tell the truth. We're going to transform the lives of everyone who sees this show.*

The show was this Saturday.

The other older punks had looked embarrassed after Sophie had stormed out to smoke, and had slunk out after her. Opal had called a break. I'd gone outside to stand with Sophie and check in, but Orsino was there in a Bite Me! sweatshirt lighting James's spliff, so I went back inside, where Jukebox was arguing with Duke and Gemma in tense whispers in the corner. It was ten minutes before Jukebox went to crouch and look at their phone. Meanwhile I tugged cables and wires around to pretend I had something to do.

Next week we would find out who the new director for Compton was going to be, and I had a feeling that Gemma already knew it would be Duke. There had been a youth-led interview process, whatever that meant. I hadn't gone, because I was working. Afterwards, Opal couldn't shut up about how cool Duke was, how he'd started a trans needle exchange in Portland and worked at a shelter in Vancouver, how he knew the ins and outs of the systems and would be a perfect advocate. And I couldn't even vent to James, because James and I were barely talking.

I wasn't sure if James had really heard what I'd said to him, in the car. I was pretty sure he hadn't, because he would have asked me about it by now otherwise. I hadn't told anyone else, exactly. I'd told Opal and Sophie they could call me Monique when we were in rehearsals together. Opal had nodded and mostly remembered, and other people were starting to use it too. I hadn't explained why. But since I'd said it aloud that one time it had started taking root like a plant, and now I was sure.

I was a girl.

It had come to me so completely in the moment I kissed James, but it had been there for months, kind of percolating. Knowing was this funny feeling—like suddenly things had clicked into place that hadn't always clicked. But it was also like suddenly realizing you're really hungry and haven't eaten in like, a million years. Of course. That was what I was. That was why I was how I was. Everything made more sense, when I pictured my future, if I was a girl. A woman? That felt weird to say, but maybe a woman. Maybe a dyke. But I liked boys. I wanted to talk to Goober or Venus, but I wasn't sure we'd get along, so I hadn't yet.

I didn't know what to do about it, but I figured eventually I would know.

Now I whispered the new words Jukebox had given us to myself to make sure I wouldn't accidentally sing the version I'd written earlier. I glanced toward the door where half the kids had gone to smoke with the older punks.

I inhaled slow and held my breath, the way that I'd been trying to do more lately, to let my lungs absorb more oxygen and send it to my brain. It didn't help. The tension in my gut stayed exactly where it was.

I felt my eyes involuntarily flick back to where Jukebox was sitting. They weren't there anymore, though their phone was still plugged in to the outlet. I looked around, trying not to look at James, sitting in the second row of seats. But then my eyes went to him, and sure enough, Jukebox was standing with one leg up on the seat in front of him, going over the script with him again. Their studded belt gleamed in the low red EXIT lights of the theater. James was trying to put on his cow-patterned pants while staying seated, wiggling them on over his skinny jeans, while looking up at Jukebox, reverently. His shirt was pushed up because of the angle of his back on the chair. His stomach was showing. I couldn't hear what Jukebox was saying.

I was going to talk to him about the kiss, and what I had been scared of, and what I needed, and what I wanted. I thought I'd be able to do it. I'd written it all out. But at school, he was always texting Orsino, and talking about Orsino, and posting about "my bf." And I was fucked up, knowing that he hadn't told anyone about kissing me.

Which meant he'd decided it was a mistake. A drunk mistake? Or maybe he didn't even remember, though my understanding of alcohol was that two beers would not do that to anyone.

Which meant that I'd realized I wanted him, and realized gender stuff about how I wanted him, only for him to realize that he didn't want me after all. And he was the person who knew me best out of anyone, and liked me better than anyone I knew, so if *he* didn't want me—

"Ian," Opal said, in a tone that told me they'd said it at least once previously.

"What," I said. My name sounded awful now. I wrenched my head over to face the drum set.

Opal's face changed. They looked at me sympathetically for a second. "Monique. I know this sucks," they said. "But we *have* to do this, you know? You *gotta* stick it. Even if this is all bullshit."

Opal had noticed how weird shit between me and James was.

"I know," I said. I leaned over to tune my amp and stood to flip the mic on the stand on. The sound system screeched, and everyone who was still sitting and talking jumped.

"Break's over," I said. "Let's try 'Actioncow' again."

James hopped up and climbed over the lip of the stage towards me. He grinned in my direction. "Let's go," he said, exuberantly.

James, to all appearances, had *not* noticed how weird shit was between us.

"James, remember," Jukebox said. "Orsino and I are going to come lift you in the middle of this number, after Monique sings '*fortitude, change.*' And I want you to go absolutely *totally* limp. You've been turned into a burger. Just let yourself be a conduit."

"Go, James!" Venus yelled. "Condu*it*!"

I liked Venus.

James did a goofy salute in Jukebox's direction and thrust his leg out on the stage, trying to do the splits in the Halloween store cow-patterned pants, lifting his arms above his head. "I'm but a limp vessel for the rock-hard word of the *worm*," he shouted to Jukebox.

"Excellent," Jukebox said, grinning with just the left side of their mouth.

Opal made a disgusted noise in the back of their throat and counted off with their guitar sticks.

"ONETWOTHREEFOUR—"

Dm Am F Fm.

The staccato tacrashthuntap of Opal's sticks on the drums and big cymbal.

Dm Am F Fm.

The pattern of the chords was familiar to me. We'd planned the song after one I'd done with Rocketpizza, based on one by Cerce, adding in extra guitar riffs for Sophie to kill on, adding stuff on drums for Opal. It was the same progression I'd played for James at Devon's house, before the show at Goat Mansion, when he'd been bouncing on the couch.

"MY HANDS ARE PLUNGED IN THE SOFT HEMI-SPHERES," I screamed. My throat hurt. "I CAN SEE THAT YOU'RE BLED BY THE WORLD / BLED TO DEATH. RED. YOUR BRAIN IS BROKEN." I almost coughed, but managed not to. I didn't like these lyrics as much. The cymbal crashed, and I felt the reverberations rising through the floor. I looked at James, walked toward him the way I was supposed to with the blocking. In the real performance, the cloth-covered wormskin draped over hoops would wind behind me, carried by Venus and Danny and flashing with Christmas lights. If we got them done in time. "YOU HAVE SEEN HORRORS. THERE IS NO ALTERNATIVE FOR YOU, THERE ARE ONLY HORRORS, UNLESS YOU BREATHE . . ."

This was the part where I stopped and Jukebox started.

Sophie's thumbs in their knitted fingerless gloves found

the right chord. Opal's tempo slowed on a slow slide and they rattled the cymbal. Their face was a scrunched mask of concentration. They sounded so good.

"REVOLUTION!" Jukebox screamed, high *Am*, from the corner of the stage.

The light cues weren't set up yet, but the lights should have changed from red to blue then.

James threw his arms up in the air like streamers, rolled his eyes to the ceiling, and fell flat on his back, the way he was supposed to. Jukebox raced over to him, bending forward the way they would when they held the shape of the fabric worm alien over their body, holding their arms around one of the hoops we planned to stretch the cloth over like they were a child pretending to drive a car. They stooped so that the hoop framed James's face, and they trembled over him, screeching.

If my mom saw this, I thought suddenly, she would think it was *so* stupid.

Which was kind of what made the parts of it that were good so good.

"Moo," James cried, and spasmed wildly with his limbs, even though he was supposed to be still now. His high voice sounded so silly against the intensity of the lyrics that everyone in the front row cracked up. The kids who were holding the banners with the corporate logos on them shook as they turned in fast circles.

I looked at James's splayed, strong legs in his cow-patterned pants and felt so tender toward him I could have choked.

"REVOLUTION!" Jukebox called again, something crackling beneath their crackly voice. I glanced behind me, not really wanting to see Orsino there, in the place he was supposed to be entering from.

Good thing, because he wasn't there.

"God damn it," Jukebox said. "Orsino, we're running the *bit*. I need you. Get over here." They looked toward the audience of the three kids who weren't onstage, who shrugged.

James raised his head off the floor and looked over towards Jukebox's boots.

"He was with people smoking outside," Sophie said, after the silence had gotten too big.

"Duke was out there, too," Barb said, standing up. "He really shouldn't be smoking with kids."

"I'll get him," James said. He scrambled across the stage, running into one of the pink plywood set pieces with his shoulder, nearly knocking it over before colliding with the door under the EXIT sign. A blinding blast of daylight flooded the theater for a second before the door slammed shut again.

"Monique," Jukebox said to me. "Go make sure they both come back. Can't trust boyfriends to get boyfriends."

I sighed and set my bass down, and followed James. I felt Opal watching me as I pushed open the door and stepped out into the haze of weed smoke outside.

"FUCK OFF. SHIT, DUDE."

I thought Orsino was yelling at me for a second, and jumped. Then my eyes focused in the light.

A few of the smokers were still leaning on the dumpster. On the asphalt below them, Duke was pinning Orsino to the ground, with his knee at the base of Orsino's spine, and his arm around Orsino's neck. Orsino's hands and knees were pressed to the dirty ground.

"SHIT," Orsino said, loudly. "FUCKING SHIT, DUDE."

"He got you," Dogman said, cackling.

"Go Orsino!" said Goober, who was sipping a dollar coffee from the corner store and sitting cross-legged on the trash can across from him.

I watched Orsino's shirt slipping up his back.

It was a second before I realized Orsino was laughing very hard.

"Say Uncle," Duke said gently, his back to us. "Tap out."

The metal door opened behind us, crashing against the outer concrete wall.

"Hey Barb," James said, across their locked bodies.

"God damn it," Barb said. She flew past us and ran over to Duke. She was smaller than him, but as soon as she yanked his hair he let go and stood up. I was shocked. I'd never seen Barb move that fast before. Or look that angry.

"Ow!"

"The fuck is going on?" Barb shouted. "Duke, what the fuck!"

Duke turned and grinned at her stupidly. "Hey, babe," he said. "You wanna wrestle too? I'm two for two."

James, his mouth open in frozen, scandalized delight, was looking at Orsino. Orsino was grinning, looking disheveled and ready for more. I suddenly realized what James saw in him. He was hot. Or maybe I'd known that before.

"We're just play wrestling," Orsino said, getting up. "Duke's good. I thought I could take him, but I guess not."

Barb looked around at the smokers, her eyes wide, her

pink hair standing up on her head. "THIS IS MY *CLIENT*," she shouted. "MY TEEN CLIENT."

"Ah, shit," Stacey said.

Duke looked between Barb and Orsino. "What?"

"Orsino," James said, over Barb's head. "Jukebox needs you inside."

Barb grasped both sides of her head. "I am a *therapist*, Duke. Do you remember that I have a *job*?"

Duke's face clouded over. "Can you tell me what's wrong?"

"This is my *client*, Duke, that I *told* you was here today, and who I said I was going to try to avoid interacting with too much, and *you* just interviewed to be the director of this youth organization!"

"We're just messing around, Barb," Duke said. "No harm done. I'm not director of anything yet."

"Hey," James said timidly. "Not to interrupt, but we need Orsino insi—"

"You're acting like a WILD BOAR!" Barb screamed.

The air still smelled a lot like weed.

"Uh, James, I need a break," Orsino said. "Barb, I'm really okay."

James looked crushed.

Barb closed her eyes and took a deep breath, stepping back toward me and James. "Orsino, I'm glad you're not hurt, but this isn't actually about your actions." She turned and glared at Duke. "Come with me. We need to talk."

She led Duke away around the corner of the building, and Stacey looked down at the ground with wide eyes as if she was on TV staring into the camera.

"Everything's so disgustingly professionalized," she said. She shrugged and started to walk back inside.

Orsino and I stood alone in the alley. The blue sky darkened as a cloud covered the cold sun.

"Orsino," I said, "why do you like that guy?"

He reached up to ruffle his bleached, fried hair. "I don't know," he said. He seemed surprised I'd ask. "He's weird. He's an older trans guy. He doesn't treat me like I'm stupid. He's nice. He's dumb. He's hot."

"Hot?"

"You know, when you see someone and you're like, oh, they're what I am, but for longer. Cool. I want to touch them."

His face was so unguarded. His eyes so dark. I knew what he meant, though I'd never felt like I was allowed to touch anyone I wanted to touch.

"I feel that too," I said. "Sometimes."

"Do you want to wrestle?" Orsino asked.

"I'm no good at that," I said.

"I'll show you," Orsino said. He spread his arms apart again, his legs the width of his shoulders. "Put your hands here."

I felt weird, but I wanted to. I moved toward him and put my hands on his shoulders. I could see what James saw in him, I thought. He put his hands on my shoulders, and pushed—hard. I stumbled back. I felt a rolling pulse in my pelvis, and my chest.

"No," he said. "Lean into it."

I laughed—I couldn't meet his eyes.

"I can't, I'm sorry," I said.

Because I couldn't. I wasn't like him. And if I touched

215

him, it would just get more complicated. I would mess something up. It would be me trying to get back at James, getting close to his boyfriend to fuck with him.

"Well," he said. He looked sad, but put his hands down. "Let's go back in, then."

We went back into the dark cave of the theater. I felt like there was a knife in my gut.

There was something that was supposed to be happening that wasn't happening, during the revolution scene where we played "Actioncow." Jukebox knew what it was, but they were having a very hard time explaining it.

"Orsino and I are going to do a psychic blast," they said. "And we need to find the chords that will pick up and reverberate that blast, and I think we have them. But what we need is the *energy*."

Danny and Francine, who had been doing their silly dance with the banners behind Jukebox during the part where they bent over James, were tired now, and were standing, banners limp. I knew my back hurt. Their backs probably did too.

"I don't know if I can do a psychic blast," Orsino said. "The way that you want. I'm not . . ." he looked at me, and back to them. He looked deeply nervous. Something had changed—inside, he didn't feel as safe, or something. I tried to gauge what I was feeling. Did I feel unsafe? I couldn't tell. I thought things were normal. But things had felt tight and weird for a while.

Jukebox had taken approximately ten minutes to get

right back to the point they were at when they'd yelled at Sophie. They turned to me.

"Monique," they said. "Play it again. Just you. James, look at him."

"His name's Ian," James said.

"I like being called Monique," I said, feeling my heart beat hard.

James rotated on his back on the floor, moving his feet so he scooted in a circle to face me.

"Monique," he said, "the aliens are killing me."

I wanted to laugh, but I bit it back. I felt such waves of tenderness for him even when he was annoying me.

The low light glinted off the broken mirror bits glued all over the set.

These *were* my people, I thought. This was the place I'd wanted to be, making *art*. Queer art. And it was queer. There was weird longing all over this place. My weird longing was a part of everyone else's.

I played the first chord, and yelled, "UNLESS YOU BREATHE . . ."

Jukebox bent over James. They put their hand on his stomach. I saw James's breath hitch.

"James, I want you to feel the pull here. There's a ship, promising freedom, promising futures. Have you ever just gotten a vision of the future, and it's glowing, and there's so much more life in that vision than you've ever even thought existed?"

"Yeah," James said, without hesitation. He was breathless.

"It feels *powerful*," Jukebox said. "Feel that."

James looked like a mouse hypnotized by a snake in an

old-timey cartoon, I thought. He smiled dreamily and wiggled on the floor. "Hell yeah," he said.

Jukebox rounded on the other kids, with the corporate banners. "I want this whole stage to tremble. This isn't about playing. It's *camp*, but it's supposed to be about that moment of tectonic shift where a whole dream changes. Your body becomes everyone else's body."

They moved their body like they were a mule, pushing the revolution in front of them.

"James is the cow, but all of you are workers looking on, eating him and realizing the horror of your existence. You're holding banners you realize you can't hold anymore. You're being told to never fight for anything because it's not important, but that's your *life*. You need to fight for it. You're realizing that that's you, that you too are about to be burgers unless you resist." They took a deep breath in. I could feel the anger crackling off of them. On the ground beneath them, James looked pleased, energized.

We tried again. I played the chords. Orsino and Jukebox heaved James up as I played the last reverberating *Fm7*, and yelled the last "REVOLUTION." But it sounded off. Maybe because I was increasingly unsure where exactly all of those ideas tied into our play about a worm.

In any case—whatever was supposed to happen, didn't.

And suddenly Jukebox seemed to snap.

"What do any of you know about the need to *survive*?" Jukebox yelled. "What, you came out after 2014 and gay marriage has just been legal your whole life and you're chill?"

Most of the kids were silent. One or two of them looked ready to start yelling things themselves.

Behind me, Opal made a noise. I glanced at them and made eye contact. "Jesus," they muttered.

Jukebox turned briefly toward Opal, and seemed about to open their mouth, but then they thought better of it. They let out a long exhale.

"Uh," Venus said loudly, drawing out the vowel sound to give everyone time to look at her. "If we're doing like, big political commentary, I think we're probably not going to be able to fit all of those ideas into a worm. Respectfully."

"I agree," Opal said.

"*You* wrote this script," Jukebox said.

"Yeah," Opal said. "But I was just trying to be like, funny and get people to *donate to Compton*. It's *funny* that James is a *cow*. We all have to dedicate our lives to do things that save the world. The show's this weekend. Can we just focus on practicing already?"

Jukebox put a hand on their heart, as if they were going to rip it out.

"The moment where someone opens to new ideas about what's possible is the moment revolution starts."

They paused, as if trying to let this sink in.

"I think the moment revolution starts is when you have a bunch of oppressed-ass people who want the same thing," Sophie said, deadpan. "For instance, *we* are all being oppressed by your loud-ass voice and all want to leave."

Jukebox rounded on Sophie again. "Well, why don't you *leave*, then?"

Sophie started for the door.

"Okay, yeah. I think we're done for today," Opal said loudly, their voice shaking a little. "Jukebox, I think you need to calm the *fuck* down." They put their drumsticks into their vest. "Like, you're putting a ton of work into this. But no yelling, okay? I don't like that shit."

Gemma had figured out there was a fight going on, and was sidling toward the stage, holding her arms delicately to either side with her wrists at angles like she was a moth that was going to fan away the conflict. She seemed like she wasn't sure how to directly step onto the stage. "Okay, okay, everyone," she said. "I'm hearing a lot of accusations and bad feeling right now. Let's step back."

Opal turned their wheels and rolled down toward the ramp and the dressing room.

In the dressing room, I grabbed my stuff and texted my mom. Opal was asking where Barb was.

"Hey, Ian," James said. He was changing his shirt and taking too long to put the new one on. I knew it was because he was proud of his scars. I let myself look at his chest a second too long. "Do you want to watch *Barbarella* with me and Orsino this weekend after the show? I miss sleepovers."

I felt tears spring to my eyes and a lump in my throat. I needed to tell him again, but I couldn't. I turned away, pretending to rummage in my bag. "No," I said. "I mean, I can't. I'm grounded. Aren't *you* grounded?"

"Only when I'm at my dad's house," James said. "My mom and him had a fight."

"She was supposed to drive me *home*," Opal said. The edge had gone out of their voice. Now they just looked exhausted. They looked to James. "Can you take me?"

James was strenuously taking off the cow pants. I watched the shape of his ass and his legs in his black underwear as he turned, extracting his feet from the fake fur. I was surprised Orsino wasn't in here with him, watching him undress. "I came here with Jukebox," he said. "I could ask if they could drive you."

Opal grimaced. They turned to me. "Not my *fave* plan. Monique?"

"I got work after this," I said apologetically. "I took a late shift because I need money. My mom's making me take the bus there."

"Wait," James said, turning to me. "Are you for real going by Monique?"

"Yes," I said. My voice was a whisper, but not on purpose.

"Cool," James said. He looked like he wanted to ask more. I turned toward Opal to avoid the question I knew was coming.

Opal had their head in their hands. "God," they said. "Today was a mess. Gemma's *useless*. Why does every adult have to be *like this*."

James had finished taking off the pants. "I think Jukebox will still drive you, Opal. It's not about you." He shoved the cow pants in his backpack and dashed towards the door in his socks. "I'll check. Be right back."

Opal waited until the door closed to tilt their head to me. "Hey, I'm sorry for saying stick it out," they said. "I think we can call this shit right now if you want. Let the fucking nonprofit fail. This is demented. The only person having a good time is James."

"No way," I said. "This is demented, but it's important."

But as I made fries and flipped burgers and stared out at the drive-through, it did occur to me a couple times that I might have chosen to get involved in literally anything else.

Chapter 14

JAMES

Ian—Monique?—had been avoiding me since *immediately* after we kissed.

I'd been in denial that it was happening, because he still texted me memes and he was half-grounded, but I realized now that ever since I'd kissed him, we hadn't had a conversation of more than two minutes one on one.

He?

Monique?

Ian would tell me if there was a trans situation happening, right? Ian was femme, but that wasn't the same as having gender dysphoria. There were infographics about it. We had both read hundreds of them.

Very possibly it took some people longer to come out than I did, but still. I would know, wouldn't I?

Monique had muttered something in the car that I hadn't heard. And like, if I asked, I would have to admit that the kiss thing had happened and was weird and my fault. I didn't really want to talk about the kiss. I knew I hadn't like, checked in exactly, or been totally consensual about it, because I'd been drunk. Ian—Monique—had been all sad and weird and had just gotten dumped, and what if that meant that I'd hurt Monique?

How bad could you hurt someone by being tipsy and horny one time? Maybe bad.

And maybe he—she?—they?— were really mad at me now, in a way they couldn't even express?

I didn't know how to deal with that.

Not knowing didn't feel *great*.

I was too nervous to text and find out what was going on.

Opal was sitting in the back of Jukebox's car while I stood there like an asshole, holding the pieces of their chair half-disassembled. I had been looking at the back of the car, trying to figure out where I could Tetris them in.

Opal was talking to me.

"But like, why did they leave? Even if they're mad they could talk upstairs or at Prancing Oat."

"Barb was mad at Duke for wrestling Orsino and giving him weed," I said. "That's *literally* all I know."

I hadn't seen Orsino anywhere either since Jukebox called rehearsal, I realized. Maybe they all had gone somewhere together to process. I texted Orsino, *hey, what's up? Jukebox is abt to drive Opal home.*

Venus and Francine, her butch fifteen-year-old friend who had showed up late, were glaring at Jukebox as Jukebox talked to Gemma under the marquis. Venus and I were maybe friends now. I tried to catch her eye.

"Today sucked," Opal said. "What the fuck was that *Star Is Born* bullshit Jukebox was doing with you, anyway? It's the music we gotta get right, not your cow antics. No offense."

"I mean," I said, "they were *directing*. Just a little, you know, queer and weird."

I'd seen a vision when they touched me on the third take we did of "Actioncow." I had been in water, hot water, and someone was naked above me, their stomach covered in mud, staring down from a grassy ledge. Then I'd seen a cloudburst, trees struck by lightning, then strange, enormous creatures swimming in the deep parts of the ocean, curling and unwinding their long blue bodies. And then—this was scary—this enormous ship, completely covered in guns, bearing down on a tiny sphere like a pink moon.

Was the moment that we needed to change hundreds of thousands of years ago? Was it millions of years ago? Was it this week? How late were we?

Orsino texted, *sorry, I took off to take a walk. Felt stressed. See u tomorrow?*

I didn't understand, but I didn't understand anything about Orsino. Weird dog bone boy. Weird beautiful ghost boy. Mysterious punk. Sad boy, deep boy.

I scooted a guitar further under the front seat and rammed Jukebox's shit more to the side so Opal's wheels fit. I worried about something falling on the wheels, but not enough to fix it. I slammed the door shut, wishing for the best, and climbed in the back seat behind Opal.

"Can I talk to you about something?" I said.

"Shoot," Opal said, though their voice was distant. They were staring at their phone.

I thought better of it. No Ian/Monique talk. If I asked, it might just cement everything and Opal would be sure I did something wrong, and one thing I knew about Opal was that they were really intense about right and wrong and hated when people were doing wrong things. Which meant I had to come up with another thing. I did have one at the ready.

"I think I have a *crush* on Jukebox," I said. "Like a big one. When they touched me I felt like, all tingly. Like I understand what the future's for." That was the easiest way to describe it.

Opal hissed through their teeth and rubbed their eyes with their wrists. "Why don't you just go *fuck* them on stage, then, James?"

They sounded the angriest I'd ever heard them.

I tried to laugh, even though I immediately felt all rotten and slimy inside. "That would sell tickets."

They glared. I realized, suddenly, how badly I'd messed things up with them. Somehow, impossibly quickly, I'd fucked up. What had I *done*?

"I thought you liked Jukebox."

"Not in a fuck-them way, James. And not really, right now. They're being a dick."

"It's just like, a crush. But it's exciting. Laying under them when they touched my stomach, I felt this jolt of like, wow, if a person like that asked me to like, kiss the ground they walked on, I would. They're so *powerful* and they wear their queerness all around in public, they look so trans and they love it. It makes me feel better about my body, to look at them."

Opal looked at me in the mirror and moaned sadly.

"What?"

"That's such a dumb thing to say."

"What's that supposed to mean?" I asked. "It's like you and Goober."

"No it's *not*. Goober is eighteen months older than me. Jukebox is twenty-seven. You're just like, all over the place, James. I can't figure you out. You were all horny at Monique, and pulled *that* shit, now you're fucking Orsino, and now you wanna get with *Jukebox* of all fucking people?"

I shrugged. I hadn't expected this. I wasn't sure exactly what Opal meant. *That shit*? "Ian's . . . has Monique been talking about it?"

Opal turned around in their seat. "James," they started to say. Their voice had the same tone as my dad talking to his old dog, and I froze. But then they stopped, looking behind me. Jukebox was coming towards the car, swinging their keys. "We *have* to talk soon," they said, just before Jukebox opened the driver's seat door.

That was ominous.

"Hey, dudes," Jukebox said, swinging through the open car door. It slammed shut with a noise like a bomb. "Sorry about the wait. Opal, hey, wanted to say sorry for earlier. Got a little intense in there. You were right."

Opal grunted, looking sidelong at Jukebox like a cat assessing a roach before looking back at their phone. I felt the earth falling out from under me. Everything could change so fast.

Jukebox grinned. "Cool," they said. They looked back at me. "James. Wanted to say that *you* were on point the whole time. I really like how into it you are. You did that take a ton. You're a trooper. You should do dance professionally."

I smiled weakly, feeling like my gut had turned to jelly.

When we got to Barb's house, it was clear that Barb and Duke's argument wasn't over. We heard Barb's voice from outside when we pulled up. Barb's house is right on street level, though the sidewalk is sloped up because the house is on almost the top of a hill. The accessibility ramp zig-zags to stay at the right grade. I opened the car door for Opal and they got into their chair with the brakes on and we went up the ramp to the stoop. Opal was about to use their keys to open the door, but then we heard a door slam inside, and they stopped.

". . . isn't the same," Barb's voice said. "It's *not* the back of a drag bar in Oklahoma City, and materially helping isn't the same as acting like you're still seventeen."

There was silence for a second. "This is a you issue," Duke said. "It's *not* a me issue. The kid's fine. I know when to code switch. That kid needs bros. He needs people who will show him people care about him in the ways that mean something."

"You do *not* know when to code switch," Barb said. "On a radical faerie commune, you can wrestle all the rogue teenagers you want, Duke, and be grubby Peter Pan or whatever and tell them you love them, but we are in a city and you have professional roles to play."

"Maybe I should just go back to Seattle, live with Ben again full time."

"So go," Barb said. "Go be with Ben. He's your partner. I have no *problem* with Ben. That is so not the issue. The issue is that you're committing to being present in a certain way for youth. Am I wrong that the job you applied for makes you responsible in a professional way for teens? Do you disagree that you have a professional role?"

"Professional role like *mother*, you mean?" Duke said, way too loudly, close enough to the window that I took a step back down the ramp. I wondered if he had heard our car. "Opal called you their *mom* to me the other day. Do you realize that?"

Opal stuck their keys in their pocket and looked at me. They mouthed, *we have to go*.

We went back to Jukebox's car.

"I can't go in there," Opal said to Jukebox. "They're fighting."

Jukebox looked uneasy. They glanced through the window at the house. "Well," they said uncertainly, "I could drive you someplace else, I guess. Or, you wanna call them and say you're outside and they gotta stop fighting?"

"No," Opal said. They were shaking now. They turned their chair away from Jukebox's car. I realized they couldn't make a decision. They took out their phone and opened TikTok, letting the speaker play. A teen was doing a one-person sketch about the musical *Hamilton*. They scrolled, and a dog wearing a hat was jumping from a truck. I watched them, knowing this could go on for a while. They were frozen, and they didn't want to go with Jukebox *or* go inside.

"Can I do anything?" I asked. I was aware of Jukebox sitting in the car, waiting to hear what was next.

"Can I stay with you tonight, James?" Opal asked. They were still looking down at their phone, frowning.

"Yeah," I said. "Probably. Let me text my mom."

I texted: *hey can opal crash tonight? Barb is having relationship issues*

My mom was probably either grading papers or watching *Star Trek*. It would be a second before she texted back.

"Let's get coffee," I said quickly. I had to stop us all from just freezing forever. I reached inside the car and grabbed my bag. "They'll be done by the time we're done. Or at worst we can stay at my house tonight." I was cold. I looked to Jukebox. "My mom can get us, really," I said. "Or Opal will be able to go inside in a bit. You're good. You can go home. Thanks for driving us."

"Cool," Jukebox said, with obvious relief. "Okay. See you dudes later. You're both amazing. Sorry for earlier."

"You're good, man," Opal said, facing away from them.

Jukebox drove off. I stood, staring at the house, and not staring at Opal.

"I am so triggered by this, dude," Opal said. "I cannot be around this."

"Duke and Barb are like, on-and-off lovers, right?" I asked. "Maybe this is just what it's about for them. Sparring."

Opal shrugged and said nothing.

"What was that stuff about Ben? Is that his ex?"

"That's his primary partner," Opal said. "He's been living with him for years. He goes to see him like every other week."

I tried to absorb this. Duke was with a *man*? A cis man, or a trans one? Was he leaving that guy for Barb?

I turned to look at Jukebox's retreating car as a cat ran across the street. "Let's go to Oakland Happyland. We can sit for a minute."

Oakland Happyland is a bakery around the corner from Barb's. It has a garden in the back that's nice to have breakfast in during summer. Most of the people who work there on weeknights are college kids. I've been eating their cookies since I was a kid. We moved down the block and around the corner slowly. Opal's chair creaked and I noticed one of the tires was getting kind of low. Opal was quiet, staring straight ahead. They were clutching the sides of the seat.

"Are you okay?"

"Not really," they said. We paused on the path to the door of the bakery. "I hate when people yell. I really, *really* hate when people yell. My aunt and my cousin would fight all the time like that, just in circles. And Jukebox was yelling earlier."

Opal did the thing they do when they're stressed and rubbed in a little hard circle with their fingers just behind each ear.

"Sometimes people argue," I said. "It's no big deal. It'll pass." I took a couple steps forward toward the bakery door so we could move inside and not talk out in the cold.

We got two big spiral chocolate and vanilla cookies and two vegan gingerbread dinosaurs and two cups of black coffee that tasted like it had been percolating since Bikini Kill broke up. I paid. We sat eating while the college kids who worked the counter danced to Grimes in the back, washing dishes. We were the only people in the cafe.

I texted Orsino, *hey, hope ur good. jsyk, if Duke acts weird and distant at you it's because his girlfriend got mad at him for wrestling you. He likes you.*

Orsino texted back, *lol. I have therapy w her tomorrow.*

No mention of what he was up to. I like-reacted to his text and decided I wouldn't ask anything else. I could ask something, but then I'd have to deal with taking care of him *and* Opal, and I only had room for Opal right now.

I texted my mom, *can you come get me and Opal at Oakland Happyland? We went to their house but Barb and Duke are fighting and its awk.*

Opal sighed. "I hope that this doesn't ruin him working at Compton. I was so excited." They sipped their coffee and winced.

I got up and grabbed a container of half and half and one of soy creamer from the counter. The soy separated in Opal's cup and came to the top like little tiny particles of tofu. "He'll be fine," I said. "Nobody's going to tell the board. We aren't like, McCarthy."

"I guess," Opal said. They put their head down on the table. "I just wish any adults would take any responsibility. They were so distracted with their shit that they didn't stop Jukebox yelling at everyone today. Now Barb's forgotten I exist, and the show's in *two days*, and it's going to suck."

"That's not true," I said, but I didn't know that.

Opal didn't answer.

"What did you need to tell me about Ia—Monique? Is she like, trans now?"

"Why don't you ask *Monique*?" Opal said.

Somehow I could not do that. My best friend—well, besides Opal—and I couldn't send one damn text.

If Ian was a girl, what did that mean for what I'd felt? What did Ian feel? Monique. Monique. But what if Monique was just doing a drag thing? Or a kind of they/them thing? And what if the kiss wasn't the issue, but something else about how I treated them?

What did I want? Did it have anything to do with what Monique wanted?

I just wanted to be in bed together again, holding each other and watching *Star Trek*.

I scrolled through Instagram and looked at Dogman's new tattoos and Stacey's video of hitting a bong. Opal dug their notebook for English out of their backpack and flipped to the back, where they wrote song lyrics. They started scribbling, not looking at me. I was worried that if I said anything else they'd snap at me, like they had earlier. I got out the book I was trying to read—Samuel Delany's *Nova*, which was about evil oligarch princes in space—and then put it down again and pulled out my homework for Chem. I'd been flunking every test since I stopped doing all the extra exercises. Before that I had been relying on cheating off this girl named Norma, knowing that eventually this would stop working, because we were not friends. Now that Norma had started sitting across the room from me, I had to stop bullshitting. I started working on a problem with my calculator.

"Are you still failing Chemistry?" Opal asked unhelpfully, after a while. I realized a couple quizzes were poking out of my science folder, with the red 62/100 and 45/100 showing bright at the top of the page.

"Yeah," I said.

Opal's phone buzzed. They looked at it, rolled their eyes, and showed me the screen. Barb had texted: *hey, in a processing convo with Duke. It isn't anything you need to worry about, just wanted to let you know.*

"I have divorced parents," I said. "Just because she's fighting Duke doesn't mean she doesn't love *you*."

"Dude, you talk all the time about how your dad doesn't love you. I don't want to live through Barb's queer premarital divorce," Opal said. "This is stupid."

We sat there for a little longer, doing homework.

My mom pulled up ten minutes later, wearing her housecoat over a T-shirt that said PJ'S LAST STAND: GINGER'S, FEB 28 2003. It's a short drive from her house to the bakery. We could even have walked home, if she hadn't texted back. We got Opal's chair in the car; my mom tried to hug Opal, but Opal didn't hug back. They looked like they were mad.

When we got home, my report card was on the table, open, next to a pot of soup on a cork coaster. I got a sinking feeling in my bowels.

"I'm gonna shower," Opal said. "Thanks so much for getting me, Thea. I really appreciate it."

"Totally," my mom said. "If you need me to call Barb or anything, let me know."

"Not right now," Opal said. They slid out of their chair

onto their knees and moved to the linen cabinet to get a towel. "But thanks."

"Are they okay?" my mom whispered to me, after we heard the fan go on in the bathroom.

I shrugged. "Rehearsal was bad today, and Barb and Duke have been arguing all night. They're having a bad time." And they're pissed at me, too, I thought, but I couldn't talk to my mom about that, or she'd be desperate to give me advice. I didn't want that.

The stew was chickpea pumpkin, thick with garlic and celery. I got one of the big blue bowls and scooped myself a sloppy pile of it, hoping my mom wouldn't say anything about my report card. I perched on a stool by the kitchen counter, turning my body away from her.

"So," my mom said, as soon as I sat. "You're having some trouble with the AP classes."

"Ugh," I said. "I *just* got home. The show's this weekend. I'm really stressed."

"Okay," she said, slowly. "But it's late, you know? You didn't let me know, and I got this in the mail today, and it was a surprise. It's almost the end of the semester. Can you talk to me about what's been happening?"

I felt my muscles tense. I knew that my mom was trying to be responsible, but I couldn't take this right now.

"I hate school and I'm dumb and transphobic people make me depressed," I said, shoveling soup. "I don't know. I haven't been able to focus. Noah and people still act like they got me. Chem's the worst. Noah's in that class. I'm sick of my teachers, and I'm sick of the principal, and I can't talk to any of them, because they all hate me for being trans."

My mom went to the teapot and put it on. "Noah's the guy that says stuff to you, yeah? Do you think you'd do okay in regular Chemistry, if we tried to switch you?"

"No," I said. "I won't get college credit then."

"Well, you won't get college credit if you fail the test, either," Mom said. "I just want to consider our options. It seems like you're having a rough time in school in general, these days. I'm wondering if it's healthy for you to keep going."

"What?" I asked. I hadn't expected that. "Are you saying I should *drop out*?" Mom had dropped out of high school, but she was also a teacher. I didn't think she would think it was an option. It wasn't an option. Dad wouldn't let me.

"I'm saying community college classes online might work better for you. I don't want you to be depressed. I don't want you to go back to the kind of place you were in a couple years ago. It scares me."

"I'm fine," I said. "I'm even, I'm doing great. You don't need to bring up my cutting every time. I don't do that anymore."

"I didn't say—"

"I'm better. I have friends." Except Opal and Monique might both be mad at me, which actually put the number of *close* friends at something like zero. Now Orsino was my closest person. And I didn't know how to talk to him either. "I just hate school."

"Okay," Mom said. "I mean, I hated school too at your age. But I just dropped out, and then it took me years to figure out what I wanted, and more time to make up my lost ground. I want you to have options."

"Dad wants me to make school work. If I don't apply to eighteen colleges by January he'll eat me alive."

My mom sighed. "You have to stop worrying about what he thinks. I'll talk to him. He knows you're my kid too, and that I have different values than he does." She poured tea into her cup. "Let's talk about it this weekend after the show. You're tired now. We'll need to decide something about classes soon. I'm here for you."

I suppressed a groan.

You're supposed to be grateful for a mom like my mom, but I couldn't make myself be grateful. I felt annoyed. I didn't want to think about the future, or to think about planning it in a normal way. I couldn't believe in the normal future, where I went to school and then worked some kind of job and got older and had to deal with stuff. I didn't want to think that the things that felt impossible weren't.

Opal and I went to sleep in my bed; they rolled over near the wall. I could hear from their breath that they weren't asleep yet, but sensed that they didn't want to talk.

I tried to read about the evil princes in *Nova*. Everyone used tarot cards to make decisions, which felt realistic. The main character's name was Mouse, and he seemed like he was in love with this older man he'd known on earth, but he had to leave him behind to go on the prince's crazy mission. I sensed he'd never see him again. There was no ideology in the book; it was about a world where guys with money ruled everything, and that was just the way it was. Or was it a critique?

I could hear Opal listening to music.

If they were mad at me, it was okay, I repeated to myself, and realized it was a lie. If Opal was mad at me, I had no idea what to do.

I lay in bed thinking of everything going wrong forever. Our show was okay. It might make a little money, and save Compton, just like Opal wanted. But what would Duke do in five months or a year? What if he wrestled more teenagers and Compton got a bad reputation?

I had ruined my friendship with Monique by wanting to fuck—and now that I was thinking about it, maybe it was because I wanted to see Monique as a guy because it meant I was a gay guy. I wanted gay men so bad. I projected on Monique. Shit.

Opal was saying that it was weird to want sex the way I wanted it. Was that fair?

What if Orsino realized that he didn't want to be with me? Did I want to be with him? I did—he made me feel excited. But there were ways I felt like we were puzzle pieces from different sets.

Last week he'd shown me the freshly cleaned bones of his dead dog sitting in a blue bucket behind Jukebox's house, and told me that she'd been named Agatha, and that his dad killed her. I'd asked him to talk about it, and he just shook his head. That seemed fucked up. But I couldn't get away from him. I wanted more and more of the salmon and explosions and blooming flowers; when I touched him, they would come out, red and blue and sweating and sparking and awesome, and I'd feel close to him. And the things that came after the visions were real. There was the dinosaur or whatever, and the water, and the fish, and the flowers. There were sounds like music that stretched the muscles inside my cheeks so it felt like I'd hurt myself smiling. Sometimes I saw the dog, in his mind, running fast across a red field. Orsino's hands were hot on my sides.

When he touched me, I knew that he loved me. These pictures froze me, stuck with me, got stuck to the roof of my mouth, tasted like blood. Whatever his thing with the aliens was, he had something real that was bigger than I could wrap my head around when I got close.

Was that enough?

Monique was a visionary like Jukebox. Monique had plans for the band. Monique made music that made me feel wonderful. I could *talk* to—her?

If she talked to me ever again.

Jukebox had a vision too, of living outside what was supposed to be normal, that included sensation and beauty and life. Jukebox's vision buzzed through me. I wondered what Jukebox knew that Orsino didn't.

Opal thought Jukebox was being crazy and righteous and stupid.

Did Opal have some other vision for the show, for the world, that I didn't understand? Was that why Opal was mad at me?

What if they never told me?

In the morning, Mom drove me and Opal to school. Opal resisted getting out of bed, and I felt like doing the same, but my mom needed to get to her school and refused to let us make her late. She shoved travel cups of coffee at us. I threw on black sweats and my biggest black sweater and big Docs, feeling like a big crusty bat. Opal and I didn't speak on the way to school; when they went to their locker, I tried to stop them.

"Can we talk later?" I asked.

"I guess," they said.

In History, we had a quiz that I'd forgotten about. I had remembered about half of the notes I'd taken last week and got to glance over them for two seconds before Mr. Garden told us to put our materials away. I drew Orsino's dog in the margins when I ran out of answers. I remembered, turning it in, that I had a test in Chem that day too. I felt myself falling further and further behind.

On the break between third and fourth period, when I was hurrying back from my locker, I texted Opal: *wanna smoke with me after school before rehearsal?*

Not really, they replied. *We do need to talk, but I'm not up to it yet. I'm just kinda mad at you still. You're being basic as fuck, you know?*

Shit.

Can you tell me what's wrong? Is it the Monique thing?

No. Think about it.

I felt my entire stomach knot like a plastic bag. I stood staring at my phone for a second, then ran for the nearest bathroom. The bell rang. The two doors stood in front of me; I went into the boys'. It was empty. I stood over the toilet in the far corner that always smelled like piss and waited to retch. I couldn't. Tears were in my eyes. I gasped for breath, feeling my chest constrict. I couldn't figure out what to do. I stayed in the bathroom all through fourth period. My brain, on some level, knew this was dumb. My stomach was wrapped so tight around my guts I couldn't breathe. I typed up a long, convoluted reply to Opal, then deleted it because I could tell it didn't make any sense. I tried again:

I know I've seemed like i don't care about the Barb stuff, or I'm not as good of an ally as I should be, but i just don't want to always be focusing on the ways y .

I think i'm just like, naturally really sexual and i'm realizing it now. I'm confused about what you mean about Monique and I know Jukebox is kind of intense but i think you need to g

I know I've been weird with Ian but I thought he

Orsino and I aren't really wor

Then the bell rang. It was lunch.

Nobody saw me leave the bathroom, but heading down the hallway afterward, I turned a corner and passed Noah and his friends sitting on the floor. They'd been on their phones, but they looked up when I walked by.

"Lookin' scary," he said to me. He snickered; his friend Ross next to him smirked.

"You can choke on my dick and eat shit, Noah," I said.

"You mean choke on your vagina."

Something inside me snapped. I turned.

"I've never fucked with you cucks in my whole life, but you're always asking for a fucking fight. The fuck is up? You can have a fucking fight, if that's what you want."

He laughed with his friends, in that way people laugh

when they're pretending they haven't done anything to you. "Woah," he said. "Are you on your period or something?" He lifted his phone. I could tell he was taking a picture of me, or a video.

"Come at me right now if you want to fucking fight," I said. "Stop recording and try me. I got suspended, now I'm back. I'm not scared of you, or your country-ass homophobic bullshit. You scared to get your ass beat? You can fight me for real or you can shut up."

The freshmen girls sitting at the other end of the hall stood up and moved away down the hall, looking back over their shoulder nervously.

"Great. We'll tell Coleman."

"Great. I don't *want* to be here. Just get me expelled and get on with your fucking day."

He and his friends laughed, a little awkwardly. He kept holding his phone up, staring at me through the camera, I knew.

I stepped forward and grabbed his phone out of his hand, threw it down the hall. It skidded on the carpeted floor. It wasn't damaged, but Noah leapt up and shoved me out of the way like I'd thrown his firstborn child as he ran to pick it up again.

"What the fuck, you psycho," he said. He turned to look at me, his face a mix of rage and disgust as he pocketed his phone. He started toward me abruptly, but if he thought I was going to fall back, he was wrong.

I swung my fist. It hit his chin. He staggered backward.

"Oh yeah, I'm the psycho," I said. "You're the one who's *obsessed* with me."

Noah reeled back, looking shocked, but then he came at me again with his other arm. I punched him in the gut. He bent over.

I tore off my backpack and threw it at him. I felt a rush of cold pleasure watching him step hastily to one side, like it was a bomb.

"You're all a bunch of musty junior-cop pieces of back-woods dick cheese," I yelled.

I felt the sourest rush of adrenaline color my vision red. I hurled myself forward, swinging; Trevor caught me and threw me off of Noah. I got in one good punch.

"Psycho bitch," he said. "Chill the fuck out, man."

I grabbed my backpack from the floor and walked down the hall, my spine rigid. I had to leave. I rounded the corner past the computer lab and shoved my way through a group of kids by the side exit, kicking open the door.

I didn't know who to call. I couldn't talk to my mom. Not my dad. *Not* my dad.

I called Jukebox. Three rings before they picked up. They had my number from Opal, from back when Opal liked them.

"Hey," they said into the phone, sounding confused. "James?"

"I'm sorry," I said. "I just got into a fight at school with some transphobic idiot. Can you pick me up? I'll send you my location." I was breathing hard. I didn't know what I was doing.

There was a long silence.

"Uh. Sure," Jukebox said. "I'm rehearsing with OVID right now, but I can dip. I'm sorry that's happening, little bro. You okay?"

"I'm okay," I said. "I just cannot go back to high school ever again."

They laughed. "Me neither, bro. Okay. Hold tight. Is there somewhere you can walk to that's not your school?"

"It's just cow fields," I said. "There's a roadside coffee stand like a mile away."

"Oh, you go *there*. I went to Tumwater too. Nah, just stay put if you can," Jukebox said. "Or, I don't know. Go to the office and wait?"

"Meet me in the parking lot behind the big square building," I said. "Nobody can see me over there." I didn't want to talk to Principal Coleman, didn't want to call my mom. In my head, I mapped Noah's route to the office.

Nobody found me in the forty minutes it took Jukebox to get there. I was crouched on a cinderblock behind the portables.

I saw I had texts from my dad, and wondered if he somehow already knew, but when I got the guts to open them, the texts read:

I heard from your mom you're failing chemistry. Something you forgot to tell me, I guess.

She says you're considering online school. I want you to know that it's still important to get your grades up this semester.

We can talk later about your habit of lying to me.

Jukebox's car made a distinct crackling, rumbling noise, and when I heard it, I managed to look up. They didn't lean out, just put one long tattooed arm out the window and waved. I could see through the windshield that they were wearing sunglasses.

"You know," they said, "you're the second teenager I've rescued from transphobic redneck bullshit this month. Had to grab Orsino from his dad's like this just before we started the show."

"Thanks," I said, buckling myself in. "I'm sorry. If I had a car I'd go by myself, but my dad won't let me drive."

"Sucks, man," they said, looking over their shoulder and pulling out of the parking space they'd careened into at a strange angle. "It's sweet I'm the one you call. Makes me feel good."

"You're a real one," I said. "I knew I could count on you."

We drove through the dry green-and-brown fields around my school, the wrong way for them to be heading back to the highway. I was quiet for a second, feeling the panic I'd felt a little earlier start to go down, replaced with a freezing dread that just sat at the bottom of my intestines, waiting for me to get back to it.

Jukebox's little mustache and sparse chin hairs were catching the weak winter light and their mullet was pulled back into a little ponytail. Their red corduroy jacket had patches on it, but otherwise it looked exactly like the John Deere one that a kid in my English class had. If they hadn't had so many tattoos, they could probably pass for one of the redneck teens at my high school. But the jut of their chin and the lines around their eyes showed they were older than that, and tougher. On their neck there was a thin blue tattoo of a line curling in on itself over and over, then twisting like string under the collar of their corduroy jacket.

"You must think I'm super dumb," I said.

"Nah," Jukebox said. "High school's fucking dumb. Did you hit anyone?"

"Yeah," I said.

"Oh well," they laughed. "I could circle back, get someone with my car."

"No, you don't need to. Where are we going?"

They smiled. "Well, now I've ditched band practice, I gotta go walk this rich guy's Goldendoodle for twenty bucks."

"Cool," I said. I felt a delicious parallel. I'd driven Orsino, and now Jukebox was driving me, through the countryside, the same way. I let myself feel their eyes on the side of my face and entertain a picture of them leaning over and kissing me. I felt a spark like an echo of the one from when they'd touched my stomach dance up through my throat. I reminded myself that I was a dumb teenager who was just tagging along, making them help me skip school.

I had a jolt of guilt. I should tell my mom where I was going. I ignored it.

We passed the frozen yogurt place that shares a plaza with the Washington State Department of Corrections office. The wide asphalt parking lot sat full of cars.

"You know," Jukebox said, "I'm really glad you saved me from having to make an excuse to get away from Stacey. I've been bugged out at her lately, she's been bugged at me. You know how she is."

I thought about Stacey's white pants and tried to find something to judge her for, to show Jukebox that I understood them. I knew she did acupuncture.

"She has those white pants."

"Stacey's just like this, big city kid."

"Exactly," I said, though I didn't know what they meant.

"She went to NYU, you know," Jukebox said. "She talks like she's rough and from the bad part of Oakland or whatever. I used to fight with her all the time about money. She's so damn cheap, even though she's rich. Her parents are dentists."

I thought, guiltily, of my dad's house, the Japanese maple in front exactly like every other beige boxy house on the block. "I mean, she can't help her parents, I guess," I said. "What are you fighting about now?"

Jukebox laughed. "Just my alien album. She thinks I'm being intense. But that's how I write now. I don't know. I thought I had a vision, and I'm trying to stick with it. I've been stuck for so long, and the alien stuff, with the Gothpel of Worm and all that, it's so rad. What you all are making is so rad and it just seems like the fire at Goat Mansion ignited everything, for all of us, and now there's *all* this art with young queer people. And I'm moving faster than usual, and it makes Stacey and Robin mad. I'm so bossy."

"I kind of like when you're bossy," I said. "I know not everyone does. But it means you're committed to it. You take it seriously. A lot of the time, Gemma and Natalie seemed just glazed over. They'd just be like, 'oh, that's nice,' whenever we did a project."

Jukebox laughed. "I lost my shit a little bit yesterday."

"Opal hates people yelling," I said. I looked out the window at the roads changing, getting narrower. We were going to Yelm or something, I guessed.

"I think they think I'm being literal, with the revolution thing," Jukebox said. "Orsino too. But I'm not like, crazy. It won't happen in a *single* second. But we had these beings tell us that there's this other future that we can open a door to. But—well. I guess I should ask you. You're keyed into it."

We swung a wide turn under some trees, hidden suburban developments on either side.

"Keyed into what?"

"The visions. The futures. They're from the aliens. They gave them to me and Orsino. You get 'em, right? You got one yesterday." They said it casually, but their mouth was tight on the corners in a weird way. "I mean, tell me if I'm crazy."

I thought of what Orsino had told me about the visions. "Yeah," I said. "I get them. When Orsino touches me, I get these images and feelings of being animals or stars or plants. And then sometimes they come true. Yesterday, when . . . you touched me. I was in a pool, looking up at someone. The water was hot. We were in a forest. It was the future. I knew, like, that there was nothing bad anymore, that we were okay. It was the future."

For a second there was just the noise of the car. "You're not pulling my leg, right?" Jukebox said.

"No," I said. I felt the memory of the sparks dance in me again.

Jukebox let out a delighted bark of a laugh. The car swerved slightly on the road, and I found myself gripping the windowsill, like my dad did when he taught me to drive. "I *knew* it," they whooped. "Wow. Jeez. I've gotta pull over somewhere."

We pulled over, next to the empty Spooner's berry field. The taupe sky seemed to hang lower without the hard black trees to cut it up. Jukebox's car curved into the dirt parking lot, looking over the blank furrows where there were strawberries in the summer. They turned off the car and immediately reached over and hugged me, tight. I froze, nose in their red corduroy shoulder feeling their arms crushing me, pulling against my seatbelt.

"James, you're a miracle," they said. "Robin's been telling me I'm insane." They pulled back. "Sorry," they said. "God, that's so exciting. Like, I know what's real for *me*, but nobody else. Robin thinks I'm imagining it, just copying Orsino's visions and going crazy again. But you felt it from *me*. That means the ship gave me the powers, too. All those visions are mine too."

I tried to follow. "Was yesterday the first time you'd . . . channeled your visions?"

"I felt that spark yesterday. And now—" their face changed.

They opened their car door, and I crawled out my side, leaving my backpack in the seat. We walked together down the road into the empty berry field. The stand that's open in summer was boarded up. They led me just a little way down the hill, past the point where we'd be visible from the road.

"Give me your hand," Jukebox said. "Here." They took my hand in theirs, gently, and opened my palm. "I don't know if it makes any difference, but I'm going to touch your heart line." Their thumb came down on my palm. I watched their mouth purse, their nose wrinkle as they concentrated. "For me, what it feels like is this sudden sense—this certainty—

that we can change things, that we have to make a future for you to live in, that atoms and leaves and birds and air are flowing parts of this great whole, and that it all has meaning, because it all continues. It's promise."

I felt a shock, again, as their fingernail dug into my palm. There was an explosion happening in space, thirteen hundred years from now and also at this very instant.

Chapter 15

ORSINO

"Don't bring any more dead things in here," Stacey yelled when I opened the door. "I don't want any fucking dead crap in the bathroom, or the laundry room, or the basement, or anywhere."

"I left it outside in a bucket," I said. I took off my coat and hung it up on the folding chair inside the door where all the other coats were. "I'm sorry for the one time."

Stacey didn't seem to be paying that much attention to me. It was because Robin was freaking out. They were both standing in these kind of tense positions, facing off across the cracked tile of the living room.

"I know they're your friend, but I can't fucking *deal* with this anymore," Robin said to Stacey. For a second, I thought she was talking about me, but then I realized that she was talking about something on her phone screen. "I just don't have the skills to deal with this level of like, BS. This is like my fucking scumbag dad."

I went to get peanut butter and crackers from the cabinet in the kitchenette and poured myself a cup of the cold coffee from yesterday that Stacey had in the coffee pot. I took it into the orange living room where Robin and Stacey were and brushed off an area on Stacey's coffee table to eat, moving all the scraps of fabric and tarot cards into a pile in the basket for yarn and magazines that she kept next to the couch. I'd been trying not to think all morning, even though I knew I had a lot to think about. Now this was happening.

Robin was showing Stacey something on Instagram, I knew. I wasn't sure exactly what it was.

Stacey looked confused and annoyed. "I'm saying I'm worried about their mental health, and I hate that the band is both all they ever want to talk about and something they don't seem to understand involves people besides them. I don't understand what exactly *you're* upset about."

Robin shrugged. "I guess I thought we'd be talking more about moving in together for real. I'm applying for jobs and everything. But it's like I don't exist to them at all."

Stacey squinted at Robin, as if assessing her, and went into the kitchenette. She reached for the coffee pot. When she saw it was empty, she turned to me.

"Orsino," she said. "Did you drink my coffee again?"

"It was cold," I said. "Sorry, I thought it was game."

"It's my *special* coffee," Stacey said. "It's expensive. I would appreciate if you didn't drink it in the future."

I tried to keep my voice level. "Do you want this back?" I held out my mug. Whatever it took to get tensions down.

"No," Stacey said. "Your mouth has been on that. I can make more." But she made no move to. She came back into the living room again and looked at Robin and crossed her skinny arms.

"Robin," she said, slowly. "Jukebox has always been a little that way with girlfriends. I hate to break it to you, but they are not in their marriage phase of life."

Robin glared at her. "That's such a fucked up thing to say to me. I moved down here to be with them and support their art. I deserve more than a cursory glance every seven days."

"You don't think I feel that way too? I'm producing and editing these fucking songs! Jukebox takes my labor totally for granted. What I'm saying is, with you, it's like, that's the way they're always gonna be. They're a fuckboi in relationships, because it's always about their art. That's something you were going to run into sooner or later. But right now, it's about their art but they don't even want to be meaningfully involved in the discourse that art involves. They're a steam engine rolling over everyone else, and fuck my needs."

Robin put her hand to her forehead, the way Mom does when she's stressed. She was still looking at whatever was on the phone. "This thing with the teen show is really making me mad. They treat it like it's the only thing that matters."

They both looked at me. I was frozen, with a dry peanut butter cracker half-swallowed in my throat. I slowly lifted my mug of stolen coffee and wet my throat enough that I could get the cracker down.

"I don't understand why they ditched practice today," Stacey said. "We aren't tight."

Robin let out a guttural moan. "No shit. What the fuck is happening?"

"My question too. They're trying to get that stupid kid's

band a deal at Lone Popper like it's vital for the salvation of mankind. Why not invest more in *our* band?"

Robin's face got tight. "Monique Fatigue's good."

"Shit, sure she is," Stacey said. She leaned back on the couch and looked at the ceiling.

I shoved the last three peanut butter crackers into my mouth and drank the rest of the coffee, then went back to the kitchenette. I wanted to be someplace else. But even if I went into Jukebox's bedroom I would still be able to hear their voices. I stood in the kitchenette. Behind me, I heard the sound of Stacey hitting her bong.

"What *I* wanna know," Stacey said, "is what's so fucking *important* right now. It's the *day* before this kid show. I *moved* my shift so we could be together and practice the set so we'd be all ready tomorrow, and then they dipped."

"I want to go *home*," Robin said. She hugged a yellow, cat-patterned pillow. "It's so clear they don't care about this relationship anymore. This is fucking psychotic. I can't be here."

Stacey grimaced.

"I can't *be* here," Robin said. "They're going to come back. What do I say to them? How do I look at them? They're just thinking about themselves. I'm just like, the stuffed animal they forgot about."

"I'd offer to drive you back to your mom's, I guess, but my car's in the shop," Stacey said. She sounded angry, but I wasn't sure if it was at Robin or Jukebox.

I didn't want to say anything. I texted James, *hey, can you hang out in a little bit?*

Robin and I went to the gas station on the corner so she could get toilet paper for the house. It was an excuse to walk someplace, I knew.

"Everything I know is falling down around me," Robin said.

Robin hadn't really talked to me in months. It had only ever been Jukebox, taking up all the space between us. I felt really tired. She'd never asked how I was doing in all the weeks we'd been here.

"We could call Mom," I said. She probably couldn't get us until tonight or tomorrow, I thought. Because of work. And I didn't like the idea of going back to Tacoma, away from everyone else. But it also wasn't like we could stay, now. I wasn't sure how to talk to Robin about this.

"We absolutely *can't* call Mom," Robin said. "Not now. Not right now. She's got so much on her plate."

"Okay," I said.

"I'm an adult," Robin said. "I lived without Mom for three months when I ran away. I have to figure this out. I can do it. I'm just sorry you're in it with me. I know you like Jukebox, and they're like, a trans mentor person for you."

I hadn't told her about the time Jukebox had made me hurt Dad. I knew that if I told her, there would be an argument. Robin didn't believe the visions were real; she would think it meant I'd punched him or something. She might be mad at me, too.

Dad had sent all of us a string of angry texts the day after it happened in a group chat. He'd called me a crazy retard again, and called Robin a dyke. He didn't say anything about the visions, or about me grabbing his arm.

I wasn't sure if that meant he didn't remember. He had sent pictures of the dug-up place on the lawn. Mom had replied, *no proof Orsino did that. These insults are great material for court tho, xoxo.* Mom had called Robin and told her to block his number, and then texted me privately to say that it hadn't been a good idea to take Agatha. But they didn't know that I'd really hurt him. I wondered if he had nightmares now, too. I hoped he didn't. I didn't like to think about my dad dreaming about blood all night.

I hadn't tried to talk to Jukebox about it, either. They asked me about my visions with James almost every day, and I told them about it—how nice it was. Jukebox got happy and excited when I told them about the rivers of fish that might be the past or might be the future. I'd been living at their house since they brought me back from my dad's. Sometimes James was there, and he and Jukebox talked. My nightmares had mostly gone away, and I'd tried to pretend that everything was fine for the last few weeks. I'd talked to Barb. I hadn't told her anything about the visions.

They had really done a lot for me. That was true. They'd sat next to me after nightmares.

Onstage at rehearsal yesterday, I could see James always turning toward them. Between that and Barb yelling at Duke, I hadn't been able to deal. I left and walked down on the pier, trying to hear the water, and hear the voices of the animals who were dead on the beach and seeping into the soil. I hadn't wanted to be around anyone, or see anyone. I had only texted James a couple times last night, but I thought about him until I fell asleep.

I knew Jukebox didn't want to hurt James. They didn't want to hurt any of us. They wanted to be the same thing as us, to make a new world together. And I knew James liked them.

"They're obsessed with controlling this show that's basically for kids, right, not that you're a kid, Orsino, but it's high schoolers. And they're really into it in this way that seems like it's just about their ego. Like, they want you all to think they're cool. And I'm—" Robin stopped. She stared ahead at the traffic light and the dirty sidewalk ahead of us.

I looked where she was looking, and I saw. Jukebox's car was stopped at the light across the street. The blue sedan with the dent in the front bumper in the shape of a 7. If they were looking, they could probably see us. We couldn't see them, because the glass was dark.

"Are they going home, you think?" Robin asked. "Where *were* they?"

"I don't know," I said.

The light changed. The car came towards us, and I could see, through the front window, that someone was sitting next to Jukebox in the car. Jukebox wasn't looking at us as they passed. I couldn't be exactly sure, but the person sitting next to them in the car looked like James.

I looked at Robin, to see if she had seen. She hadn't.

"Ughhh," she said. "Now I can't even go back to grab my *stuff*. They're going to be there. I gotta call Stacey. I can't do this." She froze, and I heard her breathing faster.

I grabbed her arm and tugged her towards the parking lot where the Groc Out was. "Let's get toilet paper and go back to the house and get our stuff," I said. "They're not going to eat you. You have to talk to them. We can always go over to Dogman's house or something after."

Robin followed me as I led her by the arm. "I'm so sorry," she said, again. "This has gotta suck for you. This just has to suck for you."

"It doesn't," I said. "Let's get a snack, too. Let's get cookies and soda or something."

We went in, and I used my mom's credit card to pay for the toilet paper and cookies and soda. Then we sat on the curb while Robin took deep breaths and texted Stacey.

I got a text from James.

Hey! I'm at ur house lol. Jukebox grabbed me from school. Where are u?

Robin looked over my shoulder.

"What?"

"I don't know," I said. It was after the time when James's school let out, but only barely. "I don't understand either."

What happened? I texted James. *Why are you with Jukebox?*

Just fun stuff lol. Got in a fight at skewl.

"So they went and picked him up? Why didn't his *mom* come?" Robin asked. She was still reading over my shoulder.

"Let's go back," I said. I texted James *coming back from the store with Robin. Wanna go on a walk with me for a second? I think some stuff is abt to hit the fan between Robin and Jukebox.*

"Don't say that," Robin said before I sent it. "He might show them."

"He wouldn't," I said, but I deleted the last sentence before I hit send.

As we walked across the yard, we saw Stacey coming towards us, pinwheeling one arm into her white pleather jacket.

"I'm getting the fuck out," she said. "Call if you need, but I can't be here for this." She looked at me. "Orsino, it's weird if you go in there. You need to stay out here too."

"I'm getting my boyfriend," I said. "Jukebox picked him up from school."

"Of course," Stacey said, throwing her arms in the air. "*That* makes sense. Obviously." She turned away from us and walked quickly down the sidewalk we'd just come by.

Robin, I could see, was already almost crying. But she looked determined. I went up the steps and leaned through the front door.

"James," I yelled through the screen. "Come outside, come walk with me."

He bounded up to the inside of the door, beaming, and flung it open, leaping out and wrapping his arms around me. "Orsino!" he said. "I have to talk to you about what just happened."

I felt how warm he was, and smelled his sweat. He was salty, like the mud at low tide.

"Come on," I said, looking down into his eyes. "Let's go walk. You can tell me." I hoped whatever it was was actually good. He looked so happy.

"I gotta get my backpack," James said, and ducked

back inside. He reemerged with a backpack that seemed strangely full.

Robin was coming up behind us on the steps. Her eyes were red, and I wondered if James saw. James ran down the steps ahead of me. I turned and made eye contact with Robin before she went into the house. She did a weird little salute.

"See you in a bit," she said. "Dogman's. I'll text."

"Yeah," I said.

James was practically skipping ahead of me down the sidewalk, the opposite way from where Stacey had gone. I had to walk fast to keep up. He was walking toward the crosswalk that led to the neighborhood with the elementary school. I wondered whether he had left his backpack in the house, and if so, whether I could make him go get it alone when this was all done.

"James," I said, "there's something I need to talk to you about, about Jukebox."

"Oh my god," James said. He jumped up and pulled a hanging brown leaf off a tree that bent over the sidewalk. "Me too. Me first, okay?" He suddenly stopped and threw his bag down on the ground. "Look at this. Jukebox made me this."

He drew it out. It was a coat, covered in shards of plastic mirrors, broken apart and then superglued back on. I saw my own face in it, frowning and upset and pink.

"That looks dangerous," I said, as he put it on and twirled. It caught the faint sunlight through the clouds and sent dancing lights over the sidewalk and the road.

"Isn't it cool?" James asked. "It's for the show, obviously.

It's for 'Actioncow'. The moment I turn into a burger, I transcend."

We were near the elementary school playground. The cold wind was too cold for my jacket. I was walking behind him, and he'd turned around and was walking backwards, hands in pockets, grinning at me. I felt ill.

"Okay," I said.

He laughed. "So, my day started like shit, right? Opal's pissed at me, and Monique might be trans and is also mad at me for not knowing, right? So I was really upset earlier. And my dad was texting me, and like, all this shit. I don't know. Monique's right to be mad but I don't know what to do, and I don't know why Opal's mad but they're probably kind of right. So I fought this guy at school today, right? And I had to leave. And I called Jukebox. And they picked me up and we met a Goldendoodle, and talked about the vision I had yesterday, in the theater. And they knew it was real, right? And Jukebox gave me this mirror coat."

I stumbled after him down the little slope that leads to the field by the elementary school. The mirrors sparkled too much for my eyes to be able to completely follow him. On the other end there were some kids playing soccer. James led me toward the playground, where all the play sets are made of rope suspended from metal.

"Wait. Why is Opal pissed at you?" I asked.

He turned and shrugged. He looked upset, but I couldn't tell how upset. "They won't tell me. I think Opal thinks it's weird that I'm so into Jukebox. They're pissed about Jukebox yelling at everyone. But like, Jukebox is just directing. They want it to be good art."

"Jukebox is being kind of intense," I said. "I've been . . . Look, James."

"You missed the point," James said. "Jukebox and I just *did the thing* together. With the visions. *They* can do it to me too."

"The thing?" I asked. I thought about the last time I'd kissed James, and the feathers of sunlight that had come up under my skin as we'd looked down on a dome filled with flowers.

"Like, a really big vision. Only it's . . . different from your visions. I don't understand it. But they can show me things about the future."

There was a shriek from the other side of the field as a child fell down.

I took a deep breath. "That's uh, part of what I need to talk to you about, James. I'm feeling weird about the show. They keep talking about this thing, and I think I know what they mean, they don't want to hurt anyone, they want it to be good and show everyone the same things that like, you and I see, when we kiss. But I'm worried. We sort of fought my dad at my dad's house, and they hurt him with the visions. I'm worried something like that will happen again. They like you, but they don't see you. For them it's about them receiving something to change the world."

James frowned. "I feel seen by them."

I sighed. "I just don't know how to talk about it. There's fire. There's this spiky warship, hovering near the moon, trying to fight these other aliens, because they want to end empire or something. And there's all the pictures of our future and past, and the aliens in the small ship want us to get the right ones. But I don't know what to do with any of that."

"They do see me. I *want* the visions." He put one leg up on the rope play toy and hoisted himself up with his hands so he was looking at me upside down. "You're not like, jealous, right?"

I looked at him and tried to understand what was happening for him, right now. I couldn't. I came up blank. "No," I said.

"It wasn't like, a sex thing." He set his jaw. I could see that he was upset, and fighting tears too. I also felt like crying now. "I mean, I kind of have a crush on them, but it's just like, an older friend crush."

Something crashed into my heart at top speed. I felt like someone had thrown a chair at me. "Uh," I said.

James flipped off the play toy and sat on the rubber-paved playground asphalt in front of me.

"Like, I have these intense fluttery feelings around them, right, but it's different from what I feel about you," he said.

"Okay," I said. "I didn't think it was the same." I was feeling more and more confused. My heart felt flattened. But I had to go on. "James, I need to tell you something else. You know how Jukebox has been acting really weird to Robin lately?"

"Weird how?"

If he hadn't noticed, I couldn't explain. "Robin's about to break up with Jukebox."

James furrowed his brow. "What? Shit. That's . . . that can't be right."

"We're going to go stay at Dogman's for a second, but—

well. I don't know. We might move back to Tacoma. It's been a really weird day. This all just happened."

"What?" James asked again. "Tacoma?"

"I'm really confused. James, I'm sorry. I'm just having . . . can you hug me?"

He leaned forward immediately and put his arms around me. Even though I was so upset, I felt my heart slow a little. His elbows hugged me at the points in my ribs where it hurt the most. I wrapped my arms around him and hugged him back.

"I don't understand," James said. "You wouldn't like, leave, right? That would be awful. I would hate that."

"We may have to," I said. "Robin doesn't really have a job."

"She could get one," James said quickly. "I can help. I can like, go around and ask if people have jobs for her. There's gotta be places." He kissed my neck, but it was too fast, and it tickled me. "And if you did have to move back, you'd still be down here, right?"

"James, please," I said. I couldn't think what I wanted to say. *Shut up? Be quiet?* I wanted him to be quiet, to pause for a second and hold me and think about what I was feeling. He was skipping ahead, like it didn't matter if I had to go back to Tacoma and only see him whenever I could get someone to drive me. He had to just sit with me. He had to hold me. That's what boyfriends were for. "I don't know. I just found out all this. I don't know what's going to happen."

"Oh," he said. He held me tighter. "Yeah. Right. I'm sorry." His arms around me were good. His face against my cheek was good. "It's okay, Orsino. We're going to be okay. I'm sorry everything is . . ." he stopped. He didn't seem to know what to say.

I felt the first tear well in my eye before I could stop myself. I knew it *wasn't* going to be okay, or not with us. I felt embarrassed and rotten. I clutched James' back and sobbed. Overhead, the sky was beginning to get darker, even though it was only four in the afternoon. I looked up and saw the warship lowering its guns, and it was tearing through the barrier between the future and the present. There was a shade of red over the trees. The soccer practice was ending, across the field. I pulled back and looked at James. His clear brown eyes looked back at me. I suddenly saw that his cheerful mood was kind of fake. It had cracked, and now he looked deeply miserable. Part of it was this news. Part of it was something else.

"I'm sorry," he said. "I don't know how to talk." He paused. "But like, if you're moving back with your mom, you'll still be here for the show, right? You can stay with me this weekend. Robin too, probably."

"I don't think I'm doing the show anymore," I said. "It would be too weird."

"But you have to," James said. "We *need* you."

I felt myself scowl. "Thanks, James, but like, you don't. I don't do anything."

"We need *your* visions," James said.

I felt so mad. It was the worst thing he could have said. I wanted to be wanted for anything else. What did he understand about anything?

"I don't want to do them for a show," I said. "I've been

telling Jukebox that. They won't do anything. They won't make any sense. I can't use them."

"But you could do what the aliens are asking you to do. You could share them."

"I don't know what that means. The worms didn't have any clear plan. Jukebox is the one who seems to know anything about what the visions are for. And you've got Jukebox. They like you. They give you fluttery feelings. I'm just some redneck weirdo who you like because I'm trans too and I make you see stuff when you kiss me."

"That's not true," James stuttered. "You're . . . you. You're amazing. You . . . have dreams. Your skull art is amazing. And . . . your body feels so good against mine. The way you kiss me feels so much better than I knew kisses could feel, and you're so beautiful. You don't *know* how gorgeous you are." He hiccupped.

"I mean, thanks. But that's three extremely vague things." I stopped, and thought about what he'd said, before. Monique. Jukebox. The way he'd said I was an alien, the one time. The way he'd been creeped out by my art. And the way he was looking at me now, in total confusion. I wouldn't really have cared, as long as I knew he was here for me. But he wasn't. He wanted my problems to disappear, so I could focus on him. Suddenly, there was an obvious, cracked-glass hole. There's a kind of low you don't know exists until you feel it. "I don't think we really *get* each other," I said, and as I said it, I knew it was true.

James was quiet for a long moment. "That's not true," he said.

"I don't get you," I said. "My problems aren't like yours."

I *wish* I got you."

I sighed, my arms still around him.

I wanted to understand James.

I held him as tight as I could.

As I slid into James's head, then, dragging the ocean
with me, I resisted slipping into him and becoming him
inside the vision. The warship and the small pink ship
were both full of the shiny, wet bodies of the worms and
their blue shining many-scaled eyes, but I ignored them. I
was looking at his mind, trying to hold our selves separate
enough to look and be conscious of looking. I had never
tried this before. It felt like slipping over the edge of a
rocky cliff on a steep trail, having to run faster and faster to
avoid falling. James was panicked, still, and I could feel his
panic around me. I knew what he was afraid of, now, but
his feelings didn't all make sense to me. Parts of him were
too small to see, and parts curved away from me as my
attention turned toward them. I couldn't see everything,
just like you can't really see *everything* in Olympia from the
roof of Jukebox's house on the hill. I got waves of imprecise
images that I could try to catch and experience. Memories
bubbled like soapsuds around me as I fell into him; I could
see Opal's face, red and yelling, a year ago, with blue hair.
I could see the blood on the tiles of James's mom's bathroom, feel the dark feeling James had felt waking up every
day. I could see James's body like it was my body, curled in
bed under a purple blanket. All this was shot through with
lines of current feeling like thin ropes of fire, or the metal
coil of a red-hot burner on a stove. I could feel his fear
about Jukebox, and his fear of Opal's anger, and his fear

that Monique wasn't talking to him either. I could feel his terror of being alone.

The warship tore through. Above us, I could hear it. It was as big as a comet, as big as a small moon. I felt certain that if I looked up I would see it.

I could feel that it felt good to him when I held him. But I also felt that he thought of me as someone who had come to heal him. At least right now, he wasn't thinking about what I needed, or what things had hurt me that I wouldn't be over for years.

He thought of me as being cold, calming down something that was too hot. A salve. I knew it was different than that. I knew I was way more fire than water.

The warship let out a blast of fire that changed the color of the sky above us. I looked up and saw that it was there, next to the moon, a small spiny thing like an anemone. I saw someone else look up and scream. It wasn't just us. It was there, shooting—not at Earth, but at the worms that had been speaking to me. I could not see the small pink ship. I was still holding James.

I let the ocean overtake both of us, icy as the underside of a glacier.

The blank, wide, saltwater world was a well of secret small sounds that you didn't hear until you had been there a minute. There was a hot fissure of lava opening far beneath us, turning to rock, venting through cold water. There were crashing waves and small bacteria and protozoa in the water, and they danced this way and that. It was a time before anything big existed except the rocky land rising out of the sea. But life was bubbling forth, growing and moving ever faster. It was going to get more complicated. It was going to get harder. We were there just at the start of the acceleration, when the sound was just at the edge of our perception. James and I were one being, in the ocean, part of the ocean, sinking. The sky was far away but we could see the light through the water.

James and I were clutching each other on the asphalt of the playground, him wearing the sparkling mirror-coat; the memory of the deep wide sea was spreading around us. The oil-bubble of consciousness in the ancient ocean grew a little beyond me and James; we were floating in the thing that had come before us.

Then I saw it again. An older, gray-haired James, shirtless, pushing my body down on the edge of a future-beach. The sun was rising, and his skin glowed, wrinkled and marked with freckles and scars. I smelled salt.

But this vision was complicated; it didn't exist yet. As I reached for it, the oil-bubbles of consciousness started to break apart. I realized that the futures weren't real yet. None of them were real yet. And they could disappear.

The mirrors spun small microcosms like light all around us and then let us go.

I knew I had to go.

The clouds above us hid the moon, but I knew where it was. The sky was purple. The warship was no longer there. Neither was the pink ship. But I had pulled the aliens through to another time—I thought.

I turned and started walking back toward Jukebox's house. Under our feet, the grass was different—stiff and long, with sharp edges. Beach grass. Marsh grass. The children's playground, and the road beyond, was covered in wet sand and dry dunes. It smelled like seabed. A bird called.

"Wait," James said. "Wait, Orsino. That was amazing. There's something I can't—I don't know how to say it."

"I know," I said, over my shoulder. "That's the problem."

"I need you," James said. "*We* need you."

"I don't want to do the show," I said. "You'll be fine." The shadows had gotten longer. I didn't know exactly where I was going.

"Orsino!" James called after me, but he didn't follow me.

Dogman's, I thought.

I texted Duke as I walked. I wondered if he'd understand what I was feeling, or what I was supposed to do next.

Chapter 16

MONIQUE

Barb texted me, *do you know where Opal is? Worried about them. Are they with you?*

I was on my couch with Mom. She had been quizzing me on Japanese adjectives so I could get my grade in Japanese up to a B+ by the end of the semester and keep my 3.85. In the background, *Diners, Drive-Ins and Dives* was playing on the TV on mute. My mom likes Guy Fieri. She had made us hot chocolate, and mine was still sitting on its coaster. I was picking at crumbs between the cushions with one hand as I watched her hands shuffle the flashcards. She was wearing her big Christmas sweater with ducks in Santa hats on it; she'd put it on after finishing hanging little wreaths and wall-hangings and ornaments all over the front door and along our hallway, and now I knew she'd be wearing Christmas stuff until January, after we got back from visiting my grandma for Parrandas.

I ignored the text.

"What's this one?" Mom asked, holding up a flashcard

with katakana that I swore I'd looked at an hour before. I could read it, but I tried to remember what it meant.

My phone buzzed again.

James isn't texting back. Really sorry to bother you.

I glanced down at my phone screen enough to see Barb's message, and went to unlock my phone, but my mom cleared her throat.

"Kosekose," I snapped, looking up at the katakana.

"And what does it mean?"

"Crying or fussy or vexatious," I said.

"Vexatious," Mom said. "Wow. Okay, next one."

I steeled myself.

"Mom, I'm sorry, but I just looked down and saw this. Barb doesn't know where Opal is," I said. "She's texting me. I'm sorry, can I call Opal really quick? The show's tomorrow, and I'm worried about them."

My mom looked discomfited. "Weird. Where do you think Opal is?"

"I'm not sure," I said, but I had two guesses. "I'm going to call them."

"Okay," Mom said. "Fifteen minutes. Let me know what's happening."

I ducked into my room, leaving my mom with the TV and her little angel statues. I felt bad. The phone rang four times before Opal picked up.

"Hey, what's up," they said. I could hear noise in the background. It sounded like they were with a few other people. I could hear plates, and music.

"Barb's texting me wondering where you are," I said.

"Oh, shit," Opal said. "She noticed."

"Of course she noticed," I said. "She lives with you. She cares about you. Are you at James's?"

Opal laughed. "Hell no," they said. "I couldn't even if I wanted to be. He ditched school early today. I'm at Dogman's. He picked me up from the coffee shop after I took the city bus downtown after school. Barb called me three times already and I didn't pick up. You'd think she'd get the hint." Opal sighed. "I guess she's done yelling at Duke."

"Should I tell Barb where you are?" I asked. "Or just tell her you're safe?"

"You don't have to do anything," Opal said. "Monique, I gotta tell you this. I was going to text you. Guess who's also here at Dogman's. *Both* fucked up and emotional."

"Who?" I started composing a text to Barb as I listened. *Opal's safe*, I wrote.

"*Orsino and Robin*. It's like, drama day over here. And they're waiting for *Duke* to pick them up. Dogman's making popcorn and I can tell he's like, how did all these people get in my house. But I'm already settled in so he can't make me leave."

I felt my heart hiccup.

"Why are they there?" I sat down on the floor, my back against my bedroom door.

"Jukebox dumped Robin, or vice versa, I can't tell, and Orsino broke up with James. Like, just now, at the same time. The *night* before the show. I can't handle it. I cannot imagine what everything's gonna be like tomorrow. And I'm *really* glad I'm not talking to James right now, because I can *not* deal with him."

"Wait, what?" I asked. "Orsino broke up with James?

Why?" I was trying very hard not to feel a rush of excitement. Bad Monique. Breakups are *bad*.

"Because James is in love with Jukebox or something," Opal said. "Which is also why I'm pissed at him. But that's not why Robin and Jukebox broke up."

"James is in love with *Jukebox*?" That didn't make any sense. Unless it did. James had been looking at Jukebox a lot, with big melty eyes. I hadn't understood. I thought about Jukebox touching James's stomach and felt a raw, nasty jealousy prickle up my neck. And then another, weirder thought. What if something else had happened between them? Would Jukebox *do* that? They were like twenty-eight. They wouldn't do that, right? "What are you talking about?"

"He told me yesterday he had a crush on them, and I guess he told Orsino now too. Which like, okay, he has a thing for inaccessible older gays, whatever, me too, but Jukebox is being a *dick*."

"Is James *with* Jukebox?"

"I don't know. I don't *think* so, not like that," Opal said. "Do you think they would do that?"

"I don't know," I said.

"Jukebox did apparently pick James up from school today. Maybe? I don't think anything's happened. Though you're right, it's creepy. I just can't believe James watched them yell at everyone and thought that was okay."

This was a lot. Why was everything always so much?

"I mean," I said, "Jukebox was being nicer to James than to us. I can see how that would make James feel good, because he's not in theater or band or anything. He's getting recognized. I felt really good when Jukebox was telling us we were good last month for the first time. And James *likes* performing. I think this is like, a big moment for him." I thought about James. I should text him, I thought.

"Oh, fuck off, you're just in love with him," Opal said. "He's not being a great friend right now to anyone, especially you."

"Did you guys fight?" I asked.

"I don't know. All this shit's going down with Barb where I'm sure she's annoyed with me for being there, and I depend on her to live, and Duke might move, and James *knows* I don't have money for college apps and so have everything riding on financial aid and complains about how his dad is making him go to college while he bombs all his classes on purpose, and it just feels like he doesn't care. And it makes me think all the times he pretended to understand were just him playing along." Their voice cracked.

I wasn't sure what to say to that. I still felt weird hearing Opal get scared like this. I couldn't figure out how much of their anger made sense to me. I felt irritated with James, too. And hurt.

"Are you okay right now?" I asked. "I'm thinking about it, and I haven't been around for you much either the last few weeks. I've been all wrapped up in show stuff too."

"I'm *fine*," they said. "You're good, Monique. I'm mad at James."

"Sure," I said, "But still. I haven't been here. I've only talked to you about band stuff."

"You're the reason I'm *in* this band. And Monique Fatigue

and the Dusties is the best. Before you ditched Devon, I was just a kid in my basement playing drums. You're putting the work in at practice, and you make me a better musician, and even though you don't have anything to do with Compton, you're helping save it. You're a cool rock star. But James isn't doing any work except being cutesy and funny and anxious about our school's bathrooms or whatever, and he's acting like his shit's the biggest in the world. He's been acting like a dick to you too."

"He's not being a dick to me," I said. "He just isn't into me. I'm sad about it, but it's not like that's evil." I had been talking myself through this very methodically.

"Here's the thing. This is what pisses me off," Opal said. "He has wanted to date you since we were *fourteen*. He wouldn't shut up about it. But then when he gets the chance, he acts like a fuckboy and messes with you and then ditches you and then starts messing with Orsino the same way."

"Uh," I said.

"Like, I told him not to try anything with you, to leave it alone unless you showed him you liked him back. But I thought you didn't like him like that. But then you did show him you liked him, and he's already on to the next boy, and the next . . . Like, what?"

"What?"

"Shit, I shouldn't have said that," Opal said. "God. But like, look. You don't *want* to date James. He's just like, following his gay dick or whatever right now."

My mom knocked on the door.

"Is Opal okay?" she asked. "Are you okay, Ian? You need anything?"

"Hey, I gotta go," I said, trying to talk quietly so my mom couldn't hear. "I'm really sorry. Keep texting if you want. I'm glad you're okay. This is a lot, but we'll get through the show tomorrow and figure it out then."

In the morning, my mouth was dry.

Gemma had told us to show up at two, even though the show was at seven. My mom dropped me off, and even she thought it was ridiculous.

"Even band kids don't do this early," she said. "See you after work, baby. I'm excited to see the show, and all your hard work. Even if it's the weird music. Maybe we can go for ice cream after. If you're not all just collapsing with exhaustion."

I laughed. She didn't know I'd collapsed with exhaustion about three months ago and had been running on fumes since.

There were posters all over the lobby that someone's cartoonist friend had drawn.

THE GOTHPEL OF WORM: A COMPTON HOUSE ROCK EXTRAVAGANZAAA! they read. FUNDRAISER FOR LGBT YOUTH. FEATURING—and there was the list of bands, with OVID at the top. There was a GoFundMe link underneath, and then drawings of aliens and worms. Mickey was the only one in the lobby with me as I stood and looked at the posters. She was wrestling a vacuum cleaner.

"You need an Ativan, girl?" she said, turning to me as I sat down for a second near the little gate that led to the concession stand. I realized my arms were crossed in front of my face and I looked psycho.

"No," I said, through my arms.

I stood up and went backstage, squaring my chest.

Obviously, there was a problem with the mics. Acorn, who was in charge of lights for reasons nobody had explained, was already upset because someone who volunteered at the theater had moved all of hir gels into a locked room, and it was unclear when the person with the key was coming by, so we couldn't run lights. And the volunteers had taken down the neutral signs in front of both the bathrooms. Sophie and Francine drew new ones, which said WORMS and WORMENS, but then they got into an argument about whether that still enforced gender binary.

Sophie stormed over to me, and Francine went to get stickers out of her bag to put up everywhere.

Opal and Dogman arrived with stale bagels. Orsino wasn't there.

"My name's not on the poster," Opal said quietly, wheeling up to me and Sophie in the backstage hallway, bagels piled on their lap. "I guess that means I can't be held accountable for anything, huh. Even though I wrote it. Maybe that's good." Their face was the kind of sarcastic where I knew they were exactly as pissed as they'd been at rehearsal.

I wanted to fix stuff for them.

"We can put your name on the posters," I said. I ran and got a Sharpie from my bag. Opal watched.

"No, don't do that," they said.

But I ran through the doors to the lobby and wrote their name—WRITTEN BY OPAL—under the title anyway.

I came back and showed them a picture. I could tell it made them happy; their sarcastic smirk got slightly less sarcastic. I felt brave. One tiny act of graffiti.

"Have you talked to Barb?" I asked. Last night, Barb had texted me effusive thanks for confirming Opal was okay.

"Yeah," Opal said. They looked down at their shoes. "She said she was worried about me."

"She cares about you," I said again. "Even if she's a mess."

"What, so I owe her something?" Opal said, challenging me.

I didn't like where this was going. "No," I said. "I know it's rough to have to trust her good faith, and all that."

"What do we think it's gonna be like when Jukebox and James get here?" Opal asked, changing the subject.

"Oh," Sophie said, "probably bad. Hey, Monique."

"What?"

"What pronouns are you using these days? I've been meaning to ask."

"Oh. Uh. She. Is. Fine." I managed to choke the words out. They felt like tacks.

"Cool. I'll tell James before I beat him up on your behalf, yeah?"

"Monique is unfortunately anti-violence," Opal said.

I was looking forward to seeing James, even if everything was going to shit, though I didn't want to tell Sophie or Opal that.

As more people arrived, the noise of everyone talking and rehearsing got louder. We had amps plugged in onstage and backstage; since Jukebox wasn't here yet, nobody was telling us what to do, and so we were practicing both places.

As I sat with Sophie in the backstage hallway and tuned my bass, the magic of the show space started to get to me a little. The black hallways were covered with posters of bands that had played here and shows that had come through. The props piled in the hallway were covered in silver spray paint and green splotches of wax and mirror shards and orange stripes of cellophane, and the kids who had shown up on time were getting them ready, arguing over where to put them. Some of the pieces were hanging from the ceiling. They didn't form a coherent picture, but they made a kaleidoscoping weird glittery overwhelming crisis of color when you looked at them—that was better than anything our high school had ever done for a play. I had on my fishnets, and Opal and Sophie were dressed all in black and were going to do makeup with fishnets over their faces, to create scales. The worm costumes were stacked in a corner, and the kid named Danny kept plugging in and unplugging them to make the Christmas lights inside them light up and flash. Francine had dressed one of the big set pieces with all these neon-green star stickers she got at the dollar store, and was now distributing a roll of stickers she'd stolen from the supermarket that said RIPE. She stuck one on my forehead as she walked by, doing her butch-swagger thing in her big tennis shoes, not smiling, putting RIPE stickers on the wall every few feet. I peeled the sticker off and laughed, and she gave me the smallest little smile.

Sophie smiled too. She'd brought her clippers. "Who

wants to get buzzed?" she hollered down the hallway. Gemma stuck her head through the door nervously, then relaxed when she saw the clippers.

Venus got half her head shaved while the rest of us were changing into costumes. Purple sequins, giant Halloween masks, big cardboard pieces that got scooted from one side to the other, fitting over different people's heads.

Sophie and Opal played through our two songs three times each. We sounded good; Goober had been upstairs with Acorn, and she tore down the stairs towards us, whooping.

"Little rock!" she yelled. "Dynamite!"

Opal's face lit up for the first time.

Acorn found hir gels, and the light from the front of the stage was suddenly flooding back towards all of us, pink, then yellow, then the vivid, vivid, red.

Jukebox and James walked in at the same time. James waved at me, looking a little nervous, and then ducked into the bathroom. Jukebox was wearing their blue denim vest over their orange tank top, and big black boots with silver studs running down the sides. They looked pissed.

"Where the hell is Orsino?" Jukebox said to me and Opal. "I need to talk to that kid."

"He's not here," Opal said, loudly enough that Emu Union, talking on the other side of the curtain, shut up for a second. "He quit the show. You made him feel weird."

Jukebox frowned. "He knows I was counting on him," they said. "I'm not gonna lie, I'm really disappointed in him." They squinted at me. "Monique," they said. "Do you have his number? We should call him."

"Uh," I said.

"I heard you treated Robin like shit," Sophie said, coming up behind Jukebox and leaning on their shoulder with her sharp elbow. "Orsino's really close to his sister. I think you need to give it a minute, bro."

Something seemed to snap. They brushed her arm off their shoulder. "Don't *bro* me, kid. You don't know shit about me and Robin."

"Sophie," I said in a warning voice that came out as more of a whine. "We can do this after the show, okay? But we gotta get along right now."

"No, we fucking don't," Opal said, turning to frown at me with an icy stare.

Jukebox stood over Opal and me and put their hands on their hips. "Who exactly did you *beg* to help you get all these bands together?" they demanded. "Who went out of my way to help you? And you know this whole show is based on my visions."

"No it isn't," Opal said. "I wrote it."

"I saw you note that on the signs out front," Jukebox sneered. "Sure, you did the script. But you only wrote it because you wanted me to be involved."

Opal had been nervous and upset and scared a lot lately; I knew that was all still there. But as Jukebox's eyes turned hard, theirs did too. I saw them turn to stone.

"I know about you and James," Opal said.

"What?" Jukebox was completely disarmed. Their taut neck muscles suddenly slackened. "What about me and James?"

I tried desperately to make eye contact with Opal, but they didn't look at me.

"I saw you touch his stomach in rehearsal, and I know you picked him up from school, and he won't shut up about his crush on you. You took advantage of Robin because she's a small-town baby dyke and doesn't know any better. She's like, years younger than you, right? Now you're shooting for jailbait." Opal's eyes flashed. "That's low shit, man."

Jukebox looked at us, frozen, and—for the first time since I had met them—completely small and terrified and confused. Their arms fell to their sides. Not in an angry way—they looked like someone had just unexpectedly kicked them in the stomach. "That's not," they said, and they shut their mouth again and swallowed. I was scared by how scared they looked. They looked over their shoulder towards the edge of the stage, where Gemma was talking to two punks from Emu Union who were smoking indoors between runs of their set. "No," they said. "No, that's not it. I really promise that that's not it. That's *not* what's happening."

"Of course not," Sophie said, glaring at Jukebox. "Which is why you won't touch him or lay a finger on him for the rest of the show or ever again, right?"

I knew Sophie was doing this because she hated Jukebox, not because she wanted to protect James. I nervously looked toward the door of the bathroom where James must be getting into costume.

Jukebox stared at Opal, and then at Sophie, their expression turning from rage to fear, back and forth, like a clock's hand that's stuck between two seconds.

"Do you believe in the visions?" they demanded, turning to me. "Do you understand what I'm trying to do with them?"

"Don't drag her into it," Sophie said.

Jukebox looked at me, almost pleading. "You felt it, at your first show, didn't you? Where you ruled so hard. I saw you and I felt transformed. Your music was good, right, but normally it would have been just good music. It was more than that, because Orsino was there, having his visions of the ship coming down, the messages from above, and it was also because of James. Didn't you feel the rush of the possible futures? James felt my vision, he saw this future that I saw after the ship took me. It was real."

I looked at them. I could see the whites of their eyes, and I suddenly realized that they didn't think they were trying to pull one over us. This was what they believed in. I thought about the first show at Goat Mansion, the feeling I'd had on stage, like the world was pink and glowing and I was going to lift up the roof myself, like the ghost of every queer person who had ever been in that room or any other was singing with me.

"Uh," I said.

"No, she doesn't know what you're talking about, because it's *insane*," Opal said. "You're saying you have some magical special bond with James about the aliens that speak to you?"

"You believe me, right?" Jukebox asked me. "You don't have to believe all of it. Just that—the thing I'm doing with James isn't about—it's about this future that he can see, and I can see it too, and we need to make this show work, because we need to share that vision."

I almost knew what they were saying, but there was something in it that I couldn't grasp. I hadn't seen the visions they had seen. Why hadn't I?

Unless those *were* the flashes, what I had seen at their shows. Was that what they meant? But those had been so short, and uncertain.

I knew we weren't the only people in the hall, and I glanced over to the corner, where Venus, fiddling with her phone, was obviously listening in, and Danny was staring openly.

"Can we fucking cut the energy crap and the vision crap?" Sophie asked. "Jukebox, you signed on to do this project to fundraise for a queer youth group. You're screaming at people, you're touching stomachs, whatever. You need to cut the shit. Whatever visions or energy you're interested in is not *happening* here, because you have *ruined the vibe.*"

"You're the one who's ruined the *vibe*," Jukebox screeched, their voice raising again. "Coming out here accusing me of child sexual abuse or some shit, after begging me to be part of your fucking kids' show! Whatever, I'm over this!"

Gemma looked over at us, and started to approach. She looked desperately harried. At the same moment, James opened the bathroom door.

"What is going on over here?" Gemma demanded.

Opal and Jukebox started to talk at once, and Sophie yelled something over both of them. James froze as he closed the bathroom door. He was wearing his cow pants. He made eye contact with me over their heads. I looked away, down at the floor.

"Jukebox," Gemma said, "please come with me. We're supposed to start in like, an hour. We can't do this."

"Who's we? *You* haven't done *shit!*"

"What's going on?" James asked, walking over.

"James, what the fuck have you been saying about me?" Jukebox said, turning to James.

"Nothing," James said. "What?"

"Opal's saying shit about you and me," Jukebox said. "That I'm grooming you or some shit, or we're doing something. Makes me feel like there's confusion."

"Oh," James said, turning red. He looked at Opal. "Opal, you know I didn't . . . Nothing's going on. I was just talking about how I felt. Uh . . ." he floundered. I felt my guts drop, watching him.

Opal sighed. "I *hope* nothing's going on. James, you're allowed to crush on people. But it's their responsibility not to take advantage of you. I'm just calling it like I see it."

"They're *not* taking advantage of me," James said.

Jukebox looked at James. "Yeah," they said, "because I haven't done shit to you. Whether you have a crush on me or not, nothing's happening. You got that?"

James looked startled. Jukebox went on.

"There's *nothing* going on. Don't go around telling people we're involved or whatever. That's not okay. You're just a kid. I thought I could show you something that means something to me, teach you something about the world, cuz you don't know shit yet. That's it."

Venus, Danny, and a couple members of Emu Union who had poked their heads around the corner were all staring at us now. I could see that in the corner of my vision. My gaze was fixed on James's face, and the horrible expressions happening there.

"I didn't say . . . I didn't . . . what?" His forehead crumpled, and his cheeks were turning red. His mouth twisted.

Gemma's jaw had dropped gradually as Jukebox spoke. Now, with a rigid grip, she reached out and seized Jukebox's arm.

"We need to step out," she said firmly. She turned to Opal. "I hope *you're* happy," she said.

"This is such bullshit," Jukebox hissed. They turned to look at me, and their expression changed a little as they met my eyes. Briefly, their eyes took on another gleam, like they'd found an ally. "Monique, this is bullshit, right?"

I wasn't sure what expression I was making. I was still feeling overwhelmed, thinking about how I knew that when they talked about visions, they were telling the truth. And I had been looking at James, and seeing the hurt and fear and betrayal in his face.

"I—I think we'd all better chill out a second," I said. "I don't know."

"Exactly," Jukebox said, looking at Opal and Sophie. "You kids need to chill. I'm out of here."

They turned and stormed out, Gemma trailing them.

I felt the same pressure in my spine that I had felt at both the other shows I'd played this year. I knew it wasn't just on me to make it work; I knew we *could* do it alone. It was us who had pulled through before, with less rehearsal time and less lighting and worse sound. This was a disaster. But I needed everyone to move now.

I had a superpower. I could use it. I could pull myself together for as long as it took to do this show.

James was actively crying.

I couldn't let that distract me. Not yet.

"Guys," I said. "Gemma's right. It's like, five thirty-eight. The show is in an hour and twenty minutes. And I think we need to count Jukebox out. Which means someone else is gonna need to sing their parts. And we need to get people in costumes."

I said this loudly, and most people paid attention. It was different from the shows in punk houses; most people here were kids, or were punks out of their element. They were ready for someone to tell them what was happening.

"Wait, no Jukebox?" Sadi from Dirt Mama called, from near the door to the lobby. "What's going on?"

I gave a helpless shrug. "We just need to have backup," I said. "They seemed like they were leaving. Someone who knows Stacey, can you tell her?"

There was a worried murmur among Dirt Mama and Emu Union.

I heard a distant door slam, and wondered if that was Jukebox exiting the front lobby.

"*I'll* do Jukebox's parts," Venus said dramatically. She rose to her feet from where Francine had been giving her an undercut. Long strands of her blond hair fell to the floor around her pink boots. "I can scream as good as anyone."

This announcement was met with silence, but I knew a savior when I saw one.

"Cool," I said. "Let's have you run through on a speed run with everyone." I turned to Francine. "Hey. Francine. Leave the clippers. Can you go get the people who are smoking and the kids who are up in the lights area to go get into their costumes?"

Stacey clattered in in her white coat at six; Venus came up with her, followed by Danny and Francine, and told her about the change. She grimaced, but then fist-bumped Venus.

"Long time coming," she said. "They've been real weird lately. Not any of your fault, whatever they yelled at you. We'll get this show on the road somehow."

James was covering his eyes with one hand and gathering cables in the other, as we moved the music equipment. I got too close, running by to try to clear the way for the six-foot whale float that the Species Parade people were dropping off, and he turned to speak to me.

"We didn't even *kiss*," he said. "Me and Jukebox. Please believe me."

"James, please hold that thought," I said.

We could not get into it right now. Not right now. The whale float was coming, and someone had left a pizza box in the way, and a forty-year-old guy with white dreads was asking Duke to make sure that none of us would hit it or climb on it, because it could break if we did that. After we got it into the wings, I gritted my teeth and charged up to where Acorn was working on lights to check in. As I went, I put on the silver coat that I'd pulled from the costume bin of donated clothes from older queer people.

Acorn was putting the gels in order; someone had opened the cabinet. Xie looked up.

"Well, you look amazing," xie said. "This is amazing, Monique. You're growing up and into it. I heard your EP, too. You all rule. I want you to play a house show at mine soon."

"Thanks," I said. "I'll ask my mom. Look, do you need anything before the show starts?"

"No," xie said. "Well, yes. I need water, probably. But I have all the light stuff. You're really taking charge, huh?"

"I gotta," I said, and, even though the breath wasn't totally back in my lungs, I scrambled down the ladder again, my shoes sticking to the metal. At the bottom, I found Goober. Her bright blond hair was pulled up into a messy bun, and she was wearing dark lipstick; I was struck, as always, by how pretty she was. I knew why Opal liked her. I liked her too.

"Hey Goober. I'm running all over for a minute. Can you get water for Acorn?" I asked. "If you have a second?"

"Sure, Monique," she said. "Hey, have you seen Opal? I wanted to say something to them. I chickened out earlier." I saw she was holding a folded piece of pink cardstock with writing on it in one hand.

I pointed behind me in the general direction of backstage, where Opal had been. Then I ran to carry the costume crate to the kids who were just arriving through the back door. There were five of them; they were all about fifteen and from the GSA in Tumwater. They looked nerdy and small and excited; they were wearing the things they thought were cool, to have on under the lab coats. One kid had on a Weird Al Yankovic shirt. Another was sticking fake flowers into the back of her collar. I looked up from them and made eye contact with Orsino, who was standing in the doorway.

He stepped inside awkwardly, hands in pockets. He looked down at the floor, and then back up at me.

"Hey," he said. "Monique."

I bit my lip, trying to keep myself from glancing around for James. I felt like screaming. I found myself suddenly picturing a tearful reconciliation between them. If it was destined to happen, I couldn't stop it. "Hey," I said. "I thought you'd dropped out."

He studied me, not blinking, for a minute. I felt a little like a laser was trained on me. "I did," he said. "But I was thinking. And I thought I needed to do something. I realized, I mean. Can I talk to you for a second?"

I sighed and stepped away from the GSA kids, who were grabbing handfuls of beaded bracelets to put on underneath their lab coats, to spill out at the audience at the end of the show. I could hear Duke's voice over the intercom:

"House doors are opening in fifteen. Get the pizzas off the stage. Raffle sellers, please come get a basket."

"Sure," I said. "Do you need me to find James?"

"No. I just need to—just talk a second. Back out here?" Orsino gestured with his thumb to the exit.

I looked at my phone for the time. We absolutely had to be running stuff with Venus in five minutes.

"Three minutes," I said. "It's busy here."

Outside, the alley was cold, and colder still in my crop top and thin papery silver jacket. I crossed my arms across my chest, and stared at him. He didn't look angry. He looked upset, and maybe sleep-deprived. But also certain about something. He had something to say. To me? Why?

"So," Orsino said. "I broke up with James. Maybe you know that. I hung out with Opal last night."

"I know," I said. "James is upset." I wanted to say something else—but I realized I didn't really know anything about Orsino, other than the fact James had wanted to be with him instead of me. I didn't even *really* know what they'd broken up over.

Orsino nodded. "He upset me, too. I don't know. I just need someone who has time for me, who wants to learn about me for real." He looked up at the blue-purple sky; it was getting dark, even though it wasn't five yet. "I talked to Duke earlier, at the coffee shop. I need friends. If James wants to be my friend, that's cool. But he and Jukebox were both looking at me like I was something else. Like, this magic thing. And it just made me lonely . . ." He trailed off.

"I'm sorry. What do you need from me?" I asked.

"You're the star of the show," Orsino said. He spoke calmly, though he looked a little worn down and exhausted. "Not Jukebox. You made the music, and made this happen, really. You and Opal. I don't think I could do this onstage. But Opal was worried about the show, and . . . I don't know if it's really important, but I feel like I should try. I think I finally figured out how to do the psychic blast thing, that Jukebox wanted. Last night with James was weird, but I figured something out. About how to change the timeline. I need you to give me your hand for a second."

"My *hand*?" What was going on?

"After that I'll go," Orsino said. "I mean, just like, I'll take off from backstage. I won't start anything with James. That's not why I'm here."

My mom would have said, at the point when someone starts talking about a psychic blast, that's when you get out of there.

I hesitated, but there was nothing else to do. I held my

hand out. Orsino nodded, then reached out and took it in his. His hand was bigger than mine, his palms calloused and warm. The Xs I drew on my hands before every show stood black and boxy against his pink skin. I noticed that his nails were short, and had black underneath on the forefinger. He had little white hairs up the back of his hand.

He closed his eyes and concentrated, and squeezed my hand in his, hard.

I waited, feeling his pulse. Inside the theater, something clattered like a drum kit had fallen. I looked around at the door. If someone had knocked over Opal's drums—

After a second, he opened his eyes. "Did you, uh, feel anything?" he asked.

"No," I said. "Am I supposed to?"

He frowned tightly, and closed his eyes again. "Mmm-hmm. Hold on. Let me try again." The edges of his mouth pulled down. I felt the bones of his knuckles against mine. If anyone saw us, they'd think we were having a tender moment. "I wonder if I can."

I felt myself smiling, despite everything being absolutely crazy. I lifted my other hand and held his hand between my two. "I have no idea what you're doing," I said. "But I *want* to understand. James cares about you. I know he does. And I know there's something there, that I don't get. I *can't* get. But I want to."

He opened his eyes and looked at me.

"No," he said. "You get it."

He smiled, with his tongue protruding just a little bit through slightly crooked teeth. I found myself staring into his gray irises.

I thought: I would like this boy to kiss me.

Then he leaned forward and kissed me, just as the shock hit me.

It felt like when you're cooking and the oil leaps up and hits you.

A door dilated.

I wasn't sure exactly what I was seeing at first, but it felt like fire. I felt the world turn, and a sideways jerk, like gravity had shifted for a second. A glowing beam hit me in my stomach, shot through me; with it came the images of everything that had ever happened, to me or to anyone else. Threaded through them were feelings of long, legless bodies twisting down circular pathways inside of a ship, gazing down through screens and through other instruments. They knew Orsino, had known him. I watched him leap through tall yellow grass when he was round-faced and had long white-blond hair and a fixed, immovable scowl; I felt his happiness at the attention of his dog, and I knew her name.

Agatha.

I felt the dreams that had come after, dreams of different futures and pasts. The purple worms with many eyes had been trying to speak to Orsino, show him the visions. They were running from a large black spiny ship. Split-up pictures like distorted images on holographic cards. *Already everywhere.* Mass graves of bodies, small cement cells with hard yellow light.

But there were thousands of doors. Through the doors, there were worlds where humans had never existed and there were still dinosaurs everywhere, and worlds where humans stopped existing and the world spun on without them, nuclear waste rolling under new growths of trees. They looked all different ways. The fish leapt in the river.

One long, flexible form bent around other lilac, velvet-smooth, furrowed alien bodies. They called like they were billions of miles away. They were ghostly, and they were also warm against my skin.

We don't know that it is possible to invite in another future.

But the ocean expanded, and the roads turned to gardens, and the salmon returned.

A long purple-glimmering tail flashed quickly across a panel of unintelligible controls, and a joy shot through me so bright and sharp it made my cheeks hurt, my belly ache.

I had a picture of a flower bursting open, salmon running upstream, leaves falling. The ground trembling, the stars spinning—

I stepped back and dropped Orsino's hand.

I felt too dizzy to panic, or to fall down. The wall of the theater felt cold and the rough cement dug into my skin through my thin jacket.

Orsino watched me. He looked unsure of whether to touch me. His big, wide face was flushed red, and he had a scowl on, which I realized was just the way he looked when he was paying attention. I was breathing hard. I thought about Jukebox, and their obsession with the visions. I knew why, now. My legs shook. I felt the beat of my heart. Down the alleyway, I heard someone call to their friend across the street, and the noise of a car.

"Sorry," Orsino said. He looked scared, but also still, and his jaw was set, waiting for me to respond.

The world had shifted. I knew something I hadn't known. What next?

I breathed in through my nose, the cold air hard in my lungs. "That was . . . Oof. God," I said.

"I don't like Jukebox anymore. But I think they were right about needing to tell people. They think that the music at the show can change something. I don't know if it can, and I knew it would sound crazy. I know that. I *have* known that. But I thought you could try to pass some of this on tonight. Just try."

I was dizzy. I was having so much trouble believing in anything I had felt and understood and known about him a second ago, while he was touching me, now that it was over. It was like I had been pressed against him with his blood flowing into my heart, and now we were on opposite sides of a room again, separated by glass. How could I have been inside him? But I knew I had just felt it. I remembered the blistering feeling I had been breathing and swimming in only a moment before—he had been so lonely for so long. I knew what that loneliness was like. And I knew what finding someone else—finding James—felt like, after everything had been awful for so long.

I loved him because he knew.

"It's so unfair," I said, before I thought about it. "It's too *big*. People will think you're crazy. It's too much, too elaborate."

"It's pretty gay," Orsino said, in a voice that sounded so flat and so serious that it took me a second to realize he was joking.

I smiled when I realized, and he smiled shyly back.

"The reason you did this is so I could perform it, right? I don't know how to do that."

He nodded. "I have no idea. I didn't get that far. I guess just play, and think about it. I'm not a musician. If it doesn't work, that's okay. I realized that too, talking to Opal about the show last night. There's a lot of false starts to things, but it's not the end of the world. There's only starts. Even if we fail, there's everyone else in the world to try. But the thing is that I have to try." He smiled. "Thanks. For letting me. I know . . . well."

I made a gesture, and suddenly we were both laughing. It came over me first, in a wave of giggles that hurt my stomach and ribs. I bent over, and I could hear Orsino laughing too, kind of high and wheezy. It seemed incredibly stupid that I had been so afraid about things that were so small, a few moments before. The stakes were unimaginably high in the world in general. The aliens knew that, and we did too. But it was possible to change something, create better futures, over years, with other people, maybe. I felt how large the universe was, and I felt the love and uncertainty and fear of the beings who were speaking to us, asking us to show them how wide the future was, hoping that we would start to repair something.

I thought about the show, and how everyone was inside, moving cardboard and costumes and lights, preparing to exclaim weird things and play loud music into the dark theater. A dozen nervous GSA teens, a dozen punks who weren't completely sure why they were there, and an audience of—who? Our parents? The punks' friends? How many people would watch? If it was anything like punk shows, people would have smuggled in beer. They would be making fun of us as much as they would be with us. People's mouths would probably be too close to their mics. There would be unintelligible shrieking. And half the people watching wouldn't know what we were doing, no matter if we pulled everything off exactly the way we'd planned.

"We should find James," I said.

"I don't know that I can go back in there," Orsino said.

"Yes, you can. You don't have to go onstage. Just talk to James with me."

I shoved the door open and ducked back inside, towing Orsino. I could feel that everyone backstage was moving fast. I could smell the sweat, too. Opal and Goober were right inside the door; Goober was saying something to Opal, and Opal was smiling wide. That was a relief.

"Okay, babes," I said, loudly, steering Orsino through the mass. "Let's get this fundraiser going."

Chapter 17

JAMES

When everyone started moving fast, carrying instruments and cardboard set pieces and plastic-bag jellyfish filled with Christmas lights in different directions, I took Francine's clippers and ducked into the bathroom again.

We'll prove it to them, Jukebox said had said in the car, when they picked me up to drive me here. *That the messages are real. You'll help me show everyone. You're the key.*

The look on Jukebox's face was frozen in my head. And what they'd said to me just now. *You're just a kid.*

What was going on? I hadn't done anything. I hadn't said anything. I wasn't trying to hurt them. Would people blame me for Jukebox storming out?

Would Jukebox blame me?

I started to text them: *Hey, I have no idea what Opal was talking about—I haven't said*

I deleted it.

I thought about the way Jukebox had touched my stomach and grabbed my hand, and how they had held me, last night, when I went back to their house crying to grab my backpack.

Was that not okay? It had felt okay, more than okay.

I imagined, briefly, posting a call-out post to say that Jukebox had wanted to manipulate me and use me sexually. What were the things I would even include? Stomach touch, lack of boundaries, helping my friend's band? Those weren't predatory, right?

That was just being part of the same community, working on a show together. They hadn't done anything to me. I'd *liked* the stomach touch. I'd liked them holding my hand so tight it hurt.

Even though I knew that Jukebox didn't want me like that.

Unless—

I wasn't going to think about it. I knew that it was complicated. Now I would never see the visions we could have made happen.

I plugged the clippers into the wall and turned them on. The outlet, along with every other inch of space, was covered in graffiti in dozens of colors of paint and Sharpie. I recognized lyrics from The Mountain Goats, names of local bands, anti-police slogans. The light was covered in graffiti too, which made the room dim. Too dim to cut hair by. I looked at myself in the mirror. My eyes were puffy, and a red zit on my chin stood out. I was wearing the mirror coat and the furry cow-patterned pants. I had smeared eyeshadow on in the bathroom earlier.

The insect buzz of the tiny motor was drowned out by the noise of everyone outside, getting ready for the show. I held the cold clipper blade, no guard, to my head, and swiped a long swath down my skull, letting my hair fall into the sink. I turned my head to look at it. It didn't look bad. I did it on the other side. I had to do something dramatic; I had to shave my whole head. Because Opal had looked at me like that, and Monique wasn't talking to me, and Jukebox had yelled at me. Because everything was crazy, and I had no friends and no boyfriend, and I was dressed like an idiot in a broken-down local theater's bathroom, getting ready to clown onstage for people who didn't like me anymore. I pushed the blade over my head again. I would never get to feel that the future was good. I would never feel how the oceans had felt millions of years ago, or feel Orsino kiss me. I thought of the last vision Orsino had sent me, last night, of us older, and of the vision Jukebox had given me, in the car on the way here. That one had been a feeling of sunlight, of warm leaves reaching up. I had heard their voice, calling from around the side of a hill, on a warm day; I had walked past a road overgrown with flowers.

I had to stay focused. If we could do the show, we could save Compton. Even if everyone there hated me, that was worth doing. Right? The gay kids having somewhere to go. I had to think about them. I had to chug along, be good, pull it back.

I glanced down at my phone, where the seventeen texts to Orsino still sat unread in my messages app. I had sent them even after my mom had advised me not to. I had tried calling him, too. He had picked up, said, "Look, I don't want to talk yet," and hung up again.

I opened my messages to Monique, and saw the last text I had sent three days ago, which was a screenshot of

Barbarella in a fur coat with the caption *you should do this look*. Monique hadn't responded either.

Hey, I texted Monique. *I don't know what's going on, but I wanted to tell you that I love you, and that won't change. I don't know if you're mad at me but I want to be your friend forever, and whatever it is you're mad about, I want to fix it. Please let's make up after the show.*

I sent it, and then realized how pathetic it sounded. I grew nauseated, thinking of the reply Monique would inevitably send back. *I'm done with you, James. You don't pay attention to anyone but yourself. I can't believe you'd make a move on me like that when I was upset. You manipulated me. I can't believe you're taking over the show, even though you don't have any talent.*

"I *hate* myself," I said in the mirror. I felt the first wave of prickly hair particles under my collar, settling in under the weight of the mirrored jacket. I shrugged the jacket off onto the floor, with a clatter. Underneath my shirt, the hair particles shifted. It was unbearably itchy, so I took off the shirt too. Then I had to look at my torso in the mirror— my scars on my chest that I liked so much, and the scars on my arms that I liked more than I wanted to admit, and my hips that I hated, and the acne on my shoulders. My chin too round, my forehead too big, my nose off-center. I was a weird-looking kid. I couldn't play music. I couldn't do school. I couldn't do friends. I took another swipe at my head with the clippers, and another feathery furrow dropped into the sink. Another, and another, and another. Around my ears, to the back of my neck. I looked at myself in the mirror, raggedly bald, like a cat with mange. I bared my teeth. Were they yellow, or was that just me drinking too much coffee? Did I have cavities? Were my lungs this gross? I imagined my ragged teeth and my horrible breath, ten years from now. If I kept smoking, everything about me would get uglier.

If the future was ugly, I could be too.

That was punk.

I was still crying, through this whole thing. I had a lump in my throat. I knew I had to get myself out onstage in thirty minutes, which meant I needed to have something gritty and hard inside me by the time I left this bathroom. I tried to focus on becoming gritty and hard. I told myself I didn't care that my friends were mad. I didn't care that I'd lost Monique, and lost Orsino. I didn't care that Jukebox thought I had betrayed them. I didn't care that Compton couldn't deal with my actual problems. I didn't give a shit.

Maybe I was unlovable, deep down. So what? I would get people to love me anyway, by dancing, or making art, or just being a cunt. Why did I need to prove I was good? I could just be a shithead, but fool people, for a little while, until they realized I sucked and moved on.

Behind me, there was a knock at the door.

"Use the other bathroom!" I yelled. The hair I'd cut off was all over the sink. I wondered if the theater's plumbing was good enough to absorb it if I threw it in the toilet. Better not risk it. I grabbed a fistful of black curly hair and stuck it in the trash. It sat on top of the paper towels, and some spilled back out onto the floor.

"James? Are you okay? We need to go on soon. They're starting the raffle."

It was Monique.

"I'm fine," I called. "I'm shaving my head."

"What?" The doorknob rattled. "James, let me in."

"No," I said. "Go *away*."

"James," Monique called. "I got your text."

I choked on my breath. The doorknob was still rattling. I reached back and opened the door.

Monique was in the costume we'd planned at Garbage Barge, and had the same scaley black and silver makeup as Opal. Monique's curly hair was pinned up with a headband that had two silver antennae on it.

"Oh, James," Monique said softly, looking at me. "Why'd you cut your hair off? It was so *cute* that length."

"Don't tell me what to do," I snapped. "Tell me what your deal is. Are you a girl, or what?"

Monique's eyes closed. "Yes. I'm . . . yep. I am a girl." Her eyes opened.

"Why didn't you tell me?"

"I did. You didn't hear me."

"Why didn't you tell me *after*?"

She put her hand over her eyes for a second, then looked up at the ceiling. "I fucking told you once, that should be enough. You should know it's hard to get the words out."

A sob welled in my throat.

"Also, your boyfriend's here." She thrust her thumb over her shoulder.

Orsino stuck his head into the bathroom.

I hiccupped. "The fuck?"

Orsino came toward me, which made me step back,

because it was overwhelming to smell him again. "Hey," he said. "It looks good."

"I didn't say it didn't look good," Monique said, leaning against the sink. "It just looked good *before*, too."

Orsino smirked at her, which confused me. He kissed me once, briefly, then drew back and looked at Monique with an expression that had a lot more in it than I understood.

Monique pulled a paper towel out of the dispenser and handed it to me. "We'll work together," she said. "To clean up. We'll be done quicker that way."

I accepted the paper towel. Orsino took another one, and stooped down to the floor, scooping up handfuls of hair and throwing them in the trash, pushing the layer of hair and paper towels down into the bag. I ducked under the sink and wiped the line of hair that had fallen under it.

"You don't have to do this," I said to both of them. "I can do it. I can get it. It's my mess."

"You have gotten me out of so many before-show nerve attacks," Monique said. "Now this is *your* first stage fright moment, and you've just gotten fucked with, and you're just going kind of crazy with it."

"What are you doing here?" I asked Orsino.

He turned around, leaning backwards into the trash can to push the paper towels down so there would be room for my hair. I was on the floor, and I realized I was kneeling in front of him, hands full of my own hair, looking at his stomach. I looked up at his face. I realized I couldn't ever be anything except soft inside, or do anything except want.

"I'm here because I like you," he said. "I don't know if we can ever be together, but I like you."

"And I'm here because I need to get our fucking cow on the stage," Monique said. She threw away a wad of hair. "And because I love you, you dumb son of a bitch."

"I'm sorry I ruined the show," I said. "Now that Jukebox isn't here, it'll be a mess. And it's because of me."

"Cut it with the melodramatic shit, James. That's not true," Monique said. "It doesn't have to be whatever thing they were imagining. I promise it's still going to rule."

"Opal's pissed at me," I said. "And it's because of how I acted to you. I didn't ever talk to you about how I felt, or ask about how you felt. I made you kiss me, that time, and then I didn't talk about it, and I made it seem like I was just using you for sex. And then I was with Orsino and wanting you and Jukebox both. I know that's shitty. I'm sorry."

Orsino breathed out and looked at Monique, as if he was waiting for her to say something. I felt so pent up I might explode.

Monique threw another hunk of my hair in the trash can. "I'm glad you're thinking about how you might have made me feel. It just was confusing for me, and I wasn't really over Tristan acting like a dick, so it hurt more. But you're not bad for being a slut. And Opal isn't really pissed at you because of that."

"Neither of you's been talking to me, though," I said.

Monique sighed. "Opal's mad at you because you haven't paid a lot of attention to them lately when they're having a hard time," she said. "That's between you two. But I'm not that mad at you. We're friends. It takes way more than making out in a car or you liking a dirtbag punk to stop being friends. Miss Sinead O'Connor." She reached out. I thought she was reaching for my hand, until I realized I was still holding the hairy paper towels. I handed them to Orsino, who was reaching out for them too, and he threw them away.

"I won't try to make out with you again." I tried to make it sound like a joke.

Monique stood by the trash can, looking at me, biting her big lower lip and breathing out a little breath. The glitter on her face reflected the dim bathroom light. "I mean, you could if you *wanted* to," she said.

"What?" Her face was very close. Orsino was right there, looking at us.

"But you do need to tell me what you want out of it. It's fine if it's just a hookup, but I can't be over here expecting romance and getting a hookup, you know? I can't get played with that way. So think about what you want, and then tell me."

She said it in a fake-casual tone. She lowered her eyes.

There was a long silence, during which I could hear that someone was yelling something about Francine being stuck in the ladies' powder room.

"We could *all* make out casually right now, and see how it feels," Orsino said, abruptly.

Monique and I both looked at him.

He shrugged, as if he had suggested something normal and not world-order-collapsing.

"You guys want to. I think you actually probably need to. I was freaked out by it, but I'm not anymore. And I realized I want to kiss both of you. Just a thought. If it works."

Orsino's broad, nearly unreadable, placid face looked seriously at Monique. I felt sweat prickle under my armpits. My brain barely had time to keep up; she reached across me and drew him in, so they were both huddled against me, their bellies pressing mine, and then their mouths met.

"What?" I asked.

I watched a very pretty girl kiss a very pretty boy.

Monique turned her head so her breath was against my cheek. Her face was the same face I had dreamed about for years; her lips nearly brushed my ear. Her dark brown eyes sparked like there were fires inside. She was the same as always.

"You know? Maybe chaos is good. If you want to, James, we can probably stay in here a couple minutes before the whole world collapses out there," she said.

I didn't make a verbal response. But I moved my face forward so my lips brushed hers, and then clung to the back of her hair. The tears on my face got on her face. Her hair was getting longer; my fingers tangled in it. I felt myself start to cry; when I pulled back to cough and wipe my nose on my sleeve and laugh with a hysterical building pressure, Monique kissed Orsino again. He drew his chapped lips along her jaw and anchored there on her mouth, holding her face in his hand. Then he turned to me and pressed his lips to my neck, and Monique turned back to me and was kissing my forehead, and then Orsino was kind of biting me, a little, and rubbing his hands on my stomach under my shirt, and Monique kissed my cheek like she was experimenting and then put her mouth on mine again, and her tongue found mine, and I pushed back, because what else could I do? I wanted, wanted, wanted, and the wanting was all that was holding me up.

"I love you. You're so important to me," I said, when I pulled back. Orsino was still biting my neck. When I said I loved Monique, he bit harder.

"I love you too," Monique said. She was crying too. "Shit, man, you've been my best friend for years."

"I don't want to lose you."

"I don't want to lose you either." Her hands were in my hair. "I hate not talking to you. I was just scared to explain, because we kissed, and it was weird, and you're gay, and I thought explaining I was a girl right after you kissed me would ruin it."

"I'm gay but I can still kiss a girl," I said.

She looked down at the dirty bathroom floor and laughed, her face flushing. She wiped a hand up her face. "You're a stupid dumbass," she said. "Fuck you."

"Or I'm bi," I amended.

"That's not—you can be gay," she said. She whacked my shoulder with a hand. "Calm down."

Orsino pulled back from my neck. He held me between him and Monique, his hands still on my clammy stomach. "This has been a crazy time," he said.

"Orsino. I love you too. I've been really weird and bad to you, and I don't want to be," I said to him.

I felt my ribs creak as he hugged me, hard, and pressed me against his chest. "I really like you, James," he said. "I haven't known you that long, but you're kind of important to me."

"You are too."

Monique was laughing through her hands. "I love gays," she said. "We're such freaks."

"I think maybe we aren't meant to be like, capital-B boyfriends right now," Orsino continued seriously.

I was crying again, and I tried to contain it. "I'm sorry," I said.

"I'm not used to getting close to people, and I couldn't figure out how close you wanted to be. I gotta be honest, I've been feeling kind of insane lately trying to act like I know what's going on. And I am kind of mad at you still."

I was trying to cry in a mature, grown-up way. "It's been confusing. It's my fault. I'm sorry."

"I want to be friends. After we cool off. I mean it."

"Okay," I said, into his shoulder, feeling the world spin.

"I don't mean that as a fuck-off thing. I mean like I actually care."

He drew back and looked at me really seriously, and then snorted and started laughing.

I didn't even care if he was laughing at me. I knew I must look dumb. But his laugh sounded so good. He drew me into a hug, and Monique hugged me from the other side. She was also hugging him. I was between them.

There were no visions, just the feeling of their bodies on either side of me.

The world stilled in the heat and pressure of the embrace.

"Okay, we probably gotta go," Monique said, finally. "Or we're going to miss the aliens saving the world."

She pulled away and straightened her hair a little, then looked in the mirror at her blurred makeup. "Oh well," she said. "It is what it is. Come on, Sinead."

"I'll go to the audience," Orsino said. "I don't really want to be backstage, it's really, really noisy." He pushed past me and opened the door for me and Monique. I studied him to see if he was upset—this was an insane thing we had just done together—but he seemed at ease.

Monique took my hand.

"Wait!" I said. I ducked under the sink and grabbed the mirror coat. I knew who should wear it. I shook it, so my hair fell out of the seams onto the ground.

I knew my makeup was smeared, but I let Monique drag me along the cement-floored hallway into the wings.

Duke jostled past us, nearly knocking me against the wall.

"We've made a quarter of our goal from the raffle before the show already," he shouted to Monique.

I bumped into three kids carrying signs, and the two kids carrying the body of the first worm sculpture, made of pink sheer fabric, then I stumbled towards Venus, who was wearing the orange sweatshirt she'd come in with. I thrust the mirror coat at her. Above us, I could see the rustling, lit-up jellyfish puppets, dangling, ready to fall from above. Acorn had said xie would run those. There was a float of a whale that must have been dropped off by the Species Parade people at the last second; I tripped around it and pushed myself against the wall, closer to Venus.

"Wear this," I said. "It'll look rad."

She looked down at it. "Was this even in the costume pile?"

"Jukebox made it," I said. "But you can change its energy. You'll rule."

Onstage, Natalie and Gemma were closing off the first raffle sale. Duke was out there with them. They were saying something about the board, and then something about the business sponsorships, and about recurring monthly donations and new programs. Duke saw us in the wings and suddenly raced offstage towards us.

"Does anyone wanna say anything cool about Compton?" he asked. "We're stalling. Mush isn't ready yet, and we gotta do two more minutes."

I felt the tears still on my face, and froze up. I couldn't say anything, I knew.

"I can," Opal's voice said from somewhere in the dark.

"Awesome," Duke said. "Come on."

Opal pushed their chair onstage, Duke walking behind them. Gemma, looking relieved, handed them the mic.

"Hey all," Opal said to the dark audience. I couldn't see how many people were in the theater, but a scattered cheer went up. "Thanks for showing up to save this organization. Buy raffle tickets. Give to Compton every month. This group is how I found out I wasn't alone, and it still is how a lot of gay and trans teenagers find out they're not alone." They took a breath, and I heard Barb's voice give a whoop from the front seats.

"Go Opal!" she yelled.

"I started a band this year," Opal said, "with my friends Monique and Sophie. I love music. Music is what gets me through shit. And when the grants dried up for Compton, I thought music could save it. So we wrote this show with some other people, because Olympia has been a punk place forever, and we made this happen. It's ours. We're gonna show you what queer youth are capable of. Please give us money, so we can keep making art and talking to each other so we don't die." They paused. They seemed to think for a moment. It was silent in the audience. "And so we can fight the power."

Another cheer, from four or five scattered voices.

"That's all," Opal said. They turned around and came back to us in the wings.

And then the lights went down, and I watched. I remembered the structure of the show, from our script and our rehearsals, but the lights still surprised me. They blinked red, glowed, grew brighter in the all-black of the theater. I felt a shudder go through me, and a slight spark.

Emu Union's song was a rattling, drum-heavy crash; it woke up the audience, who had been sleepily sitting down in the seats that started ten feet back from the stage. A few of them stood and moved forward, stood at the front of the stage, jumped up and down, as the jellyfish dropped and the booming bass crackled in the antique sound system. Blue light bloomed, then red; the whale float was rolled forward onto the stage. Two band members seemed surprised by it, and the sound died for a second before they remembered where they were and finished the song with a scream. Behind me, Danny and someone else, whose name was maybe Jolene, scrambled forward in the long fabric-covered body of the worm, onto the stage, racing back and forth as the whale float spun in circles, and the drums and snares landed like rolls of thunder, and the lights flickered blue.

"They have always watched, waiting for the time they could unite with us," Ron from Emu Union called, over the last dying bass line. A thrumming throb from his own guitar crescendoed, and briefly drowned him out. Danny and Jolene stomped from one foot to the other, rolling the worm's body, shaking it around as the rest of the stage went dark and the whale was wheeled off the other side. "The worms wait to share their wisdom . . . but watch us fall."

A crash, and scattered screams came from the audience. There was applause, too, from the people still sitting down. The worm continued running around on stage as the next band got ready to come on. The change between bands had to be faster than it was at punk shows, and I could tell moving that fast stressed everyone out. But the audience loved it. I could see through the shadows, from where I was standing on the edge of the stage, that more people were coming forward, standing in front of the stage. They were moving like they would have at a show—pushing against each other. I could see a couple people holding forties that they'd somehow snuck in. I could see people's hair moving up and down.

How many tickets had we sold? Would it be enough?

Everyone who had been waiting in the wings was involved in the next part, except the band members who were about to go on; we had to throw our bodies around crazily in the red light. The lyrics were about the dawn of war and patriarchy. I heard my heart pounding in my ears. We raced around in the red, as Mush played loud noises, rumbles, crashes, unwinding and insane small high noises. The lights were red, scarlet, bright bloody-pink, deep purple.

We brandished props—swords and big silver arrows. We didn't have fake guns, but there was a machine-gun sound that Mush's synth girl played. One by one, we fell as the shots rang out in the theater. The hard floor on my back was cold and grainy.

"They're killing each other," Venus's voice rang out. Her voice was high above us, coming over the speakers. Venus herself was backstage. "We have to do something. We have to tell them that they can stop it."

Danny and Jolene in the worm costume dived across the stage again, in a swoop of hoops; they tripped against each other. Francine, who was lying down on the ground, reached up with one hand; Danny reached down and pulled her to her feet, and she hung on the worm's back as they snaked off the other side of the stage.

I barely caught my breath before it was the scene where cows were getting turned into hamburgers. We were using Acorn's projector to project a meat grinder on a bedsheet above the stage and having me run across the stage, then around the back of the stage, then across, again and again, as all the cows, because we only had the one cow costume. Each time I reached stage right, a crunching, grinding noise sounded over the speakers, and the meat grinder on the screen changed colors. I tried to appear the same each time I ran across the stage; we'd talked about needing a consistent stage picture. I was getting out of breath. Sandy Thong was playing their song.

Bottle-broken
Ground up
God I'm choking

Girl I'm choking
Ground up
Four degrees
Rotten meat . . .

The music was good; we were running around like animals. What would they be thinking? Would they all want their ticket money back? Would they understand how important this place was to us?

Just the experience of being here, of screaming, of dancing, was better than what was outside.

The music faded. The projection on the screen above the stage changed to a knife, and then to the meat grinding. Cow-me froze, staring up at it in horror, and dove away behind a piece of cardboard, breaking the cycle of running back and forth, and the song drew to a close with one ominous bass chord that drew out and out and out.

It was my turn. How was I going to do this? I thought about Jukebox, and the visions. Without that, what was it? A weird dance?

The spotlight shone on me as I crawled back out from behind one of the set pieces, still panting from racing back and forth; I saw Monique and Opal and Sophie hustling to get into position as Sandy Thong's guitarist ducked through a curtain. I heard a laugh from the audience as I crouched onstage, staring up at the spotlight as it turned green, lighting up all the hairs on my arms. My stomach churned. We hadn't practiced band changes enough; we hadn't run it enough.

Monique's voice tore through me.

"MY HANDS ARE PLUNGED IN THE SOFT HEMISPHERES," she screamed, rasping. My throat hurt just hearing her. "I CAN SEE THAT YOU'RE BLED BY THE WORLD / BLED TO DEATH. RED. YOUR BRAIN IS BROKEN."

The spotlight flashed on me, and Jolene and Danny came out in their worm costume, swaying side to side next to my arms. They nudged me, and I swung my arms over them, one over each. They hauled me to my feet. Venus was coming out wearing the mirror coat and the trailing cape that Jukebox was meant to wear. The lights around the spotlight changed to purple, and the cymbals crashed. Opal was staring at me.

I felt a shock, and the world turned sideways, the floor coming up around the edge of me, the sky swirling in the direction of my left ear. An electric current ran through me—

—Lightning flashed, and something began swimming, far underwater, at the dawn of time—

"REVOLUTION!" Venus shouted, wrapping one arm around me.

My heart pounded inside my skull. Something was stretching around my brain, pulling tighter, like a rubber band ready to snap.

Stacey, standing to one side, played a chord on her guitar, which was tuned to a high, crisp twang against the crash of Monique and Opal and Sophie.

A jet of blinding purple light shot through me as the guitar and bass swelled into the audience. I felt a ripple, like I was standing up to my chest in the sea, too close to a riptide. I imagined being pulled under the water, my knees scraping the ocean floor, my blood merging with saltwater. I felt myself stagger into Venus; she staggered into Jolene

317

and Danny, and we all fell. We hit the floor together, under the rippling tide of sound and feeling.

In my head, I saw the earth underneath us, cracking under the weight of the theater, and the bones and bugs trembling with the sound; I felt the echoes of every movement that anyone had ever taken on the stage resounding back into me, shaking my teeth.

The worms' twisting bodies, purple and soft, in the ship by the moon—

The possible future full of blood and darkness, paws hurting as we stamped the ground—

The hot water flowing over me and a touch on my back—

Music and people, voices in a chorus between small fires on a beach—

Holding a baby—

Roads overgrown with plants, houses with tin roofs, forests thousands of years old, not in the past, but in the future—

A face with just eyes—

I turned back to look at Monique. Her eyes were shut, and her face was contorted with the force of her noise. The arc of her body leaned forward, toward me, toward the audience. I could hear her on the high notes, mixed in with the noise of Sophie's guitar and Opal's drums; her voice was almost just a scream. I felt myself disappearing into it, floating above the ground. My feet lifted for a second in the green spotlight, and I was pulled into the air. I felt the hair all over my body stand up; my stomach jumped. My feet were off the floor. I couldn't put them back down. I reached for Venus, who was still clutching me, staring. She let her hand slip, and I rose further, for an instant, and hovered, a foot above the floor. Then her face became a face with many beautiful eyes, and speech which I couldn't understand but also could.

The future is not yet fixed.

There was a screech, impossibly loud, like a scream from a dying animal right next to me, and I saw cords around where Opal was playing spark white and blue and green.

The theater went completely black. The spotlight that felt like it was holding me aloft disappeared.

Monique was still singing when her mic cut out with a thud.

I fell back to the floor like I was made of lead. My foot landed at the wrong angle, and a pins-and-needles shudder went up my legs and seemed to snap the vise around my head. I fell against Jolene again, or maybe Venus. Venus was clutching my wrist. There was a long moment of silence, and then a scrambling in the dark. I could hear the adults backstage whispering, trying to find the light.

Onstage, I felt unable to speak. I couldn't raise my voice. I couldn't even make a small sound. Everything around me buzzed like it was coming apart; my face felt stretched wide, hurting, in a grin. My heart pounded. I felt around in the dark, touched the hands and sides of other kids who had been onstage. Someone let out a high giggle.

I heard Duke's voice, from the side of the stage:

"Hello, everyone! We seem to have an electrical malfunction! No big deal. We are going to take a brief break. Please find the exit strips on the floor between the seats. You can meet us back inside in fifteen minutes. We think we can turn the breakers and bring back the lights."

In the dark, the audience laughed, and then began to

applaud, raucously, and whistle and hoot. I couldn't tell if they had thought it was part of the show or not, or if they had felt what I felt. I heard Monique gasping behind me, taking deep breaths.

To us, Duke said: "Stay where you are. We'll get flashlights here in a second."

I sat in the dark, hand on someone's hand, breathing. Someone laughed, and someone else moaned. I couldn't make any sound, still; my legs ached. I was motionless until a beam of yellow light found us. I saw Duke's black shoes shining against the mottled black stage, and looked up at his shadowed face.

"Follow me," he said. We got up and followed him, holding onto one another's clothes.

In the alley behind the theater, we gathered in our costumes while Mickey and Duke tried to find the breaker in the basement. The sky was dark, and it was cold; my bald head made me more exposed to the icy wind. It still smelled like dead fish.

"We'll be back on in a second," Duke said. "I'm gonna say we skip the rest and go to the raffle prizes and call for pledges, and if we get the sound equipment to work again we can have the last band play as an encore."

My teeth chattered. I looked around and saw Monique and Opal coming out the door behind me. I turned to Opal.

"That was a really good speech, at the start," I said to them. Words felt odd in my mouth. I felt like I shouldn't have a mouth.

They looked at me hard for a second, and then smiled, their white teeth shining against the dim yellow light in the alley. "It was, wasn't it?" they said. They brushed their hair back from their face, and pointed at my head. "Nice haircut, Caillou."

I touched my prickly goose-bumpy head. I had done that.

Monique looked as shaky as I felt, but she smiled. She reached out and pulled me to her, in a hug. "He's not Caillou," she said. Her voice sounded so hoarse and weak and crackly. She heard it too and wheezed with laughter against me. Then she tilted her head up to look at the sky.

"Look up," she said to me, quietly. "Look at that."

I looked up. I could see deep blue sky, half-hidden by clouds. "What?"

"There was a light up there, moving."

I squinted into the blackness. The glow of the city blotted out the stars.

I wasn't sure if she was messing with me. I pushed my head against her shoulder again. She put her hand on the back of my head. I was sure Opal was giving her a look, but I didn't care; I could feel her cheek smiling against me. She was so warm, and she smelled like sweat and pleather and her lemon-scented hair gel.

Maybe I hadn't learned any lessons at all, but I would. She would too.

Someone must have found the breaker; there was a screech inside from all the mics and instruments being left on.

During the raffle, I sat next to Monique and Opal and Sophie backstage. We were waiting to come out for the encore. I thought to check my phone for the first time. There was a text from Orsino, unread, on the home screen. I opened it.

You did great onstage. Talk soon ok?

Compton Youth ...
Yesterday at 2:55pm · 🌐

UPDATE: WE MADE 140% OF OUR GOAL!!!! AND
WELCOME TO DUKE AND JADE!

Dear Community
From the youth and volunteers at Compton, we want
to say THANK YOU to everyone
who turned out for our GOTHPEL OF WORM ROCK
MUSICAL last saturday and dug deep into
your pockets to support your local LGBT youth
organization. Our gorgeous performance
featuring local bands can be found on Vimeo. Wait for
the exciting ending, when the lights
cut out due to an electrical issue!
Between tickets, raffle prizes, monthly donors, and
one-time donations and support from
local businesses, we have managed to actually
EXCEED what our yearly winter gala was
estimated to pull in-- —by 40%!! We made a total of
$10,231, mainly from monthly donors,
whose names, if they choose, will be included on our
Sponsor page. While we still count on
grants and other sources of income for our programs
throughout the year, our rock show's
income means we are out of the danger zone and in
the clear until May, and are able to
announce our first three months of programming for
January-March.

Next, since we have two new directors (GOODBYE
GEMMA AND NATALIE!!!) we will be
hosting a Restructuring Queer Camp-Out with youth
and board members in the last week of
March, where Jade and Duke, our new directors, will
speak with youth about their visions for our
space and programs in the future while staying at the
beautiful and affordable Duck's Feet
Cabins on the Olympic Peninsula. Learn more on our
site.

Other upcoming programs will include a Self-Care
Workshop night, a Tarot Card
Workshop with Duke and Jade, and—for the first time
ever—a Youth Skate Night. Watch this
space for dates and times!
We will also be reopening our Clothing Donation Day,
to assist people who may need
warm winter clothes or camping gear.

Have an amazing holiday season with your chosen
families! LGBT POWER!

👍 James Goldberg and 102 Others   54 Comments

👍 Like   💬 Comment   ↪ Share

Jukebox January ⋯

Yesterday at 8:24 PM · 🌐

Hey, if I haven't reached out to you, just know I'm
going through a really rough time right
now. I am trying! There is a lot going on in my life. If
you want to know what's going on, DM me.
I am trying to avoid conflict-oriented spaces online.

All I have to say is—I'm going to keep telling the truth,
and spreading visions of a better future. If
you're with me, you're with me. Some days I feel like
giving up, but we can't give up.

👍   0 Comments

👍 Like   💬 Comment   ↪ Share

JAMES

"Hey," he said, as I rolled up with my bike on the board-walk. It was kind of a misty day, and the air near the pier smelled like salt and mud.

"Hey," I said.

We looked at each other for a minute, and then I hugged him. I wasn't sure if he would push me away, but he didn't. He hugged me back.

I got an image of a bright red bird and a flower opening.

"It's been a bit," Orsino said. "Your hair's still gone."

I had kept shaving my head every two weeks. After the initial shock of having no hair, it felt kind of cool to be bald. Monique joked that me and Sophie should start a Baldies Union.

"Male pattern baldness hit me early," I said. "Your hair, like, went green."

"It must be the lichen," Orsino said. He paused and sat down on the bench he'd been on. I put the kickstand on my bike and sat down next to him. It felt really weird, I thought, to be doing this. I didn't know what came next.

Orsino reached up to his collar and pulled a necklace from inside his sweater. It was a seashell with a moon snail hole through it, on a long string. "Look what Robin got me."

"That's cool," I said.

"Robin says it's a protection charm, but it's just a shell," Orsino said. He pulled up his knees. "But I like it. She found it in the library parking lot, where the shells were that one time. I got her a necklace too, with some beach glass. We drove out to the coast last weekend."

"Wasn't it cold?"

"Yeah," Orsino said, and grinned. "Robin has this friend named Crab now, who goes surfing at Westport. He has like, a wetsuit. We went with him and looked after his dogs on the beach while he went in this like, freezing cold water. He's a weirdo trans guy from like, Vashon. We all looked for stuff on the beach. I found a bunch of dead stuff."

He smiled at me, and I felt a weird pang of guilt mixed with longing. "That sounds sick," I said.

I wasn't sure when to show Orsino the drawing I'd done of him. It was in my backpack, which was shoved in one of the bags on my bike. I also didn't know if he'd like it. I glanced toward my bike.

"So," Orsino said. "Spaceships. Do you want to go to Robin's house?"

"Yeah," I said.

I thought about asking him if he wanted to ride on the back of my bike, but that felt like maybe too much. I also wasn't sure if I could steer good if he was on the back, and my tires had already popped twice since I started biking every day. So we walked. The place Robin was living at was a little house on the west side, almost directly across the sound from where Oakland Happyland was. It wasn't far from Monique's place either. As we walked, we passed a cop on the street who was walking purposefully toward some kids sitting against the front of a closed store.

"Hold on," Orsino said, and he stopped. "I'm going to try to stop that cop."

That sounded like a comically bad idea, but I didn't say anything. He leaned casually against the traffic light pole, closing his eyes like he was trying to remember something. I watched the cop. I felt something like a wave rippling through me, but I might have just been imagining it. The cop, fifteen feet away, suddenly froze. The kids were looking at him with some degree of nervousness. Orsino's hair spiked up a little on his head, I thought, but that also might have been the breeze.

The cop looked around like he was suddenly unsure. His legs shook a little. He walked back to his black-and-white car and got in.

When Orsino touched my shoulder, I felt a little spark. "Okay," he said. "We can go."

"Did you do something?" I asked.

"I showed him what it was like to be a marmot in the mountains hundreds of years ago," Orsino said. "I think." He paused. "Marmots have like, predators and stuff, so it's kind of a scary one. You smell the mountains and all the tunnels you make. Marmots don't bother people sleeping outside." He shrugged. "I think the really scary ones wipe me out too much. Who knows what difference it makes. But I keep finding more images. The deeper I go."

We walked toward the bridge. I thought about how much I didn't understand.

"I've thought about you a lot," I said.

"Me too," Orsino said. "I mean, I've thought about you."

I knew that wasn't everything, but I also thought now might not be a good time to push talking about it.

"I'm so glad Jukebox moved," I said.

"Yeah," Orsino said. He trailed his hand over the wet railing on the bridge, where mist had beaded up. "I hope someone around them can like, help them. I don't think they're like, trying to hurt anyone." He wiped his hand on his shirt.

I considered this. "If everything had happened differently. Do you think the visions thing would have worked the way they wanted them to? In the theater?"

"I don't think it would have been nothing," Orsino said. "But I don't think it would have done everything they wanted it to." He shrugged again. "I knew that, and then I wasn't sure, because they made me feel like I'd been misusing my powers and not helping. But then I realized they thought they were more powerful than they were. Nobody's that powerful alone. They were looking to lead everyone, not work with people. I was so alone for so long I didn't realize I could work with people."

On the porch of Robin's house there was a coffee can full of cigarette butts. I'd been trying to stop smoking. Orsino stopped and smoked on the stoop before we went in. I didn't say anything, just watched him. Then we went to Robin's room. She was at work downtown. She had a new job at the pizza place. Her room was small, and her mattress was on the floor, but she had a desk.

"We found a kitten under the porch," Orsino said. "We took it to Goober, since she knows people who want cats."

He showed me a picture of the cat on his phone.

"Cool," I said.

"My mom wanted us to bring it up to Tacoma, when I go back for the weekend next time," he said. "But she only *thinks* she wants a cat."

He started getting out the stuff for our stick and pokes.

"I thought I'd do red ink for mine," he said. "But I have blue and purple and black too."

"I want purple," I said. I wasn't sure how close to stand to him.

Orsino had calligraphy ink and regular embroidery needles and sewing needles that he soaked in isopropyl alcohol and then passed through a candle flame. He wrapped them in thread before he dipped them in the ink. We'd texted about the best way to do stick-and-poke tattoos, but a lot of the supplies that were recommended were expensive.

"I did this one on myself," he said, pulling up his sleeve. "The dog."

It was a little picture of a black dog running, in outline. The lines were sketchy, but you could tell what it was. It looked healed.

We drew the outlines in pen. I didn't know how sterile this all was, but I took my chances. Orsino drew the flying saucer on his arm first, and then copied it on mine, up near my bicep.

"You sure you want the same one?" he asked.

"I know I do," I said.

Orsino looked at me. "You're sure."

"Some things are forever," I said. "I always want to have you in my life, but even if that wasn't true, I wouldn't want to forget anything."

Orsino hadn't really smiled yet, but now he did.

The needle pokes hurt, but not more than doing testosterone injections. Orsino's face hovered a few inches from my shoulder as he jabbed the purple needle just below the first layer of skin, following the drawing's shape. I held on to my own leg.

It took maybe half an hour. The tattoo wasn't super big.

"We might want to go over them again in a week or two, once they heal," Orsino said. He wiped off the ink. I looked at the tiny flying saucer, holding its shape against the red skin behind it. "We gotta keep it clean. Wipe it with alcohol."

"Now let me do yours," I said. "I'll be careful, I promise."

Orsino held onto the edge of the floor mattress as I started on his arm. I tried to poke the way he had poked, through just one layer of skin. It was harder than it looked, and I winced every time the needle seemed like it went in deeper. Orsino looked away from my face after a minute.

Halfway through, I paused to wipe the ink away and look at the ship. It looked wicked and bloody on his big arm. I felt like I was opening a wound. "There's a lot about you that I still don't know," I said. "You've been through stuff that's super bad."

"I think you have, too," Orsino said. "I've had good and bad stuff."

"Your bad stuff is worse," I said. I stuck the needle in. "Just like, you know, objectively."

"Maybe," Orsino said.

The sun came through the window. Downstairs, we heard one of Robin's roommates come in and slam the door. I stuck the needle in five more times.

"I'm almost done," I said. My back hurt from bending over. I liked the way his arm looked, still. As I put the needle in again, I got a flash of a vision. Rolling on a beach, over and under another body. Sand everywhere.

"I kind of like how this feels," Orsino said. He gave no sign that he had had the vision. Maybe it was just me. "Did you like how it felt for you?"

I could still feel the slight sting of my tattoo. "Yeah," I said. "Definitely."

I thought about the picture of me in the future again, from the first time he kissed me, where we had both listened to the water. I touched the tattoo on Orsino's shoulder, and it flooded back to me—the roar of the waves and the window, open wide. Orsino's eyes met mine, and I felt him again, inside me. The window in the vision opened further than it had before; the wind whipped my face and Orsino's face at the same time. I got a flash of the ship, like a white hole in the sky.

"Alien boys," I said, and grabbed his hand like we were on a union poster.

Orsino smiled. His big hand squeezed my small one. "Alien boys."

I rode my bike home at three, so I could get my car and go pick up Opal from school, and go hang out with Monique and Sophie.

ACKNOWLEDGMENTS

This book was written on stolen Lenni Lenape land and is set on stolen Salish land. Anyone who has grown up in the Puget Sound has watched the horrifying changes global warming has wrought there in living memory. Settler colonialism is an ideology which produces death; it alienates people from life systems and history and kills specific groups of people in order to extract short-term value from labor and land. This author believes in the restoration of rights to land to the land's original inhabitants and a restoration of wild ecosystems so we all have a chance at a future where our air is breathable and power isn't so majorly and fatally consolidated.

Thank you to Lauren Hooker, Tal Mancini, and Claire Zuo at Seven Stories for your work getting this book into shape. Thank you to Ruth Weiner for figuring out how to promote it.

This book could not have been written without the advice and critical feedback of Jeanne Thornton, Andrea Lawlor, Hannah Fergesen, Peyton Thomas, and Stephen Ira.

Jeanne especially. Jeanne, thank you. You have now helped two of my books become better and more effective versions of themselves. You are also a genius and a credit to the goddess Brigid.

Thank you to Rachel Carns, Radio Sloan, and Nomy Lamm for authorizing me to use lyrics from The Need's rock opera *The Transfused*. Without *The Transfused* and the music culture of Olympia in the early 2000s, I would not exist in my present form and neither would this book.

I would like to thank Nicholas Shannon, my partner in life, for hearing me talk for hundreds of hours about this book patiently and enthusiastically, and just hearing me out about all of it. Thanks to Jolene, my girlfriend and big wolf, without whom I might not have understood Monique as well as I needed to.

Thank you to the early readers who gave me honest feedback, especially Blu and Noah.

I would like to thank Luis Galvan for his eternal encouragement and his modeling of future possibilities for me. You're one alien I'm speaking to. Thank you to Aalon for being my lover and friend over many years and treating me as family. I hope to always live up to it.

I would like to thank Kale Mays for material education and spiritual wisdom about history, divinity, and climate crisis that has influenced my writing.

I'd like to thank Stonewall Youth circa 2010-2014 for its Queer Rock Camp, weekly support groups, punk mentorship, lending library of books which I sometimes stole, etc. When I was quite young, Stonewall allowed me to witness and be party to much confusing intracommunity queer conflict, which prepared me for much of queer and trans life. This sounds bitchy but it's also earnest. Queer youth groups help us survive and they also help us see each other, get disillusioned with each other, care for each other, lust for each other, and get mad at each other. They help us make art. The people who want us to not have those things want us to die. Stonewall made me believe in the possibility of queer family and queer love more powerfully than everything else, even at moments when we are all insane. Thank you to my friends from that time, even if our lives have taken us to different places.

Thank you to Seven Stories for taking another chance on some weird YA and for making my book a book in the world.

ABOUT THE AUTHOR

Hal Schrieve is a children's librarian in Manhattan and the best part of hir job is facilitating comics and creative writing workshops with young people. Hir first book, *Out of Salem*, was longlisted for the National Book Award for Young People's Literature. Hal's comics are featured in *We're Still Here*, an all-trans comics anthology, and the zine Very Online. Hal's comic *Vivian's Ghost* was on the shortlist for *Comics Beat*'s 2023 Cartoonist Studio Prize Award for Best Webcomic. Follow Hal at @howlmarin on Instagram and @hal_schrieve on Twitter.